FALLING HEAD OVER BOOTS

Falling Head OVER BOOTS

A TENDER HEART TEXAS NOVEL

KATIE LANE

To my loyal readers, thank you for all the encouraging emails, comments, and love you've given me over the years. Every time I sit down to write, I'm thinking of you.

"Duke Earhart believed in picking out a woman like he picked out a filly. Look for strong teeth, long legs, and a sweet disposition."
−Tender Heart, Book Four

CHAPTER ONE

❧

I MPOTENT?
He was NOT impotent. He was a strong, virile bull that just needed a little motivation. Yes, that was it. Motivation was keeping him from being the acclaimed stud everyone knew him to be. The female population didn't stir his blood. Didn't prime his juices. Didn't fill him with a raging desire to pursue and conquer.

Females could do that to a male. One second, they could make you feel like the king bull of the herd, and the next second, they could make you feel like a castrated steer.

Zane Arrington's hands tightened on the steering wheel, and he had the sudden urge to put his fist through the window. Instead, he took a deep breath and tried to get control of his temper and his wayward thoughts. And if he was good at anything, it was control. He'd been controlling his emotions for years.

Where was he? Oh, yes, he'd been thinking about Ferdinand, and why the prize bull he'd paid a half million dollars for wasn't doing his job of impregnating the herd. It couldn't be impotency. The bull had proven himself to be a damn good producer— which is why Zane had bought him. Ferdinand's prize bloodline was going to enrich the herd. That was if Zane could figure out what was wrong with the animal's libido. He had tried everything from vitamins to hormones, but the bull flat refused to mount one heifer. Zane's sister Becky thought the bull just needed more time to adjust to his new environment. And maybe she was right. She did seem to know a lot about males. She had half the male population of Texas panting after her.

It made absolutely no sense to Zane. He loved his sister, but she was the biggest pain in the butt this side of the Pecos. She was too opinionated, too controlling, and too competitive for her own good. He liked his women to be soft-spoken, reserved, and sweet. Just like . . .

He shook his head. No sir, he wasn't going there.

Becky. He was thinking about his sister Becky and how he was going to kill her for not checking in like he'd asked her to if she was going to be late. But asking never worked with Becky. She was hardheaded just like their daddy. Zane was more easygoing like their mama. Which is exactly how he'd ended up babysitting his little sister. He should've flat refused to let her move back to the ranch after college. He should've sent her to Austin to live with Mama and Daddy so they could've been dragged out of their comfortable bed at all hours of the night. And he planned on reading his inconsiderate sister the riot act about that . . . as soon as he made sure she was okay.

Since Becky loved to dance, his first stop was the only bar in town. The Watering Hole was never busy. Not only because it had the worst food in Texas, but also because most folks were home by eight and in bed by nine. So he wasn't surprised to find only a few vehicles in the parking lot; none of them his sister's brand-new half-ton pickup. He wheeled his own half-ton around and was about to look elsewhere when the owner of the bar came out the door with one of the regulars. And in Bliss, you never got away with just a wave. Especially if you were an Arrington.

Zane rolled down his window. "Hey, Hank. Hey, Jeb. How y'all doin'?"

"Fair to middlin'," Hank said. "Not as bad as most, but not as good as you." He grinned. "I saw that article about you in *Rancher's Life* magazine. I don't remember the exact words, but it was something about you being the perfect mix of the hardworking cowboys of the old West and the technically savvy ranchers of the future."

Zane adjusted his hat. "I don't know if I'd go that far." Especially when he'd wasted a fortune on a bull with no libido. Not that he was willing to spread that gossip around. He had yet to tell his daddy. Even though his father was retired, he still considered the ranch his and would be pissed that Zane had wasted the money.

"Yep," Jeb said with a sloppy grin that pretty much said he'd had too much to drink. "You've done the Arrington name justice, and the town of

Bliss proud."

The comment should've made Zane happy. He'd spent most of his life trying to do his family's name justice and the town proud. But right now he didn't feel happy. He just felt confused about how his perfect life had gone to hell in a handcart so quickly.

"So what has you in town so late at night?" Hank asked. "You looking for Becky? She was in earlier, but she left around nine with Dale Foster. I thought she was dating Jake Holmes."

"That was last week," Jeb said with another sloppy grin. "This week it's Dale."

Obviously, the entire town was keeping up with his sister's speed dating. Not wanting to fuel the gossip, Zane told a little white lie. "Actually, I was looking for my foreman Jess. He wasn't answering his phone so I thought I'd see if he was here." He changed the subject. "You okay, Jeb? You need a ride home?"

Jeb shook his head. "I think I'll walk tonight. Maybe sober up before I get home." He winked. "You know how ticked wives can get when you've had a little too much to drink."

No, Zane didn't know about that. After getting married, he'd never had a little too much to drink. His daddy had taught him that a good husband never had more than the occasional beer. And Zane was a good husband. A damn good husband.

His hands tightened on the steering wheel again. "Yeah, wives can sure get ticked at that. Y'all have a good night."

After leaving the Watering Hole, he headed down Main Street. The town was closed up tight.

Not that there were a lot of businesses still open in Bliss. Most of the buildings were vacant and had been for years. The only thing keeping Bliss on the map was the occasional tourist looking for Tender Heart.

Tender Heart was a fictional book series that Zane's great-aunt had written. It was based on a group of mail-order brides who had come to Bliss in the eighteen hundreds and pretty much started the town. The series was considered a classic and had rabid fans who showed up sporadically looking for their favorite fictional characters and for the little white chapel where all the brides had been wed. They were sadly disappointed when all they found were ordinary folks and a bunch of vacant buildings.

A flicker of light in one of those vacant buildings caught his attention, and he took his foot off the accelerator and slowed down to take a closer look.

The diner had been built in the late fifties when Bliss had been experiencing its heyday. At the time, Texas was producing plenty of oil for all the gas-guzzling cars, cattle prices were high, and the Tender Heart books had just come out and were selling like hotcakes. The diner had closed when Zane was in high school, but he still remembered the hearty home-cooked meals you could get there. The kind of meal that warmed a man's belly and stuck to his ribs.

Nothing like the cheese sandwich Zane had made for his supper.

His mind started to go down the bad path again, but he reeled it in and concentrated on the flickering light in the diner. Was that a flashlight?

Candlelight? Or maybe a fire? At that thought, he drove into the alley and parked behind the diner. He wasted no time getting out and heading to the back door. He shoved it open so hard that it ricocheted off the wall. He went to flip on the lights, but a distressed feminine shriek had him charging for the kitchen, where he found a woman flapping at the flames of a small fire with a dishtowel.

He wasted no time scooping the woman up in his arms, which wasn't that difficult. She was a tiny little thing. Although in her agitated state, she was a little difficult to hang on to.

"Put me down!" She wiggled and squirmed like a worm on a hook.

"It's alright, ma'am. I got you. You're safe now."

"I'm not worried about my safety, you knucklehead. I'm worried about the book!"

Knucklehead? Obviously, the woman wasn't a resident of Bliss. No one in town would ever call him a knucklehead. It was also obvious that the fire had made her a little delirious if she was worried about a book.

He tightened his hold and stepped out into the alleyway. "Don't be worrying yourself about a little ol' book. I'll buy you a new one. Let's just get you out of harm's way so I can call the fire department."

"I don't want a new one. I want that one!" She clipped him hard enough on the chin with her fist to knock his head back and his cowboy hat off. And Zane hated his hat touching the ground. He loosened his hold to pick it up, and she squirmed out of his arms and raced back into the diner. He caught up with her before she reached the door. He wasn't the type of cowboy to manhandle a female, but sometimes you had to take the bull by the horns. Especially if it was for its own good.

"Okay, that's about enough." He wrapped an arm around her waist and lifted her off her feet. "You can't go back in there. I don't care about your silly book."

"It's not a silly book." She kicked him in the shin, and he saw stars.

"Sonofa . . ." He bit back the cuss word as he hauled her over to his truck. But once there, he wasn't sure what to do with her. If he let her go, he had little doubt that she would head back into the diner. And if she continued to kick like a mule, there was a good chance he wouldn't be fathering any children. So he did the only thing he could think of: He pinned her against his truck. He held her arms down so she couldn't hit and straddled her legs and clamped them tightly between his.

That seemed to shock her into silence. Of course, it shocked him into silence as well. It had been a while since he'd gotten this close to a woman, and he'd forgotten how nice it felt. She really was a little bit of a thing. The top of her head barely reached the second snap on his western shirt. Although her hair added another couple of inches and brushed the underside of his chin. He'd expected the short spiky hair to be prickly, but it was as soft as the feathers of a baby chick. And her hair wasn't the only thing that was soft. Two full breasts pillowed against his ribcage, and her lower body conformed to his better than his Sealy Posturepedic.

Desire settled hot and heavy in his loins.

He wasn't surprised. He hadn't had sex in months. It was perfectly normal to feel a little randy after such a dry-spell. And maybe that was Ferdinand's problem too. Maybe they'd been offering him too many heifers. Maybe he needed to be cut off from the herd for a few weeks so he would appreciate the selection he had.

Ignoring his reaction to her tempting body, Zane held her tight while he fished his cellphone out of his back pocket. It took a while for Mike Wright to answer. He was the volunteer fire chief and got called a lot when people even smelled a whiff of smoke . . . or when they discovered a skunk in the attic.

"Hey, Mike, this is Zane Arrington." The woman in his arms stiffened up like a poker, and he couldn't help smiling. Obviously, she hadn't known who had come to her rescue. That was his fault. He should've introduced himself before he started manhandling her. He loosened his hold.

"Hey, Zane," Mike said. "What's up, man?"

"We have a little fire at the diner."

"No shit? We'll be right there."

After Mike hung up, Zane placed the phone back in his pocket. "Have you settled down enough that I can let you go without you racing back in to get your book?"

"It's too late," she grumbled. "It's probably burned to a cinder by now. And it's all your fault."

He drew back. "Excuse me? How is it my fault? I wasn't the one who started the fire."

"If you hadn't charged in like an insufferable superhero, I wouldn't have jumped and knocked over the candle I was using to read."

The gall of the woman amazed him. "And exactly why were you reading in the vacant diner in the first place? Last time I checked, breaking and entering is illegal."

She released her breath in an agitated huff. "Which is exactly why I was reading by candle-light. Now do you mind letting me go?"

Zane didn't know why he hesitated. Maybe because it had been so long since he held a woman that he was kind of enjoying it. Still, there was only one woman he should be holding, and it wasn't this woman. He released her and stepped back.

It was dark in the alley, but now that he had the chance to study her, there was something vaguely familiar about her spiky hair and pixie features.

"Do I know you?" Before she could answer, his brain finally clicked in. "Well, I'll be damned. If it isn't little Carly Sue?"

"As soon as the women stepped down from the stagecoach, cowboys swarmed around them like bees to their hive. Most were polite and shy. But there was one tall brute that had Laura Thatcher ducking behind the other women when his intense blue eyes glanced her way."

CHAPTER TWO

❦

CARLY HANOVER WAS NOT HAPPY. She was not happy about losing her job as head chef of an exclusive San Francisco restaurant. She was not happy about needing to impose on her friend until she found another job. And she certainly wasn't happy about being rescued by Zane Arrington.

Again.

The last time had been in the little white chapel. She and her friends Savannah and Emery had been checking out the famous church when a spider had dropped onto her arm from the rafters. If there was one thing that sent Carly into squealing girlie mode, it was spiders. Zane had waltzed right in the door of the chapel and witnessed her being a squealing sissy, which probably explained why she didn't like the man.

She hated showing any sign of weakness, especially to a man who thought so highly of himself.
A man who looked like he'd grown taller since
she'd last seen him . . . and even more handsome.
With his thick, wheat-colored hair, intense blue
eyes, and big muscled body, he looked like Thor in
western wear. Like the arrogant god, he was more
than a little annoying.

"Don't tell me you don't remember me, Carly
Sue." One side of his mouth tipped up, and with it,
a dimple appeared in his cheek. "I'm the one who
rescued you from that tiny ol' spider."

"It wasn't a tiny ol' spider. That thing was huge."

"Uh-huh." The slow way he said it wasn't an
agreement at all.

She rolled her eyes. "And my middle name isn't
Sue."

"But I thought that's what your friend Savannah
calls you."

"It is, but just to annoy me. Something that you
seem to excel at as well."

This time, he gave her the full two-dimpled
smile. "Now, you have to admit that Carly Sue does
have a nice ring to it." She glared at him, and he
chuckled. "Fine. So do you want to explain what
you were doing in the diner? Or in Bliss for that
matter? I thought you lived somewhere in California."

She had lived in California. But after having a
fight with yet another restaurant owner, she's been
fired and pretty much blackballed in San Francisco.
She just refused to tell that to this arrogant man
who already thought she was a loser.

"I'm on my way to Atlanta to help Savannah with her wedding, and I wanted to stop and see Emery. Unfortunately, I had a little car trouble along the way and didn't get in until late. Since I didn't want to wake Emery and Cole, and the Bliss Motor Lodge office was closed—"

He cut her off. "You broke into the diner to sleep?"

"I didn't break in," she snapped. "The door wasn't locked. And I didn't plan on sleeping in the diner so much as . . . cooking." She understood his confused look. Sneaking into a diner in the middle of the night to cook was a weird thing to do. There was no way to explain to a person who didn't love cooking how soothing it could be. Now that she was jobless and homeless, Carly needed soothing in a bad way. Luckily, she didn't have time to explain before a siren sounded off in the distance and quickly grew louder.

"That'll be Mike and the volunteers," he said. "I probably should go and see if they need some help." He shot her a stern look. "You'll stay right here?"

"Of course."

He studied her for a second longer before he retrieved his hat from the ground and headed around to the front of the building. Carly watched his Wrangler-clad butt until it disappeared around the corner, then she headed straight for the back door of the diner.

Since there was no longer any need for stealth, she turned on the light in the kitchen and hurried over to the stainless steel prep counter. She thought she'd find a pile of ashes or singed pages, but all she found on the counter was the tipped-over candle and a few burned pieces of the manila envelope. There were no burned pages. And no navy backpack with green stitching.

She had found the backpack on the prep counter as soon as she'd lit the first candle. When she'd pulled the aged paper out of the envelope she'd found inside, she knew immediately what she held in her hands. The funky t's and p's in the typed text were identical to the ones she'd seen in the chapter Emery had showed her not more than a month earlier. But it hadn't been chapter one. It was chapter six. The chapter proved that Lucy Arrington had written the final book in the series before she died. A final book that would be worth millions. Of course, if Carly couldn't find the chapter, she couldn't prove anything. Or make a dime.

She looked under the counter and on the floor, but all she found was the dish towel she'd swatted the fire with and few more pieces of burned envelope. She wanted to blame Zane for the missing pages and the backpack, but he'd been with her the entire time. Someone else must've taken them. But who? And how had they slipped past her and Zane?

While she was trying to figure it out, the front door opened and a firefighter rushed in, holding a hose that was aimed directly at the opening to the kitchen. She ducked before the full force of the spray could hit her, but that didn't stop the overspray from raining down on her like a monsoon. She grabbed her purse from under the counter, then crawled on her hands and knees to the back door. A back door that was being held open by an overbearing rancher.

"I thought you promised you wouldn't go back inside," he said. As she got to her feet, his gaze lowered and his mouth went slack. Since her t-shirt was white and soaking wet, she figured he was getting an eyeful. But she was too concerned about the missing backpack and Tender Heart chapter to care.

"I didn't promise anything," she said as she pushed past him in the sloshy squish of wet converse sneakers. She would've headed to her car if he hadn't slipped her purse off her shoulder. "Hey!" She went to grab it, but he held it over his head like he was playing Keep Away from an annoying little sister. She flatly refused to join in the game. She placed her hands on her hips. "Give it back."

He shook his head. "Since the motor lodge is closed, and I agree with you about not waking up Emery and Cole, I figure you'll have to stay at the ranch tonight."

"Thanks, but no thanks. I'll just sleep in my car." She held out her hand, but he didn't give her the purse.

"My mama would tan my hide if I let a little lady sleep in a car when I have a perfectly good guest room."

"I promise not to tell your mama."

"Still can't do it." He hooked her purse over his shoulder and headed for his truck.

She hurried after him, sloshing the entire way. "Give me back my purse, you knucklehead. And would you stop with the *little* business. I am not that little."

"You aren't that big." He took her elbow and

steered her around to the passenger side of the truck. He opened the door and waited for her to climb in. When she crossed her arms and refused, he released an exasperated sigh. "Why are you being so stubborn about this? Do you really want to sleep in a car when you could go to my ranch, have a nice hot shower, and sleep in a comfortable bed?"

It was the nice hot shower that did it. After driving the entire day, not to mention getting doused with a fire hose, she couldn't resist the idea of a hot, steamy shower. Even to spite an arrogant, controlling jerk.

"Fine. I'll stay the night at your house." She held out a hand. "But I can drive myself."

"You'll have to forgive me if I don't believe you." He left her standing there and walked to the driver's side of the truck . . . with her purse.

She released a huff and climbed in at the same time as he was. "Did you realize you're the most controlling man I've ever met?"

He chuckled as he started the engine. "Then you must not know a lot of men because everyone in Bliss knows that I'm as easygoing as they come." Before she could argue the point, he turned up the radio and blasted her out with a country song about a woman who put the "her in hurt"—whatever that meant.

He stopped by her car and got her suitcase out of the trunk without once asking if it was all she needed. It did happen to be all she needed, but he still should've asked. The firefighters were coming out of the diner when they drove past, patting each other on the backs as if they'd just prevented a catastrophe. Zane turned down the radio and stopped to join in on the male ego stroking.

"Fine job, guys. I sure appreciate you getting out here so quickly. The entire diner would be nothing but ashes if you hadn't."

Carly rolled her eyes as the guy who had blasted her with the water beamed with pride. "No, problem. Just doing our duty. What happened?"

She thought for sure that Zane would throw her under the bus, but he didn't. "I'm not sure. I was just driving by when I saw the flames. Probably some kids messing around."

"No doubt, but it's sure a good thing you caught it, Zane. A few more seconds and the entire block could've gone up in flames." The firefighter's eyes narrowed beneath the brim of the cowboy hat he wore under his firemen's helmet. "What are you doing in town so late?"

It was a good question, and Carly became even more curious when Zane didn't answer truthfully. "I'm just picking up a friend of Emery's."

The firefighter glanced in the window at her and looked completely baffled by her drenched state. "What happened to her?"

She couldn't believe the man's gall. "What happened to me is that you—"

Zane cut her off. "She got caught in a freak Texas rainstorm."

The firefighter didn't even question it. "I've been caught in those once or twice myself." He slapped the roof of the truck. "We'll finish up here, Zane."

"Thanks, and it might be a good idea to lock up the diner when you leave." He shot a glance at Carly. "We don't want any little tykes starting another fire."

She paid no attention to the dig. Her mind was focused on the diner being locked. Up until now, the back door had never been locked, which was how Carly was able to treat the kitchen like her own when she was in town. If the firefighters locked the back door, she would have to break and enter for real if she wanted to get back in. And she wanted to get back in. Maybe the chapter was still there. Maybe she'd just knocked the pages behind something in her frenzy to put out the fire.

"Here," Zane reached into the back seat and pulled out a towel and tossed it to her as he pulled away from the diner. It was tattered and a little dirty, but beggars can't be choosers. She used it to dry her hair.

He took off his hat and tossed it onto the dash, then pulled his phone out of his shirt pocket and made a call. While he waited for someone to pick up, she couldn't help but study his profile in the light from the dashboard. It was pretty perfect. His nose was straight but not too narrow. His cheekbones high and chiseled. His jaw square and dusted with a day's growth of golden beard. And his full lips looked good enough to eat. It was too bad that he was so controlling . . . and already taken.

"Are you calling Rachel to tell her I'm coming?" she asked.

The phone slipped from his fingers and clattered between the console and his seat. He stared down into the dark hole for only a second before he returned his attention to the road. "She won't mind. She's in Austin."

"She must travel there a lot. Wasn't that why she

couldn't be at Emery and Cole's wedding? She was in Austin?"

His jaw tightened. "Yeah, she travels there a lot. And speaking of traveling, are you moving? Or do you just like to drive around with lamps in your trunk and boxes in your back seat?"

It didn't surprise her that he'd noticed the lamp and boxes. It seemed that very little got past Zane Arrington. "As a matter of fact, I am moving from San Francisco."

"Did you get a new job? You're some kind of a cook, aren't you?"

"Executive chef."

"What's the difference?"

It wasn't like she hadn't heard the question before. Few people understood the difference between a cook and a chef. Still, she couldn't help being annoyed. Probably because Zane viewed her as a "little lady" who couldn't kill her own spiders or take care of a fire.

"Actually, there's quite a big difference," she said tightly. "Like a culinary degree, a year work-ing under a tyrant of a chef in Paris, another year working under a temperamental chef in New York City, three more years busting my butt as a sous chef, and the last two years working as an executive chef for five-star restaurants and putting up with arrogant owners' every whim. I'm an executive chef. Not a cook."

He glanced over at her and cocked an eyebrow. "Uh-huh."

At that moment, she had never wanted to pop someone in the mouth as much as she wanted to pop Zane. Luckily, she was distracted when they passed under the scrolled iron gate of his ranch.

Carly had never been to the Earhart Ranch, but she knew the story behind it. At one time, it had been part of the larger Arrington Ranch. But after Zane's father got into an argument with his two brothers, the ranch was divided three ways. The Arrington Ranch was owned by Zane's cousin and Emery's husband, Cole. The Tender Heart Ranch was owned by Zane's other cousin, Raff. And the Earhart Ranch was owned by Zane's family. According to Emery, Zane's ranch was the most prosperous. It wasn't difficult to figure out that was true when they pulled up to the sprawling ranch-style house.

It had a deep wraparound porch that invited people to come sit and sip a cool drink, while the multitude of windows beckoned with a warm coziness. It was the kind of house you lived in forever. Not that Carly knew about those houses. Being an Army brat, she had lived in base housing all over the world. But she had dreamed about living in a forever house. A dream that was fueled by the Tender Heart series.

Once he'd parked inside the five-car garage, Zane got out and came around to open her door. She ignored his hand and climbed down by herself. Unfortunately, her wet sneakers slipped on the running board and she fell right into his arms. He easily caught her and set her on her feet.

"You really do need a keeper, Carly Sue."

She started to correct him, but then let it go. The more she disliked the name, the more he would probably use it. He grabbed her suitcase from the bed of the truck, and she followed him into the house. She expected rustic cowboy décor in masculine tones. She did not expect modern contemporary in bright feminine colors.

She was about to tease him about the pink flowered chair with the lime-green pillow when his sister Becky came striding into the room, looking like she'd won the lottery.

"Why didn't you tell me that you and Cruella are getting a divorce?" She waved the stack of paper in her hands. "We're free! We're free!"

"It didn't take much looking to find what he wanted. Duke ignored the petite women who were trying to catch his attention and headed straight for the sturdy-looking woman hiding in the back of the pack."

CHAPTER THREE

(

USUALLY BY NINE O'CLOCK IN the morning, Zane had gotten a good three hours of work done on the ranch. He was normally up by five and out the door by five-thirty. But since he hadn't gotten much sleep the night before, he'd slept in until after seven. Now he was twiddling his thumbs while he waited for his houseguest to make an appearance. He could've let one of the ranch hands take her back to town, but after the scene his sister had made the night before, he needed to do some damage control.

His jaw tightened. What had Becky been thinking sneaking into his office and snooping through his desk? She might own a portion of the ranch, but the house was his. He'd bought it from Mama and Daddy after he was married and completely renovated it with his money—or Rachel had renovated it. Still, his sister was damn lucky he let her live there in the first place.

"Good morning."

He glanced over to the doorway of the kitchen to see Carly standing there with bed-mussed hair and bloodshot eyes. Obviously, she'd gotten as much sleep last night as he had. She yawned and stretched her arms over her head, causing the skimpy tank top she wore to hike up and reveal a whole lot of naked stomach above the sagging Sponge Bob boxers. Just below her belly button was a tattoo. He wasn't surprised. She seemed to like inking her body. He'd seen a red broken-heart tattoo on the inside swell of her left breast when he'd caught her jumping around swatting at a spider without her shirt. Some men might find tattoos sexy. Zane had never cared for them. Especially if they were silly sayings.

"Cooking is love made edible?"

She lowered her arms and looked down at her stomach. "It seemed poetic after a few shots of tequila." She glanced around. "Coffee?"

"I can make you instant, but I've yet to figure out the fancy coffeemaker."

She lifted an eyebrow. "You can't make coffee in your own coffeemaker?"

"Rach—" He cut off the word. "No, I can't." He got up from the uncomfortable spaceship-looking barstool he'd been sitting on and walked to the cupboard to get the instant coffee. But before he could pull the jar off the shelf, Carly reached around him and grabbed the bag of coffee beans.

"I never put instant anything in my body." She did a quick appraisal of the kitchen before heading for the coffeemaker.

Zane didn't have time to wait around for her to make coffee. He needed to figure out how much she'd gotten from Becky's outburst before he'd shut his sister up. But before he could subtly broach the subject of last night, the coffee grinder started to run and the scent of freshly ground coffee filled the air. It had been so long since he'd had a good cup he decided conversation could wait.

While the coffee brewed, Carly walked to the refrigerator and opened it. She seemed disappointed by what she found, and he couldn't very well blame her. He had asked Becky to stop by the grocery store on her way back from town, but his sister had ignored that request as well as the one about checking in. He had given her an hour-long lecture last night after showing Carly to the guestroom, but he doubted it had done any good. Becky had always been as wild as a March hare. He had two choices. He could put up with his sister's shenanigans or he could tattle to Mama and Daddy and get them to take her off his hands. Since he'd never been a tattler, he was pretty well stuck with shenanigans.

Carly grabbed the almost empty gallon of milk, the last two slices of cheese Zane had been saving for dinner, the carton of eggs, and the butter, then bumped the fridge door closed with her hip.

From that point on, she moved in a blur of efficiency. Butter was melted in a skillet, eggs were cracked, whipped, cooked, and cheese applied, coffee was poured, and before Zane could say Jack Robinson, she was sitting at his breakfast counter with a good-looking cheese omelet and a steaming cup of coffee with the last of his milk in it.

Not once had she offered him anything.

More than a little irritated, he watched as she took a big bite of fluffy omelet and chewed. "Mmm, not bad if I do say so myself." She reached for her coffee and took a sip. "So your wife left you."

Damn. The damage he needed to control just got a lot worse.

Trying to keep his emotions from showing, he walked over and took his favorite John Wayne mug down from the cupboard and poured himself a cup of coffee. When he turned, Carly was studying him. While everything else on her body was petite, her brown eyes were big and expressive. He could read the know-it-all satisfaction in them as clearly as he could read the mile-long grocery list on the refrigerator.

He took a sip of coffee, but couldn't enjoy the rich, strong flavor because he was too focused on keeping his voice calm and even. "Look, I'm sorry you had to be right in the middle of our family . . . situation last night. My little sister can be overly dramatic at times and assumes things without getting all the details."

Carly cocked her head like his dog Shep when he was completely baffled by something. "So your wife didn't leave you?"

He pinned on a smile. "What woman in her right mind would leave one of the best cattle ranches in Texas?"

She stared at him for a long moment, and then a sparkle of amusement entered her eyes. "Maybe a vegetarian?"

Zane didn't find that funny. "I would never

marry a vegetarian. Now if you hurry up and finish eating and get dressed, I'll take you to get your car. I have work to do, and I'm sure Emery will be excited to see you."

She cradled her coffee mug in both hands. "She doesn't know I'm coming. I thought I'd surprise her."

"You think that's wise? I hate to point this out, but Cole and Emery are technically still on their honeymoon. A surprise visitor might not be big on their wish list—especially after Cole's sister just left for that physical therapy center in Dallas and gave them the house to themselves."

A frown marred her forehead as she pursed her lips. "I don't plan on staying long. I just stopped for a couple days on my way to Atlanta."

That worked out real well for Zane. The less time she was here, the less time she'd have to gossip. "I bet you're in a hurry to see Savannah."

"I wouldn't say that. I can only take her southern beauty-pageant charm in small doses. And I can't take her fiancé at all. He's a real jerk." She set down her cup and took a big bite of omelet. His stomach grumbled. She must've heard it because she stopped and looked at him. "Did you eat breakfast?"

He took another sip of coffee. "I'm not hungry." It was an out-and-out lie. His stomach was touching his backbone.

"You should eat something. Breakfast is the most important meal of the day." She pointed her fork at him. "So did your wife leave you for another guy? Or was it because you're so overbearing?" The sip of coffee Zane had just taken went down wrong, and he fought to keep from choking as she continued. "I'd bet on your overbearing personality if infidelity wasn't one of the main reasons people leave a relationship. The grass always looks greener on the other side of the fence—or in this case, the cowboy always looks hotter on the other side of the corral. Which must make you feel pretty emasculated."

The burn of strong coffee in his windpipe had tears filling his eyes. Tears Carly completely misunderstood.

She quickly got up and patted him on the back. "That's it. Just let it all out. I won't tell a soul that I saw big, bad rancher Zane Arrington crying."

He coughed until he'd cleared his throat, then straightened. "I don't cry."

Carly rolled her eyes. "That's a ridiculous statement. Of course, you cry. Everyone cries. And it's okay to be upset because your wife cheated on you and you're getting a divorce. That's the second most devastating event after death."

The words *cheat and divorce* felt like a bull had gored him in the gut. It took a second for Zane to collect himself enough that he could speak in a casual tone. "My wife did not cheat on me and I'm not getting a divorce. She's just staying a little longer in Austin, is all." He took his mug to the sink and poured out the coffee he no longer wanted. "Now if you'll hurry up, I'll take you back to your car so I can get to work." When he turned, she was still standing there watching him with those big expressive eyes. This time he saw disbelief.

"I get that this must be a major hit to your super-sized ego. But you can't keep something like this a secret forever. Sooner or later, someone is going to let the cat out of the bag. And you would look far less pathetic if you were the one to tell people that your wife left you."

That was it. Zane had reached the end of his patience. He had tried his best to be hospitable to the woman. Hell, he had rescued her twice. But enough was enough. In two long strides, he was standing boot toe to bare toe with her.

"I'm not, nor will I ever be, pathetic. And do you know why? Because this entire thing is just a temporary situation—just a simple misunder-standing that I have every intention of fixing. So I don't need you feeling sorry for me or twisting the truth." He leaned closer so their noses almost touched. "Do you understand?"

"Perfectly." She gave him a smug smile, then sashayed out of the kitchen with a twitch of her saggy-boxer-clad hips.

When she was gone, Zane thumped the counter with his fist. This was exactly why he didn't want people knowing about Rachel leaving. He didn't want people feeling sorry for him because he couldn't keep his wife and speculating on why she'd left. Especially an annoying little pixie pyro who was afraid of spiders.

He went to grab his cowboy hat off the breakfast counter and noticed the half-eaten omelet she'd left on the plate. He glanced back at the doorway before he picked up her fork and finished it off in three bites. Maybe she was annoying, but she was a damned good cook.

"I guess you're still mad at me?"

He glanced up to see his sister. She was dressed

in her usual t-shirt, jeans, and cowboy boots. And if the mud on her jeans and boots was any indication, she'd been busier than he had that morning.

"Did you get the cattle moved to the north pasture?" he asked.

She nodded. "It took longer than normal. We had a calf get stuck in Whispering Falls Creek."

"Did you get him out?"

"Yep, but Jess ended up throwing his back out in the process. I just came from taking him to see Doc Jenkins."

"Is he okay?"

She pulled off her ball cap and wiped the sweat from her brow with her arm. "Doc said he just pulled a muscle, but he doesn't want Jess doing any heavy lifting for a good three weeks."

That was just great. As if Zane didn't have enough to worry about, now he was going to be one man short during summer haying season. And not just any man, but his foreman. A man he trusted to get the job done without having to be babysat. But there was nothing to be done about it now.

"Did you pay the doc and get Jess home okay?"

"Of course." She looked at the coffeemaker. "Did you make coffee? I thought you didn't know how to work that machine."

"I don't. Carly made it."

Becky glanced at the doorway. "She's still here?"

"Would you lower your voice? I swear you have no manners at all."

"Just because I don't pussyfoot around things like you do doesn't mean I don't have manners." She walked over and grabbed a thermal travel mug out of the cupboard, then poured herself some coffee.

"I just believe in saying what I think and telling it like it is. And I can't help it if I'm joyously happy that Cruella Deville is gone."

"Becky," he warned.

She turned around and held up a hand. "Fine. After the lecture you gave me last night, I get that your personal life is none of my business. But you're my brother. I love you and only want what's best for you."

This was why Zane couldn't stay mad at his sister. He knew that she loved him and only wanted the best for him. But what she couldn't seem to get through her thick skull was that Rachel was the best for him. They were perfectly matched. They had grown up on neighboring ranches and both belonged to the 4-H club. They'd attended school together. She'd been a cheerleader and he'd been a football player. They'd been voted homecoming king and queen. People had expected them to get married. And Zane didn't like disappointing people. This was just a bump in the road. And life was filled with bumps. He just needed to navigate around this one and get his life back on track.

He reached out and gave Becky an awkward thump on the arm. "I love you too, Beck, but I'm the one who gets to choose what's best for me. Not you."

She looked at him with eyes the same Arrington blue as his. "Okay, but if Cruella comes back, I'm moving into the little white chapel."

"I'd get rid of the spiders first."

At the words, they both turned to the doorway. Carly had re-spiked her hair and was dressed in the same cut-off jeans she'd been wearing the first time Zane had met her. Although this time she had on a top.

"Good mornin'." Becky held up her cup. "Thanks for the coffee."

"You're welcome. I could teach you how to work the coffee machine if you'd like."

"I know how to use it. It's my brother who's kitchen-appliance ignorant."

Both women looked at him as if he should have a reply to that. He didn't. He knew how to ride, rope, and manage a ranch, and as far as he was concerned, that was more than enough.

"You ready to go?" he said to Carly.

She saluted him. "Yes, sir."

Becky laughed and grabbed her cap. "I'll go let the hay crew know about Jess." She looked at Carly. "I'm sure I'll see you around. I have my new horse on stud loan to Cole, and I like to check on him every now and again—usually after supper so I can beg for leftovers."

"So that's where you were last night." Zane was relieved that his sister had been with Cole and Emery and not out raising hell.

Becky tugged her cap back on, then pulled her long braid through the back. "Dirk was there, and we got to talking and lost track of the time."

Zane was no longer relieved. "You need to stay away from Dirk. He'd a no-account drifter."

"He's not a no-account drifter. He just doesn't want to be tied down. He's really an intelligent, nice guy."

"And smoking hot," Carly added.

Becky exchanged looks with Carly, and there was some kind of female connection that Zane did not care for. His sister grinned. "And that too." She waved. "Catch you later, big brother."

After she left, Zane grabbed his cowboy hat and herded Carly toward the door that lead to the garage. "Don't egg her on. She's wild enough."

"You should be wild in your twenties—which means I only have a year left to sow my oats." She paused at the door he held open for her. "And speaking of eggs . . ." She reached up and brushed a finger over his bottom lip. For a moment, he lost his breath as heat speared through him. She smiled as if she hadn't just started another fire. "You have a little egg on your face, Rancher Zane."

"She'd thought life in Texas would be much easier than her life in Boston. But when the brute hoisted her over his shoulder like a sack of potatoes and said 'I'll take this one,' Laura had to wonder if she'd jumped from the frying pan into the fire."

CHAPTER FOUR

"OKAY, START FROM THE BEGINNING." Emery handed Carly a large glass of iced tea. "Why did you get fired from Sauce?"

Carly took a sip of tea, then fished an ice cube out of her glass and rubbed it over her forehead. "Holy crap, it's hot. If it's like this in early June, it's going to be hotter than hell in July and August."

Emery lifted her hair off her neck and fanned her face. "Cole says it's the hottest summer they've had in years. And don't try to change the subject. What happened to get you fired?"

Carly blew out her breath and sat back in the rocker. "It was totally bogus. The owner should've sided with me instead of that jackass who said his pork loin wasn't done enough. It was done perfectly with just a touch of pink in the center. But when it came back to the kitchen, I didn't argue. I made sure the next plate had no pink." She glanced at Emery. "And do you know what the guy said? He said it was too dry. Of course it was too dry. It was well-done like he wanted it!"

Emery sent her a pointed look. "What did you do?"

She shrugged. "What any good chef would do. I sent him a selection of pork to choose from."

"A selection of pork? Are we talking nasty pig parts?"

Damn. Maybe Emery knew her too well.

Carly set down her tea and tried to justify her actions. "I was just trying to please the customer. I didn't think he'd actually toss his cookies when he saw the pig's foot. In some places, those are considered delicacies. Although they are usually cooked before being served."

Emery sighed. "Well, that explains why you got fired and blackballed from every restaurant in San Francisco."

Talking about it made Carly depressed all over again. She slumped in the chair. "Not all restaurants. McDonald's was willing to give me a chance. But I couldn't afford my apartment on their starting salary."

"So what are your plans?"

"I don't know. I've tried applying for executive chef jobs in other cities, but I've been turned down flat. The last restaurant owner I spoke with said he couldn't risk his business on a temperamental chef with a bad attitude. I'm not temperamental. And I don't have a bad attitude." She glanced at Emery. "Do I?"

It wasn't reassuring when Emery looked away

to pick an imaginary piece of lint off her shorts. "Umm . . . well, I wouldn't call you temperamental. I'd call you sensitive. And as for a bad attitude," she glanced at Carly and smiled weakly. "You just have strong opinions and you don't mind sharing them. I'm sure you'll find the right restaurant."

"I wish I could afford to start my own. After spending my entire childhood moving from state to state and country to country, all I ever wanted was to put down roots in one place. Now here I am a nomad again."

"You are not a nomad. You're just in a state of transition." Emery reached over and gave her hand a reassuring squeeze. "And you can stay here as long as you want."

"I'm not going to crash your honeymoon," Carly said. "I plan to stay at the motor lodge tonight and head to Atlanta tomorrow morning." She didn't look forward to dealing with Savannah in full-blown Bridezilla mode. Of course, maybe she could throw a few wrenches into the wedding plans. As far as Carly was concerned, Savannah's fiancé, Miles, was a self-centered donkey's butt and her friend would be better off without him.

Unfortunately, Emery did know her too well.

"I don't think you going to Atlanta this close to the wedding is a good idea," she said. "Besides, I want you to stay here with me. With Cole working such long hours at the garage to help pay for Gracie's therapy bills and the new horse stables, I'm going stir-crazy from having too much time on my hands."

"I thought you were doing freelance editing and working on the non-fiction book of the mail-order brides' diaries?"

"I am. But going from being a busy New York editor, working twelve-hour days on multiple projects, to freelancing and working part-time is a big adjustment. I don't miss the stress, but I miss working with other people. The only company I get is when Cole comes home for lunch or Dirk stops by for dinner."

"Cole lets you invite Dirk to dinner?" Like Zane, Cole didn't seem to like Dirk. Carly figured it had to do with the Arrington cousins not wanting another arrogant rooster strutting around in their barnyards. Carly didn't find Dirk arrogant so much as amusing. He was like the ornery little brother she never had.

"Actually, I think Dirk has grown on Cole," Emery said. "They've been working on the plans for the new horse stables, and Dirk has been a big help. Plus, he convinced Gracie to go to the rehab center."

Gracie was Cole's little sister. She had gotten into a riding accident months earlier and damaged her spine. She'd been in a wheelchair ever since, but just recently had been accepted at a rehabilitation center in Dallas.

"How is she doing?" Carly asked.

"When she calls, she doesn't talk much about how her therapy is going. I think she doesn't want to get anyone's hopes up that she'll walk again. But Cole talked to one of her therapists, and she said Gracie's making amazing progress."

"That's good to hear. I like Gracie. In fact, I like all the Arringtons, except for Zane. I swear I've never met such a control freak in my life. No wonder his—" Carly hesitated. She usually confided in Emery about everything, but that was before Emery had gotten married. Once people got married, you were no longer sharing things just with them. You were also sharing things with their spouses. And if Cole found out about Zane's wife leaving it wasn't going to be from her. While she thought it was foolish to think he could keep it a secret, it was still his secret to keep.

"No wonder his what?" Emery asked.

She took a sip of her now lukewarm tea. "No wonder his sister is so rebellious. I'd rebel too if I had to live with that man ordering me around."

Emery glanced over at her and grinned. "She reminds me of someone else I know. Becky would have no qualms about breaking into a diner and starting a fire."

Carly's eyes widened. "You already heard about the fire?"

"News travels fast in a small town. Ms. Marble called me this morning before you got here. Although she said some kids had broken in and started the fire. When you showed up, it didn't take me long to put two and two together. I know how fond you are of the diner. Was it a grease fire?"

Carly stopped rocking. "No, it wasn't a grease fire." She glanced around before she leaned closer. "It was a chapter of the final book in the Tender Heart series."

Emery's shocked look was understandable. Not only was she a book editor, she was also an avid Tender Heart fan. The series was what had brought her to Bliss in the first place. She'd received a letter from Cole's sister saying she had found the last unpublished book in the series. As it turned out, Gracie had discovered only one chapter.

Now Carly believed she'd found another.

"I know," she said. "I couldn't believe it either when I pulled it out of the backpack I found at the diner."

Emery almost jumped out of her chair with excitement. "Do you have it with you?"

Carly hated to disappoint her friend, but there was no help for it. "Unfortunately, no. I was in the process of reading it when a noise startled me and made me knock over the candle—"

Emery eyes widened. "That was the fire? You burned up the chapter?"

Carly held up a hand. "It was the envelope the chapter came in that caught fire. That was when Zane came charging in like Captain Cowboy America and carried me out."

"Zane was there?"

"The man is everywhere." Carly scowled. "He was the one who called the fire department. By the time I got back into the diner, the fire was out and all that was left were a few pieces of the burnt envelope. The backpack was gone and there were no signs of burnt pages."

Emery leaned closer. "Are you sure the chapter was written by Lucy?"

"I'm not an expert on Lucy's writing like you are, but it certainly seemed like her voice. And the paper looked identical to the paper of the first chapter that Gracie found. Plus the lowercase t's and p's were jiggy. Although it wasn't the second chapter that I found. It was the sixth. And there was a page missing."

A strange look came over Emery's face. "A page missing? Did you notice the number?"

"Ninety-three?"

Like she was sleepwalking, Emery got up and walked inside. When she returned, she had one piece of aged paper in her hand. She held it out, and Carly felt a weird tingle run down her spine as she took it. The tingle grew when she read the number on the bottom.

"Holy shit." She looked up at Emery. "Where did you get this?"

"I found it on my wedding day in the Arrington cemetery. Cole and I searched everywhere for the rest of the chapter but couldn't find it."

Carly took a moment to read the page. The story fit perfectly with the chapter she'd found in the diner. She looked at Emery. "Well, you found it now. Or at least, we know it exists. I wonder why the person who found it in the cemetery didn't tell anyone."

"Probably because they want to see if they can find more. Since Gracie found the first chapter, the entire town has been looking for the rest of the book. Everyone wants to be the one who finds the other chapters and makes millions. And maybe that's why they were in the diner. They were looking for another chapter."

"But why take the chapter they found in the cemetery with them?"

"Maybe they wanted to use it to authenticate any other chapters that they found. Did it look like someone had been searching?"

"No. Everything looked tidy when I got there. Of course, I didn't have time to look around much.

And after the fire, the fire department locked the diner." Thanks to Zane butting his nose in where it didn't belong.

Emery carefully took the page from Carly. "Then we'll have to break in."

Carly snorted. "This coming from a woman who criticized me for going in an unlocked door."

"That was when all you were doing was using their oven. Now we're looking for the biggest literary find of the century." She held up the page. "Do you know what this means? It means that the rest of the book is out there somewhere. All we have to do is find it."

As much as Carly would love to hunt for the rest of the Tender Heart book, she needed to hunt for a job. And she wasn't going to find that here in Bliss. "I'm sorry, Em. But I can't stay—"

The sound of crunching gravel had her looking at the road that led to the ranch. At the sight of Cole's truck, Emery quickly took the page and hurried into the house. When she came back out, she no longer had it with her.

"Cole has spent most of his life dealing with rabid fans of the series," she said. "And he married the most rabid fan of all. I think he's pretty sick of hearing about the long-lost last novel. So it might be best if we keep it to ourselves."

"Mum's the word," Carly said as Cole hopped out of his truck.

Even though his hair was coal black instead of wheat blond, there was a striking resemblance between Zane and Cole. They had the same deep-blue eyes and strong, angular features. While their bodies were different—Cole's lean and rangy and

Zane's big and muscular—they had the same arrogant stride.

Cole merely tipped his straw cowboy hat at Carly before he swept his wife into his arms and kissed her. The long kiss made Carly realize that Zane was right. She had no business imposing on newlyweds.

She got to her feet. "Well, I'm going to let you two lovebirds get on with your afternoon delight. I'm going to go into town and check into the motor lodge."

Emery drew back from the kiss. "Absolutely not. Tell her, Cole. Tell her that she needs to stay with us."

Cole flashed a smile at Carly. It was lacking dimples. "You're more than welcome to stay. I think my wife is getting a little bored here at the old homestead." He looked back at Emery. "Although I've been working hard to keep her busy."

Emery swatted at him. "Would you stop already? You're making me blush."

"I like making you blush." He hooked an arm around her waist. "But that's not why I came home. I heard something today that has me a little worried." His features turned serious. "It seems that Rachel left Zane."

"It was confusing. Miss Laura didn't seem very excited to be picked by the best damn cowboy in Texas."

CHAPTER FIVE

ℰ

ZANE LEANED ON THE SPLIT rail fence and watched as his half-a-million-dollar bull stood amid a group of fertile heifers and did nothing more than nibble on the grass and flick his tail at flies. It was pathetic. Almost as pathetic as a man who couldn't keep his wife. He tried to push the thought from his mind, but he was too damned tired from working in the hayfields all day to fight back thoughts of Rachel.

It had been over two months since she'd left him. At first he'd thought it was just one of her routine trips to Austin. But then he'd received the divorce papers by special courier.

Divorce.

He still couldn't get his mind around it. He knew she'd been unhappy about leaving Austin. They had lived there for years. She and Zane had attended college at the University of Texas and gotten jobs in the city after graduation. When Zane passed the bar exam and was hired at a prestigious law firm, he'd asked Rachel to marry him. They lived in Austin for three more years after their wedding, but he never made any bones about eventually moving back to Bliss and taking over his father's ranch.

He wasn't a big city boy. He hated the noise, heavy traffic, and the skyscrapers that blocked the horizon. As an attorney, he'd sat at his desk in the high-rise building and longed for the wide-open spaces, the feel of a saddle, and the smell of fresh-cut hay.

The Earhart Ranch was his legacy. His ancestors had fought off outlaws and desperados to keep what was theirs so they could pass it down to Zane and his cousins. Just like he'd planned to pass it down to his children. But there would be no children if he couldn't talk Rachel into coming back.

"Damn, that is one handsome bull."

Zane turned to find Dirk Hadley standing at the fence looking at Ferdinand. Dirk had arrived in town six months earlier and started doing odd jobs for the people of Bliss. The women had taken to his bright smile and easygoing manner like ducks to the water. It had made the men more than a little leery—Zane included. While he didn't dislike Dirk as much as his cousin Cole did, he didn't trust the guy either. Especially around his sister, who had agreed with Carly that Dirk was hot.

Hot? More like wet behind the ears. Obviously, Carly was one of those women who liked her men young and inexperienced so she could lead them around on a leash.

"What are you doing out here?" he asked.

Dirk crouched down to scratch Shep. The dog usually didn't take to strangers, but it seemed that dogs liked Dirk as much as women did. The dog rolled onto his back so Dirk could scratch his belly. "I stopped by looking for you, and one of the ranch hands said I'd probably find you out here with your new bull." He nodded at Ferdinand. "I don't blame you. He's sure something to look at. Perfect frame, massive muscle, and an impressive set of balls that are sure to keep the womenfolk happy."

Zane glanced at Ferdinand who appeared to be napping. "Yeah, real happy. So what did you want to see me about?"

Dirk stood and pushed his battered straw hat up on his forehead. "I heard you were short a ranch hand and I thought I'd apply for the job."

If it had been any other man, he would've hired him in a second. But Dirk was a drifter, the type of man who was here today and gone tomorrow. And Zane wasn't going to train someone and then have him disappear. Nor did he want the slick-talking womanizer around his sister. From the sound of things, Becky was already spending too much time with him. Which explained how Dirk had heard about the job.

"Becky shouldn't have mentioned the job to you," he said. "I haven't decided if I'm hiring someone to fill in for Jess. Things worked out just fine without him today."

Dirk gave Zane's dirty jeans and shirt the once over. "Are you sure about that? Hay season's a pretty tough time of year. An extra hand could make your life a whole lot easier. And Becky didn't tell me about the job."

"Then how did you hear about it?"

Dirk shrugged. "You know how small towns are. Rumors spread quickly." He paused. "You should probably know that there's a rumor spreading about your wife leaving you."

It was extremely hard to keep from throwing down his hat and cussing a blue streak. Especially when he knew exactly who he wanted to cuss at. There was only one person who could've let the cat out of the bag to the entire town. Obviously, Carly hadn't wasted any time spreading the news after getting out of his truck. And to think he had gone out of his way to be nice to the woman. Well, he wasn't going to be so nice from now on. In fact, he wasn't going to give her the time of day.

"You shouldn't believe everything you hear," he said.

"I couldn't agree more." Dirk gave him a direct look. "Most folks have me pegged as a drifter, and I'll admit that I don't much care for settling down. But I'm a good worker, and you won't have to train me. I spent one summer working in hayfields where I got experience operating mowers, rakes, and balers. If you need references, all you have to do is call Cole. He seems pretty happy with the work I've done for him."

Zane didn't have time to deal with Dirk. He had other things to worry about. Like how to keep the gossip about Rachel leaving him from getting completely out of hand before he had time to fig-ure out how to fix things.

"Sorry, but I'm not hiring. Now if you'll excuse me, I need to go into town for . . . something." He turned and headed to his truck with Shep on his heels. Unfortunately, Dirk followed as well.

"If you need other references, you can talk to the people of the town—well, except for Mrs. Crawley. She's still pissed about me seducing her daughter Winnie. Which I didn't do, I might add. I didn't even kiss her. And yet Mrs. Crawley still kicked me out of the motor lodge."

Zane stopped at his truck. "I've heard about Winnie. I've also heard that you're a good worker . . . when you show up. And that's why I won't be hiring you. On this ranch, I need dependable people I can count on to show up every day. Not just when they feel like it."

Dirk stared back at him for only a moment before he nodded. "Fair enough. But would it be too much to ask for a ride into town? I hitched out here."

"I thought Cole gave you Gracie's old car for the work you did at his ranch."

"Actually, it was Miss Gracie who made the deal for her car. But I couldn't bring myself to take it."

"Why not? From what I hear, you earned it."

Dirk placed his hands on his hips and studied the ground. "I don't rightly know. Especially when I sure could use a vehicle." He looked up and shrugged. "I guess I just wanted the car to be there waiting for Miss Gracie . . . just in case she needs it."

The only way Zane's cousin would need it was if she was walking. The entire family had high hopes for that. He hadn't thought a drifter would too. Maybe he had pegged Dirk wrong. Maybe he wasn't as irresponsible as he thought.

"Get in," he said.

"Yes, sir." Dirk grinned and hurried around to the other side of the truck.

❦

ONCE THEY GOT INTO TOWN, Zane realized things were much worse than he could've imagined. Every person they passed on the street gave him a sympathetic look and a weak wave as if he were a dying man and this was his last day on earth. Even Dirk noticed and commented.

"I haven't seen so many sad faces since Blake and Miranda split up. You're one popular son of a gun."

"Too popular," Zane grumbled as he pulled into Emmett Daily's gas station. He didn't need gas, but the station was where everyone stopped to gossip. If he could plug the hole here, he might be able to nip the rumors in the bud. He didn't want them getting back to his parents. They were vacationing at their condo in Hawaii, and he hoped to have his life back in order before they got home. As luck would have it, Emmett was playing dominos out in front with Old Man Sims. Both spread news faster than Twitter.

"Hey, Emmett. Hey, Mr. Sims," he said as he climbed out. He was about to whistle for Shep, but the dog had already jumped out of the bed and was following Dirk toward the two old guys.

"Hey, y'all." Dirk pushed up his hat on his forehead and looked down at the dominos on the table. "Looks like you got a good game going. Who's winning?"

"Emmett," Mr. Sims said. "But only because he cheats."

"I don't cheat, old man. I just don't have dementia like you." Emmett glanced at Zane. "So I heard about Rachel running off and leaving you. That can't be easy on a fella."

Before Zane could try to make light of it, Mr. Sims butted in. "Did she leave with that truck driver who delivers those tasty sugar donuts to the grocery? I've never liked the looks of that dude. Anybody with a mustache that trimmed is up to no good."

Emmett snorted. "Just because a man trims his mustache doesn't mean he's some kind of a womanizer."

"Really? Then explain Dax Davenport in the Tender Heart series. That outlaw kept his mustache trimmed all nice and neat and look how dastardly he was."

Zane rolled his eyes. When the conversation turned to the Tender Heart books, it was hard to get a word in edgewise with the townspeople. He loved the series as much as anyone, and his mother had even given him the middle name of one of the Tender Heart heroes. But he didn't have time for book club today.

"Just to make it perfectly clear, Rachel didn't—"

Emmett cut him off. "I don't know if I would call Dax dastardly. True, he liked women and he was a hired gun, but I have a feeling that if Lucy had gotten a chance to finish the series, ol' Dax would've turned out more hero than villain."

"I couldn't agree more." Ms. Marble joined the circle of men. For a woman in her late seventies, she could certainly move quietly. Zane hadn't even heard her walk up behind them. Of course, she'd been a teacher for over forty years, so that probably helped. You had to be stealthy when you were dealing with a bunch of rowdy kids.

"I view Dax like Snape in Harry Potter." She folded up the front brim of the large shade hat she wore, giving her the look of a pirate. A white-haired pirate with sharp blue eyes. "He's a misunderstood hero. But unlike J. K., I'm sure Lucy gave Dax a happily-ever-after."

"I wouldn't be sure about that. Especially since only one chapter has been found." Emmett got up and offered his chair to Ms. Marble, but she declined with a flap of her white-gloved hand.

"The others will turn up."

"Not likely," Mr. Sims said. "I was here when everyone in town was searching for the damn thing. No stone was left unturned."

"On the Arrington land." Ms. Marble opened the tote bag that hung over her shoulder. "But maybe the rest of the book isn't on the Arrington land. Maybe it's right here in town." She pulled out a plastic-wrapped plate.

Ms. Marble was one hell of a baker. Due to her diabetes, she could no longer eat what she made. So she gave her pies, cakes, and cookies away— often to people who were going through hard times. Besides the occasional cookie at a holiday potluck, Zane had never been a recipient of Ms. Marble's baked goods. And while he would give his right arm for one of her apple pies, he took pride in knowing he'd never needed one.

Until now.

She held out the plate to him. "They're extra-dark chocolate brownies with pecan frosting. Chocolate is reported to release endorphins, and

I figure anyone whose wife ran off and left him could use a few happy endorphins. What got into that girl, leaving only weeks before the Fourth of July Chili Cook-off?"

Again, Zane mentally cussed out Carly Hanover. He could've stretched the truth with Emmett and Mr. Sims, but damned if he could lie to Ms. Marble. She'd been his first grade teacher and had given him a ribbon for telling the truth about sticking his gum under the desk. His mama still had that ribbon.

He cleared his throat. "Thank you, Ms. Marble. But Rachel hasn't left me . . . for good. We just had a little disagreement, is all. Nothing that can't be ironed out."

Ms. Marble studied him with her eagle eyes for a long, uncomfortable moment. If she asked him a direct question, there was no way he could lie. Thankfully, before she could, Dirk spoke up.

"I'm sure Rachel will be back in no time. Why, my aunt got mad at my uncle once and drove all the way to Santa Fe and stayed for a solid six months. She came back with a new short hairstyle, an Indian rug, and addiction to green chile. She and my uncle just celebrated their fiftieth wedding anniversary last year with the best green chile enchiladas you've ever tasted." Dirk slapped Zane on the back and smiled his contagious smile at Ms. Marble. "So you see, sometimes a little distance can help a relationship."

Ms. Marble arched a nearly invisible eyebrow at Dirk. He squirmed under the look, but Zane had to hand it to him, he didn't buckle. "You do have a point," Ms. Marble said. "Sometimes a little space is good for a marriage."

"I wish you'd tell that to Joanna, Maybelline," Emmett said. "I would love a little space to go fishing."

"Since Jojo is my best friend, I know all about how much space you take for fishing, Emmett. And I don't think you need any more." She hooked her tote bag over her bony shoulder. "Now, if you gentlemen will excuse me, I need to stop by the store and get some more baking supplies." She walked off down the street beneath the shade of her large hat.

When she was gone, Zane thought Emmett and Mr. Sims would go back to their questions about Rachel. Instead, they went back to bickering over their domino game. It looked like the gossip had been squelched . . . at least for the time being. He said his goodbyes and whistled for Shep before heading back to the truck with his pity brownies. Dirk followed him.

"Your aunt didn't leave your uncle, did she?" Zane asked.

Dirk pushed his hat back and grinned. "Nope. I don't even have an aunt—at least not one that knows I exist. But I figured you could use a wingman right about then to take some of the heat off you." He lifted a hand. "Thanks for the ride into town."

Before he could turn, Zane stopped him. "Alright. You've got the job. Show up tomorrow morning at six o'clock and I'll introduce you around." He pointed a finger. "But don't even think about seducing my sister or I'll do more than kick you off my property. I'll kick you clean out of town."

Dirk held up his hands. "No problem. Becky and I are just friends."

"Uh-huh." He climbed into his truck. He was about to pull away from the pumps when Dirk tapped on the passenger side window. He waited for Zane to roll it down before he leaned in.

"I was thinking. If I'm going to be working out at your place, it might make more sense for me to just sleep there. That way you won't have to come all the way into town to pick me up. I could just stay in your barn . . . or maybe the bunkhouse."

Zane could sympathize with his cousin Cole. Dirk was like a barnacle that once attached was hard to get rid of. But he'd done Zane a favor so he couldn't exactly turn him down. Plus, it would save him a drive into town every morning. And make sure that Dirk showed up for work. "Climb in and we'll stop by and get your things. Where are you staying?"

Dirk got in and immediately helped himself to one of the brownies Zane had set on the console. "Since I got kicked out of the motor lodge, my choices are slim. I've been sleeping in the old diner, but it seems that someone locked it up tight."

The old diner? Was that why Carly had been there last night? Was she waiting for Dirk? Zane didn't know why the thought bothered him. Maybe because just the thought of Carly made steam come out of his ears.

"Lucky for you," he said as he pulled away from the gas station, "I happen to have a key."

"When she opened the front door of the boarding-house, Laura couldn't quite believe her eyes. While all the other mail-order brides were being courted with flowers, cowboy love songs, and poetry, Duke had brought her a . . . goat?"

CHAPTER SIX

𝒞

CARLY COULDN'T SLEEP. IT WAS sticky hot, and the muffled noises coming from the other bedroom were no help. The giggles and moans didn't bother her. She was happy that Emery had found love. What did bother her were the memories the noises brought up. Memories of her own honeymoon and the man she'd thought she would love forever.

Sam Hanover had been the coolest guy in high school. He had tattoos, a crotch rocket motorcycle that he could pop wheelies on, and a tortured James Dean persona that made girls swoon. When Carly had first laid eyes on him, she'd swooned right into his arms.

Growing up with a strict military dad who enforced ridiculous rules had made her fall for an irresponsible loser who broke all the rules. And when Sam gave her a single rose with a diamond ring hidden within the petals, Carly had been unable to say no. She didn't care that she'd just graduated high school, or that neither she nor Sam had a job. She didn't care that her father hated Sam and swore that if Carly married him, he would cut her off without a second thought. In fact, all that just made her want to marry him more.

Unfortunately, her father had been right. Sam couldn't hold down a job and spent his days partying with his friends. Carly was the one who worked two jobs. The one who came home to find her husband passed out in a pile of empty beer bottles and pizza boxes. But she had refused to admit her mistake . . . until she caught Sam in bed with the married woman who lived in the apartment above them.

Completely blindsided, she packed up and left. With nowhere to go, she had phoned her dad. She apologized and begged him to let her come home until she could figure out what to do. But Colonel Joseph Bennett was not the type of man who forgave easily. His only child needed to be taught a lesson. A lesson she had learned well.

Never trust love. Or men.

After divorcing Sam, she'd continued to work two jobs and started taking college classes. That's where she met Emery and Savannah. Once they discovered their mutual love for Tender Heart, they had become immediate friends. They spent most their time at Carly's apartment. She would cook while they argued over which were the best hero and heroine. Amid the Tender Heart stories and steaming pots and sizzling sauté pans, Carly found peace from her past pain. There was something about preparing food that soothed her soul. So she quit college and started culinary school. From the moment she stepped into her first cooking class, she knew she'd found her calling.

Now she wasn't so sure.

She sat up and reached for her laptop. She scrolled through various web sites searching for executive chef jobs that she hadn't already applied for. When she couldn't find any, she searched for sous chef jobs. It was a step down, but beggars can't be choosers. She applied to numerous restaurants before she finally closed her computer. The sounds coming from the other room had stopped, but it was still too hot to sleep.

Slipping on her sneakers, she headed outside. A full moon hung high in the sky, illuminating the faded barn and the acres and acres of land that surrounded Cole's ranch house. When she'd been there in the spring, the pastures had been filled with wildflowers. Now they were lush and green. She moved down the steps and followed the dirt road that led away from the house. She knew where it would take her. She and her friends had traveled the road many times getting ready for Emery's wedding.

The little white chapel looked as beautiful as she remembered. In the moonlight, the stained-glass windows glittered like colorful art and the tall spire stretched up to the star-filled sky like a ghostly scepter. Lucy had thought up the Tender Heart series in this chapel. It was where all the mail-order brides had been married. And it was where Gracie had found the first chapter of the final book. The church sat on a piece of land still jointly owned by all of the Arrington cousins.

Carly had never met Cole and Zane's cousin Raff, but from the rumors she'd heard, he was a major bad boy. He'd spent time in jail and was the only one of the cousins who didn't care about the Arrington name.

It seemed that Zane cared a little too much. Why else would he worry about people finding out that his wife had left him? It seemed silly to Carly. On the other hand, maybe she should start caring a little more about what people thought. If she did, she probably wouldn't have lost so many jobs.

Because of her spider encounter, she decided not to go in the chapel. Instead, she headed back to the road and followed it until she reached a dead end. Not wanting to go back to Emery's just yet, she climbed through the slats of the fence and walked through a large, open pasture. She had lived all over the world, but always in big cities or on military bases. She had never lived on a farm or a ranch. And she had to admit that the wide open spaces were nice . . . even if the smells weren't.

She held her nose as she sidestepped a huge pile of manure. The sound of water drew her attention. She followed the sound to a thick line of trees. She pushed through the bushes and undergrowth to find a large creek flowing over limestone rocks into a deep pool, making a tempting whirlpool that shimmered in the moonlight.

With the heat and humidity, Carly didn't waste any time slipping off her sneakers and climbing down the rocks to the water. But before she could wade in, she heard a splash. She stepped back into the shadows of the trees and searched until she saw a dark form breast-stroking through the water. It emerged right in front her. She watched the man's toned, sculpted back muscles flex as he stood and moved beneath the falls.

Carly should've left the guy to his late-night skinny-dipping. That would have been the right thing to do. But she rarely did the right thing, and she hated to ruin her record. So she stayed and watched. From his broad shoulders to his trim waist, he was quite the male specimen. He stood there for a few moments before he disappeared under the surface. Seconds later, he reappeared and swam toward the opposite bank. As he neared the shore, he stood, the water slowly receding from his body inch by mouthwatering inch.

When his entire butt finally came into view, Carly's eyes widened. She had seen nice butts before, but none compared to this one. This guy must do some serious squats to get his glutes so tight and defined. If his backside looked so hot, how would his front side look? She couldn't help giving him a little mental push.

Come on, turn around. Just a quick little peek.

But before he could turn, she heard a rustling behind her. She whirled to find the bushes shaking. As she stared, two eyes appeared in the foliage. Not tiny eyes, but big eyes that reflected the moonlight. It was not someone in the bush, but rather something. Something that was taller than she was.

Before she could take a step back, a large black monster emerged from the bushes. Or not a monster as much as a . . . cow? She wasn't that relieved. She'd never been around cows before—at least not live ones—and she didn't realize they were so big. Or so mean looking. The cow moved closer, so close she could feel the heat of its breath on her face.

"Hi, little cow," she said in a high-pitched voice. She remembered how much she hated being called little and changed her wording. "I mean, hi, big cow." She searched for a way to make friends and could only come up with one idea. She reached out and scratched it under the chin like she did Savannah's cat. Its breath puffed out in a sigh and its eyes closed. "Well, aren't you a sweet—"

"Back away slowly."

She recognized the voice immediately as Zane wrapped an arm around her waist and pulled her back against him. The feel of those wet, hard muscles made her realize that he had been the skinny dipper.

"Let me go." She tried to struggle out of his hold, but his arm only tightened.

"Stay still. Do you want to get us both killed?"

Killed? She stopped struggling and looked at the cow. Now it wasn't just docilely standing there. Now it was stomping its front feet like it was getting ready to . . .

Carly swallowed hard. "That isn't a cow, is it?"

"City girls," he muttered under his breath as he drew Carly back into the deep pool. The water was much colder than she thought, and she sucked in a breath when it covered her breasts. Breasts that were resting on Zane's muscular forearm and jostling with each one of his kicks.

"You can let me go," she said. "I can swim to the other side by myself."

"Uh-huh," he said, but his grip didn't loosen. In fact, when they reached a point where he could stand, he scooped her into his arms and carried her out of the water.

It had been one thing to be carried by Zane when he was clothed, it was another to be carried by him when he was naked. Now she could feel every flex of his body through her thin wet top and boxers. The bulge of his bicep against her back, the swell of his pectorals against the side of her breast, and the ripples of his abdominals against her hip. He felt like one big muscle. One big, amazingly perfect muscle that she slithered down as he released her legs. Her knees were so weak that it took a real effort to stand.

"What the hell do you think you're doing?" He pointed a finger across the creek, seemingly unaware that he didn't have on a stitch of clothing. Carly wished that she was as unaware. The trip across the creek had made her too aware.

"That's a two-thousand-pound Angus bull that you were scratching under the chin like a lap dog. Do you know what he could do to you? Men my size have been killed by their bulls. Someone your size would have their bones crushed in a New York minute."

If her mind had been working right, she probably would've mentioned the fact that the bull wasn't acting angry until Zane showed up. But her mind wasn't working. It had gone into a comatose state. Her body, on the other hand, was wide-awake and buzzing with enough energy to light downtown San Francisco during a blackout. All that energy was fixated on Zane.

"And what are you doing out here in the first place?" He ranted on. "This is my land. I don't like people trespassing. Especially people who spread gossip about me and my family." A flicker of moonlight drew her gaze to the pendant that hung on a chain around his neck. It looked like an arrowhead. An arrowhead that directed her to look down. This time she took direction well.

Her gaze lowered to the one part of his body she'd been avoiding. For having just come out of cold water, it was impressive. She had to wonder how impressive it would be once it was warmed up. Like with her mouth. Suddenly, she realized that Zane wasn't ranting anymore. Her gaze trailed back up his muscular body to eyes that were staring at her from beneath lowered brows.

"What are you doing?"

It was a good question. One she didn't have an answer for. At least not one that wouldn't make her look like a sex-starved, pathetic woman.

"I was, umm, I was just . . ." She shrugged. "Checking out the goods."

His eyes widened. "What?"

"The goods." She motioned at him with her hand. "Do you think that men are the only ones who check out nice bodies? Especially when you're right in front of us and naked as the day you were born?"

His mouth opened, but nothing came out. He just stood there staring at her as if she'd lost her mind. The only thing that kept her from feeling like a complete idiot was his dangling part. It wasn't dangling anymore. It jutted out from his body like Luke Skywalker's lightsaber. For a second, she really wanted "the Force" to be with her.

"Dammit!" He cursed as he turned and stomped off.

She would've left as well if she'd been on the other side of the creek. On this side, she didn't have a clue how to get back to Emery and Cole's. So she followed the muttered cussing and found Zane standing by his pickup truck, struggling to zip his jeans over a hard-on that looked painful. She waited until he was zipped and buttoned before she spoke.

"I didn't tattle to the town about your wife."

He whirled toward her. "As if I'd believe that after all the trouble you get into." He grabbed his shirt out of the cab of the truck and pulled it on. "Go back to Emery and Cole's, Carly. Despite my condition, I'm not interested in sex with you."

She wanted to be ticked about his arrogance. But she really couldn't get too mad. She had been lusting after him. Or at least his body. Of course, she would never have sex with someone like Zane, even if he were single. He was much too controlling for her tastes. And much too responsible. Against her better judgment, she was still attracted to deadbeats.

"I guess I'll have to live with that. And I'd be happy to head back to Cole's ranch if I knew how to get there." She glanced at the creek. "I could swim back across, but I don't want to get crushed by a hornless bull."

He stopped snapping his shirt closed and turned to her. "He's plenty horny. He just needs a little motivation is all."

She stared at him, totally confused. "Obviously,

we have a major communication problem. I was talking about the bull's lack of horns on his head. Not his lack of sexual desire." She paused. "Does he have a problem in that area?"

He finished snapping his shirt with jerky motions. "Ha! As if a half-million-dollar bull would have problems in that area."

"Holy shit! You paid half a million dollars for one bull? And men talk about women's compulsive spending."

"It was not a compulsive buy. I spent a lot of time researching that animal, and he's worth every penny."

"Even if he can't get it up?"

"He can get it up!"

Carly might've laughed at his adamancy if he hadn't reached into the truck for his boots. Suddenly, she realized that she'd left her sneakers on the other side of the creek.

"It looks like I'll have to deal with an impotent bull after all," she said. When his gaze swept over to her, she smiled. "I left my shoes on the other side."

Zane released his breath and ran a hand through his wet hair. "Get in the truck. But this is the last time I'm going to come to your rescue. Do you understand me?"

"Perfectly." She pulled open the passenger door and climbed in, then waited for him to enter the cab before she added. "And just for the record, I don't need to be rescued."

He glanced over and sent her his dimpled smile. "Uh-huh."

"The storekeeper? Miss Laura had turned Duke down for dinner and gone out with the storekeeper? Hell, the man couldn't even ride a horse!"

CHAPTER SEVEN

❧

ZANE SAT IN HIS STUDY and stared at the divorce papers on his desk. What had happened to his perfect life? He had worked so hard for that perfection. He'd been the perfect son. The perfect student. The perfect athlete. The perfect boyfriend. He'd never sassed his parents, never failed a class, never missed a practice, and never dated anyone but Rachel Barnes.

And there had been plenty of women to date.

His sophomore year in high school there had been Mary Ann Schmidt, who would let guys play with her boobs for a date to the movies and a six-pack of Bud. Junior year he'd had a serious crush on Dana Woods, who had mile-long legs. Senior year it was Sarah Millhouse, who had a great personality and made him laugh. And in college there had been numerous women he'd wanted to ask out. But he hadn't. He'd ignored temptation and stayed true to Rachel. Because everyone knew that

Rachel was the one he was supposed to end up with. The one who fit perfectly into his life.

She was born and raised in Bliss. Her family was friends with his family. Her father had been a rancher until he retired, so she understood ranch life. She knew all about the long hours and the lack of focus on anything but the ranch. At least, he'd thought she understood. He'd thought she was happy doing her thing while he did his. Obviously, he'd been wrong.

He looked at the divorce papers. He should just sign the damned things and be done with it. But signing was like quitting, and Zane had never quit anything. He wasn't about to start now.

He tossed down the pen he'd been holding and headed to the kitchen to see if he could find something to eat. The pickings were slim. All that was left in the refrigerator was a jar of pickles and a variety of condiments. He pulled his cellphone from his pocket and texted Becky to see if she wanted to go to the Watering Hole for dinner. As usual, she had a date. It looked like he'd be eating burnt hamburgers and greasy fries alone.

He was backing his truck from the garage when he saw Dirk coming out of the bunkhouse. Earlier in the day, Dirk had been covered in dust from running the hay baler. Now he was cleaned up and looked like he was going somewhere. Since he'd proven to be a damned good worker, Zane figured he'd earned a ride into town and maybe some dinner.

He rolled down his window. "You need a lift? I was just headed to the Watering Hole."

Dirk didn't hesitate to climb in. "Thanks, Boss."

Zane waited until they were on the highway before he issued his invitation. "I'd like to buy you dinner for the great job you did today."

"I appreciate the offer, but I already have dinner plans."

"A hot date?"

The look Dirk sent him was pure arrogance. "As hot as they get. The woman's not only sexy as hell, but she also cooks like nobody's business." He pointed to the road that led to Cole's ranch. "Just drop me right here. I can walk the rest of the way."

Zane slammed on the brakes so abruptly, Dirk had to grab his hat to keep it on his head. "When I said right here, I didn't mean right here. The side of the road would've been fine."

He turned to Dirk. "Carly? Your hot date is Carly?" Just saying her name brought up an image that he'd been fighting since Whispering Falls. An image of a wet tank top that clung like a second skin to small breasts with sweet rosy centers.

Dirk looked confused. "Is there a problem, Boss? I thought Becky was the only woman you wanted me to stay away from. Is Carly off limits too?"

Zane finally realized how ridiculous he was acting. "No. I just didn't think of Carly as hot, is all." Dirk looked at him like he'd lost his mind. And hell, maybe he had. It was certainly betraying him with strange thoughts lately. Or maybe he just couldn't see Dirk and Carly as a couple. Dirk was an easygoing country boy while Carly was much more the aggressive city girl. She'd eat the poor kid up and spit him out.

This was proven as soon as Zane pulled up to the porch where Cole, Emery, and Carly were sitting.

Carly didn't even wait for Dirk to finish getting out of the truck before she started flirting outrageously.

"There's my hot cowboy." She stood and leaned over the porch railing. The humidity had done a number on her hair. It was no longer spiky so much as a mass of honey-blond curls that made her look innocent and sweet. Her next words completely shot that image to hell. "I was wondering when you were going to stop by and charm me out of my panties."

"Get ready to be charmed, honey." Dirk hurried up the ramp that Cole had built for Gracie and swung Carly into his arms. She didn't show any signs of resistance. In fact, she kissed him right on the lips. Dead center. Which just proved that she was too aggressive for the kid.

"Hey, Zane." Cole got up from the rocker. The look on his face was the same look everyone in town had been giving Zane lately. Damn, he hated sympathy as much as he hated aggressive women. "I'm glad Dirk invited you along for dinner. It will give me a chance to show you the plans for the stables."

"Actually, I was just dropping Dirk off. I'm going to grab some dinner in town."

Emery moved to Cole's side. "That's nonsense. You're going to eat with us. There's plenty of food." She glanced at Carly, who was still clinging to Dirk. "Isn't that right, Carly?"

Carly shrugged with indifference. "If Zane has other plans, we wouldn't want to keep him."

Her inhospitable reply pissed him off. He had rescued her numerous times and given her a room to sleep in, and she couldn't even offer him a meal? He jerked off his hat and strode up the ramp. "Dinner sounds good. And I'll take one of those beers, Cole, if you got another."

It was a mistake to stay for dinner. While he enjoyed talking to Cole about the plans for his new stables, he did not enjoying listening to Carly and Dirk's annoying flirting. It was so annoying that he stretched his drinking rule of one beer to five. But even the alcohol buzz didn't help.

"So how many hearts have you broken while I've been away, Dirk?" Carly asked as she sipped her red wine. Her beverage choice surprised him. He'd taken her for a tequila girl. Tequila and tattoos seemed to go together.

"Not a one," Dirk said. "I've been saving myself for the right woman." He took another bite of chicken and closed his eyes. "Someone who can cook like a dream." He opened his eyes and winked. "And looks like an angel."

Carly held a hand to her heart. "Why, Dirk Hadley, is that a proposal?"

"Hell yeah, it is. I propose we go for a walk so I can show my gratitude for this wonderful feast."

Zane snorted a little too loudly. All eyes turned to him. But the ones he zeroed in on were big and brown and looked almost as surly as he felt.

"Was there a problem with dinner, Zane?" Carly said his name like it left a bad taste in her mouth, which made him forget all the manners his mama had drilled into him from youth.

He shrugged. "Dinner was fine. I mean, if you like chicken in a rich sauce."

"Fine?" Her hard gaze swept down to his plate

that was pretty much licked clean. "If you don't like chicken Marsala, why did you have two helpings?"

"Just being polite." He slid his chair back. "Well, thank you for the invite, Cole and Emery. But Dirk and I should be getting back. We have a long day ahead of us tomorrow." There was no way in hell he was going to let Dirk go for a walk with Carly. She might look harmless, but beneath that Disney fairy façade was a vicious viper.

"You sure you don't want to let your food settle a little?" Cole paused. "And those beers you drank?"

"I'm fine." He got to his feet, and damned if he didn't sway on his boots and bump the table.

Cole got up "I think it would be a good idea if you drove home, Dirk."

"I don't need anyone to drive me home." Zane pulled the keys from his pocket, but only a second later, Carly swiped them right out of his hand.

"Since Dirk drank as much as you did, I'll drive you both and walk back."

That was the last thing Zane wanted. If he had to listen to any more flirting, he was going to gouge out his ears with an ice pick. But before he could argue, she waltzed right out the door, leaving him no choice but to follow. The only consolation was that Dirk hopped in the bed and cozied down between two bales of hay so there would be no more annoying flirting. But that did leave Zane alone with the viper. Not that he was feeling so friendly himself. It was the first time he'd been a passenger in his own truck, and he didn't like it. He didn't like it one bit.

"Are you sure you can reach the pedals?" he

asked as soon as he got in. She sent him a hard look before she popped the truck into reverse and hit the gas, kicking up a spray of dust and gravel. "Damn, woman!" He grabbed the dashboard, then glanced in the back to see if Dirk had been tossed out on his head. The cowboy was still there with his hat tugged over his face.

"Don't damn me," Carly said as she fishtailed out of the drive. "Damn yourself for having a drinking problem and needing a ride. I understand now why your wife left you."

Now that pissed him off. "I don't have a drinking problem. And Rachel will be back."

"You don't have a drinking problem. Your wife doesn't want a divorce. Your bull isn't impotent. And you aren't a control freak." She glanced over. "I've never met a man who is in more denial than you are. Which is probably why you have a drinking problem. Hiding from the truth takes a lot of work."

If he had been sober, he could've controlled his temper. But he wasn't. So he didn't. He let out everything he'd been keeping in for so long. "You don't know shit about me, lady. Or my marriage. Or my bull. You're just some stuck-up California girl who thinks she has everything and everyone figured out. Well, if you have everything figured out, why are you here in Bliss with no job and a car filled with a pathetic amount of belongings mooching off my cousin and his wife? If you're supposed to be this amazing executive chef then why aren't you working in some exclusive restaurant making loads of cash?"

She whipped onto the highway. "Because I'm

not willing to put up with assholes like you. And I'm not mooching off Emery and Cole. The only reason I'm still staying at their house is because they refuse to let me stay at the motor lodge."

"Because that would be inhospitable. Good folks don't let their friends stay in a motel when they come to town. But that doesn't mean they really want you staying with them. Especially when they just got married and want some time alone." He held onto the dash. "And slow the hell down!"

"Fuck you!"

She drove like the hounds of hell were after her until she reached the ranch house, then she slammed on the brakes an inch away from his garage door and jumped out without a word. By the time Zane got out, she was hightailing it across the pasture. Even as mad as he was at the woman, he didn't like the thought of her walking alone in the dark. Especially when she had a knack for getting into trouble and pissing off his bull. He glanced in the bed of the truck, but it looked like Dirk was sound asleep. That left Zane little choice but to go after her himself.

For a woman with such short legs, she could flat move. As he came up behind her, he couldn't help noticing how nicely her butt filled out her jean shorts and how enticingly her hips swayed with each hurried stride. He blinked away his beer goggles and jogged until he reached her. She wasn't thrilled to see him.

"I think it would be best if we stayed away from each other," she snapped.

"I couldn't agree more. And as soon as I make sure you get home safely that's exactly what I intend to do."

She shot him a sideways glance. "You really are the most responsible person I've ever met."

He didn't know if it was a compliment or a jab. Since he hadn't been acting very responsibly tonight, he took it as a jab. "And what's wrong with being responsible?"

"Nothing, unless you think you're responsible for the world. That has to be one hell of a job." She stopped in the middle of the pasture and turned to him. "Tonight was the first time I caught a glimpse of the real Zane."

He got angry all over again. "The real Zane is not a hot-tempered drunk."

"A few beers don't make you a drunk. I was just pushing your buttons when I said that."

Her honesty never failed to surprise him. "You seem to like pushing my buttons."

"Yeah, well, I wouldn't take it personally. I enjoy pushing the buttons of people in authority. It's kinda my thing." She started walking again. This time at a slower pace.

"Is that why you don't have a job?" Obviously, the alcohol had loosened his tongue and taken away all his manners. But she didn't look insulted when she glanced over at him. She just looked resigned.

"Pretty much. And why I can't get another one. It seems my food isn't worth my surly disposition."

It was strange how quickly she could anger him, and how just as quickly she could pull the truth from him. "I liked your chicken Marsala."

She shot him a glance. "Just liked?"

"Okay, so I wanted to drown in that gravy."

She laughed. "Is it always so hard to get a compliment out of you?"

It wasn't something he had given much thought to, but now that he did, he realized she had a point. "I learned it from my father. Compliments don't come easy from him. He's a hard man to please."

"And have you spent your life trying to please him?" She stumbled over a clump of grass, and he took her arm to steady her. She had soft skin and fragile feeling bones. His grip loosened as he guided her around a pile of manure.

"What can I say? I'm a people pleaser." They came to the fence that separated his land from Cole's, and he climbed over before reaching out a hand to help her. She ignored it and climbed over by herself. He couldn't help smiling at her stubbornness.

"My dad is hard to please too," she said once she was on the other side. "And after failing to get his approval, I settled for his disapproval."

"Wild child?"

She glanced over and quirked an eyebrow. "Butt kisser?"

He laughed. "You really know how to bruise a guy's ego."

"Again, it's my thing. All related to daddy issues. Which probably explains why I'm still single." He wanted to ask about those daddy issues, but they arrived at Cole's before he could.

She turned to him and smiled. She looked pretty when she smiled. Or maybe not exactly pretty so much as . . . hot. He mentally shook the thought away as she spoke. "Thanks for walking me home."

"I'd thank you for driving me, but you scared

twenty years off my life."

Her smile turned more impish. "I think you're one person who needs to have his chain rattled occasionally." Her gaze lowered to the open collar of his shirt, and without warning, she slipped her fingers inside and brushed his collarbone. Suddenly, he knew how a steer felt when it got branded. Her scorching fingertips seemed to sear right into his skin and mark him for life.

"And speaking of chains . . ." She pulled the gold chain out of his shirt and cradled the arrowhead in her palm. "Is this some kind of Native American talisman?" She leaned closer to examine it. She smelled of spices and herbs and flowery shampoo. The scent so captivating that he almost didn't catch her next words. "Or is it a reminder to stay on the straight and narrow—to never veer from the moral path?" She lifted her head, and her gaze locked with his. "Don't you ever wonder what would happen if you veered off that path and did what you wanted to do instead of what was expected of you? What do you want to do, Zane?"

No one had ever asked him that question before. So it took him a moment to find an answer. When he did, there was nothing moral about it. At that moment, there was only one thing he wanted. He wanted to touch Carly. He wanted to brush a finger over the moonlit flush of her cheek. To palm the stubborn curve of her jaw. And kiss the pulse that beat at the side of her neck.

Instead, he pulled the arrowhead away from her and dropped it back inside his shirt, ignoring the warmth her skin had infused in the stone.

"Goodnight, Carly Sue."

"Virgil Hansen owned a store instead of a ranch. He spoke in soft tones instead of loud bellows. He brought her daisies instead of a goat. Unfortunately, before he could hand her the daisies, Elsa the goat jerked them out of his hand and ate them."

CHAPTER EIGHT

"WHO TAUGHT YOU HOW TO jimmy a lock?"

Emery looked up at Carly and grinned. "I have two older brothers, remember? When he was thirteen, Jared wanted to be a cat burglar and forced me to be his accomplice. As part of my initiation into his den of thieves, I had to jimmy my grandmother's back door lock and steal all the lemon bars she made for her bridge club."

Carly laughed. "Why, Em, you criminal."

"Not really. I was riddled with guilt after I took them. So I made her another batch and replaced them before she got back from her hair appointment. Although I forgot the eggs and they turned out hard as a brick. If Grandma noticed, she never said a word." Emery finished removing the screws from the doorknob, pulled it off, flipped the lock, and pushed open the door. "Voila!"

Carly stared at the doorknob in her hand. "I wouldn't call that jimmying as much as dismantling. I hope you know how to put it back together."

"Of course." Emery got to her feet. "I would never leave my grandma with a broken doorknob." She followed Carly into the diner. "So where did you find the backpack with the chapter in it?"

Carly led her into the kitchen and pointed to the prep counter. "It was sitting right there."

They spent the next few minutes searching the kitchen for the navy backpack with the green stitching. They didn't find it.

"I told you it was gone," Carly said. "Which means that someone had to be here that night and they grabbed the chapter and the backpack."

Emery glanced around. "I wonder if whoever it was found another chapter. If they were searching, they weren't messy about it. Nothing seems to be different than when we were here last."

"The floor is wetter from your overly zealous fire department." Carly stepped over a puddle of water. "And maybe whoever was here that night didn't have a chance to look before I arrived. Although I don't get why they would look here when the other two chapters were found on Arrington land."

"I was thinking the same thing, but then it dawned on me." Emery pulled Carly into the dining room. "It's not about the Arringtons as much as it is about Lucy. The first chapter was found in the chapel that inspired the books. The sixth in the cemetery where Lucy got inspiration for her characters. Why wouldn't one be here where she wrote all her outlines?" She walked over and pulled a metal Coca-Cola sign off the wall and looked behind it. The disappointment on her face proved that there was no chapter there.

"But why would she hide them in different places?" Carly asked. "That seems really weird."

"Lucy was eccentric. Maybe she only wanted the fans who knew her best to find all the chapters. Sort of like a literary treasure hunt." Emery moved to a Norman Rockwell picture on the wall. "Help me get this down."

For the next two hours, they looked behind every dusty picture, sign, and neon light. Under every vinyl chair, table, and barstool. And through every shelf, box, and cupboard in the kitchen. They found nothing but a dead mouse that freaked out Emery and three live spiders that freaked out Carly.

"Okay, I'm done." She backed away from the black spidery corpse Emery had just squashed with her flip-flop.

Emery put the flip-flop back on. "I think you're getting over your fear. You didn't get hysterical like you did when Zane came charging in and rescued you."

"Zane certainly has a hero complex." She gave the squashed spider a wide berth and sat down on a barstool at the counter. "But he's not quite as big of a stuffed shirt as I thought he was. He needs to drink more often. I actually caught a glimpse of a human being." She'd caught more than a glimpse. Once he'd let down his guard, she'd discovered a man who wasn't that different from her. They both had overbearing fathers. And they were both struggling for control over their lives.

Emery sat down next to her. "Poor Zane. He's

obviously upset over his wife leaving. I guess he and Rachel were high school sweethearts and have known each other forever. Why would she just leave him after all that time?"

"Just because you're high school sweethearts doesn't mean you're meant to be together forever," Carly said. "Sam and I are a perfect example."

"That was a little different. You discovered him cheating with another woman."

"And of course, Saint Rachel would never leave Zane for another man." Carly glanced around. "Well, I guess our treasure hunt is over."

"Just because we didn't find it here doesn't mean we can't look in other places that inspired Lucy."

"What about the Watering Hole? Wasn't it a bar in the fifties? Maybe Lucy used to go there."

"Doubtful, since she was a teetotaler."

Carly shrugged. "It's just as well. I need to pack and get going."

Emery swiveled the barstool toward her. "You can't go. Not when there are more chapters to find."

"We don't know that for a fact. And even if there are more chapters, you won't need any help finding them. As an expert on Lucy Arrington, you're the one who will know the best places to look."

"But it won't be any fun without you. Every sleuth has to have a sidekick."

"Cole is your sidekick, and it's time I let you two get back to being newlyweds while I get back to being a chef."

"So you got an offer?"

Carly shook her head. "No. It looks like I've been blackballed. Which means I'll have to start a little lower on the food chain—pardon the pun. I figure my reputation isn't so bad that I won't be able to get a job as a sous chef."

"But you've worked so hard to become an executive chef."

It was true, but Carly tried not to think about all the work. She had to focus on the long term. If she could get a job as a sous chef, there was a chance she could get promoted. "It won't be forever. Once I have enough money saved up, I'll open my own restaurant."

"I wish Cole and I could help, but we're already counting every penny so we can start his horse ranch and pay for Gracie's therapy. He refuses to take financial help from Zane or my parents." Emery perked up. "But I bet my parents would love to invest in a restaurant. They couldn't finance all of it, but maybe we could get Savannah and Miles to chip in? I bet he has connections with restaurant owners in Atlanta. Or you could just ask him for a loan."

Carly shook her head. "I'm a little like Cole. I don't want to owe anyone, especially an ass like Miles."

Emery rested her chin in her hand and released her breath. "Dang, I wish we had found the rest of the book. That would've solved all of our financial worries. Instead, all we found was a lot of dirt and dust." She lifted her head and looked around the diner. "Although for being so old, this place is in pretty good shape. With a little bit of work—"

She stopped and swiveled to Carly. "What about this place? I know it's not exactly an exclusive restaurant in a big city, but I bet you could lease it for almost nothing. In fact, I know you could. And it wouldn't take that much to get it ready to open. Just a good cleaning and the booths and chairs reupholstered."

Carly held up a hand. "Whoa, Em. I don't mean to hurt your feelings, but I don't want to live in Bliss. And I certainly don't want to own a greasy spoon diner where all I serve is hamburgers and hot dogs."

It wasn't surprising when Emery didn't let up. She was tenacious when she had a plan, and it looked like the diner had become her new one.

"Okay, I get it. You want to own an upscale restaurant in a big city. But you don't have the money to do that yet. This could help you get that money. I know for a fact that people would flock here after being subjected to the Watering Hole's food for so many years. As far as what you serve, the choice is yours. You've seen *Diners, Drive-Ins and Dives*. They serve all kinds of things in diners now. You do this for a year, save some money, and who says you can't open up a nice restaurant anywhere you want."

Carly wanted to argue, but found that she couldn't. If it was her restaurant, she could put whatever she wanted on the menu. She would be the boss. She wouldn't have to put up with arrogant owners who didn't know a whisk from a ladle.

She glanced around. Emery was right. Despite some ripped upholstery and chipped tile, the restaurant wasn't in bad shape. With just a little bit of money, it could actually be a pretty cool diner. Still, opening a business was chancy.

"I'm not sure if Bliss has a big enough population to support a restaurant," she said.

"It wouldn't just be the townsfolk. Once they hear about how good your food is, you'll get truck drivers, tourists—" Emery's eyes widened, and she literally bounced up and down on the barstool. "We could play up the entire Tender Heart theme. After all, this was where Lucy outlined all her stories. You could decorate the walls with poster-sized covers from the books and pictures of Lucy."

For the first time in a long time, Carly felt a surge of excitement. "We could even name all the dishes after characters and have the Rancher's Special and Mail-order Brides Barbecue—do you think I could get Cole's smoker?"

"Of course you could. It would fit perfectly out in the back alley."

Carly got up and started to pace. "I'll need waitresses and bussers and a food supply company that's willing to make regular deliveries. I can clean and paint, but I'll need to contact upholsterers and someone to retile the floor. And of course, we'll need new dishes and some new kitchen equipment, but I could probably find those second hand." She sat down and took out her cellphone to make a list. She had barely typed out the first item when Emery released a squeal and hugged her.

"Oh my gosh, you're actually going to stay here in Bliss!"

Carly tried to calm her down. "It's not for certain. I'm just considering it. And I'm not staying with you and Cole any longer. I'm renting a room at the motor lodge tonight."

"Okay, but you'll go crazy without a kitchen."

She did have a point. Carly didn't like not having

access to a kitchen. But maybe if things worked out, she'd have the diner kitchen soon.

Emery hugged her again. "This is going to be so much fun. I'll help you however I can. I used to waitress in high school. And when we're not working, we can search for the rest of Tender Heart and you can help with the Fourth of July Chili Cook-off. I'm on the committee, and we could really use your professional advice."

"I don't think I'll have much spare time if—and that's a big if—I'm going to start up a restaurant." She set her phone on the counter. "First things first, I need to talk to the person who owns this building and see what he's willing to lease it for."

A knowing sparkle entered Emery's green eyes. "That's easy enough. You happen to know the owner."

"Really. Who is—?"

The back door flew open and banged loudly against the wall. Carly and Emery exchanged a quick look before diving beneath the counter. They huddled there and listened as hard boot heels resounded against the tile floor. The sound faded, then grew louder again until two scuffed boots appeared. They were attached to muscled, blue-jeaned legs that Carly recognized instantly.

She rolled her eyes as Zane spoke.

"Ahh, it looks like the criminal who broke in left something behind."

Carly cringed when she realized she'd left her cellphone on the counter.

"Let's see if I can figure out who the culprit is," Zane continued in an annoying know-it-all voice. "A simple, inexpensive cellphone case with a smartphone, two twenties, and a credit card with the name of . . ."

Carly crawled out and grabbed the credit card and cellphone out of his hands. "Shouldn't you be out herding cattle?"

He lifted an eyebrow. "I was until I got a call from Drew Holmes. I guess he was walking his dog and saw some suspicious behavior in the back alley. What is it with you and this diner?"

She put her hands on her hips. "What is it with you? You seem to be overly concerned with this place. Why would this Drew call you if someone was breaking in? Why wouldn't he call the sheriff? Or the owner?"

Zane's smile was smug. "He did."

"Duke had learned from experience that if you wanted to get a stubborn cow corralled, sometimes you had to change your tactics."

CHAPTER NINE

℃

ZANE FINISHED SPREADING THE WHEAT straw in the stall he'd just sterilized for his mare Cinnamon, who was getting ready to foal. When the weather was nice he usually let his mares give birth in the pasture. But Cinnamon's last pregnancy had resulted in a stillbirth, so he wanted to keep an eye on her this time around. The stall they used for birthing was equipped with cameras so he could check on the horses using an app on his phone, which meant he was in for some sleepless nights.

Or rather, more sleepless nights.

Lately he'd had a bad case of insomnia. He wanted to blame it on Rachel. Any man whose wife left him would have trouble sleeping. But it wasn't thoughts of Rachel that kept him up nights. Another woman had taken over his brain. A woman with seductive brown eyes who asked way too many questions.

What did he want?

Life wasn't about wants. It was about working hard and fulfilling your obligations. Something that Carly didn't understand. She was a nomad with no responsibilities, while Zane was a ranch owner with numerous responsibilities. One of which was just rolling her motorcycle into the barn.

Both Becky and the bike were covered in mud. But that didn't bother him as much as her lack of protective gear. She wore a helmet, but just her regular clothes, which wouldn't protect her body if she took a fall. If he spent all his time worrying about what he wanted, who would watch out for his sister and keep her from breaking her fool neck?

He stepped out of the stall. "What happened to your riding jacket and gloves?"

Becky shrugged. "It's not a big deal. I just rode into town."

"It will be a big deal if you end up wrecking. Especially on the highway."

"I didn't take the highway, thus the mud." She rolled the bike into the stall where Zane kept his dirt bike. A bike he hadn't ridden in over a year. She came back out with a grocery bag hung over her arm.

"You went to the store?" he asked.

"I had to pick up some spices." *Spices?* He could think of about a hundred different food items they needed more than spices. But before he could complain, she continued. "I ran into Mrs. Crawley at the store, and she interrogated the hell out of me about Rachel leaving."

He had hoped to stop the gossip, but it had only

gotten worse. That was why he avoided going into town. He didn't need to be interrogated in the frozen food section. "What did you tell her? I hope you didn't let her know how happy you are about it."

"I'm not happy." A smile split her face. "Okay, maybe I'm happy, but I wouldn't let Mrs. Crawley know that. I feel bad enough about letting the news out." She scowled. "That's the last time I tell Roy Fuller anything. I thought he could keep a secret, but he broadcasted it all over town as soon as we got off the phone."

Zane stopped in the process of hanging up the pitchfork and turned to her. "Roy broadcasted what all over town?"

"The news about Rachel leaving. Of course, after you peppered his tailgate with buckshot for bringing me home so late, he probably figured he owed you."

Carly hadn't spread the news of Rachel leaving. He was surprised how happy that made him. Although he still didn't trust her as far as he could throw her. She hadn't lied about spreading the rumor, but she had lied about why she and Emery broke into the diner the other day. He didn't believe for a second that she'd left her cellphone the night of the fire. A woman didn't go days without her cellphone. And if she had left it, why hadn't Emery just called him to unlock the door? No, the two were up to something. He just hadn't figured out what.

He brushed at the mud Becky had left on his shirtsleeve before nodding at the grocery bag. "Please tell me you got other groceries today besides spices."

"You know I'm not good at shopping or cook-ing, big brother. Which is exactly why we need to hire a cook . . . and soon. I'm running out of guys to take me to dinner. Or maybe I'm getting sick of having to put up with these guys just to get dinner."

She was probably right. He did need to hire a cook. His stomach felt like a hollow log. "You bet-ter not be going out with Roy. If I see that man, he's going to get more than his tailgate sprayed."

"Nope. Roy is old news. Danny Thompson is taking me to Houston to go dancing."

Zane followed her out of the barn. "Danny Thompson? Isn't he a little young?"

"He's legal. Still, I would've said no if I'd known Carly was cooking dinner for us tonight."

Zane stopped in his tracks when he noticed the Subaru parked in front of the house. "Carly's here?"

Becky looked at him with confusion. "I thought you knew. She acted like you did when she showed up earlier with all the bags and boxes of food." She held up the grocery sack. "Although she forgot the spices she needed for the beef tenderloin so she sent me into town to get them."

"Why would she cook me dinner?"

Becky's eyes sparkled. "Maybe she likes you."

He snorted. "That's doubtful. The woman loves to get under my skin."

"The perfect way to get a man's attention is to get under his skin." She headed into the house, but Zane was too stunned to follow.

Was his sister right? Was Carly interested in him? It made a certain kind of sense. Why else would a woman show up at a man's house to cook for him? And now that he thought about it, there had been other signs that pointed to her interest. The way she had looked at him at Whispering Falls like he was a side of prime beef. The way she had jumped at the chance to drive him home the other night. The way she had touched his arrowhead.

He smiled.

Carly liked him.

Why the thought made him feel so damned good, he didn't know. Maybe because since Rachel left, his ego could use a little bolstering. Of course, he wouldn't let anything come of it. He was a married man after all. And he needed to make that perfectly clear. Still, he couldn't help the strut that entered his step as he followed Becky into the house.

He intended to put an end to Carly's cooking and send her on her way as soon as he stepped through the door. He might be starving, but he wasn't about to lead the poor woman on. He did follow a moral path. And if her plan was to make him veer from it, she was in for a major disappointment.

Unfortunately, when he stepped in the door, he lost sight of his moral path amid the aroma of food cooking. He didn't know what the smells were, only that they made his stomach growl in anticipation and his head feel a little light and woozy.

He walked into the kitchen to find Carly standing at the stove, flipping asparagus in a sauté pan. Her hair was dampened by the steam coming from another pot and fell in cute little curls around her face. She wore a tight white t-shirt, cutoff jean shorts, and no shoes. Her toes were painted black of all things. They bounced in time to some pop song that came from her smartphone. He was still studying her toes when she turned and let out a shriek.

"Geez," she put a hand to her chest, "you scared the shit out of me."

"Sorry. I didn't expect to find a woman in my kitchen."

She turned back to the stove. "I thought I'd cook you dinner as an apology for breaking into your diner."

Okay, that cinched it. She liked him. There was no way this woman apologized for anything.

"Really?" he said. "I would think that Emery would be the one that owes me the apology. She was the one who took off my doorknob and then couldn't put it back on."

Carly pointed to the pie on the counter. "She stopped by Ms. Marble's and got you an apple pie as her way of saying she was sorry."

Ms. Marble's apple pie. Beef tenderloin. Sautéed asparagus. Yes, he would wait until after dinner to let Carly know he wasn't available.

IF THERE WAS SUCH A thing as a food orgasm, Zane experienced it while eating Carly's cooking. The tenderloin with the drizzle of wine sauce melted on his tongue like beef butter. The mashed potatoes with the sprinkle of chives were like a scoop of whipped heaven. And the asparagus with the touch of lemon zest were cooked just enough to still have a snap. Not to mention the dinner rolls that broke apart in a billow of yeasty steam. After taking a bite of those fluffy clouds slathered in butter, there was a moment that Zane actually closed his eyes and moaned.

Carly didn't comment, but the smug look of satisfaction on her face confirmed that she knew how much he was enjoying the meal. And he didn't care. For the first time in a long time, he felt content and satisfied. And he intended to enjoy every single second of it.

"I have never seen anyone eat like you," Carly said after he finished his second slice of apple pie. "Where do you put it?"

He wiped his mouth with a napkin and pushed his plate away. "I ate so much growing up that my mom thought I had a tapeworm and kept taking me to the doctor. Finally, he convinced her that I just have a fast metabolism." He patted his stomach. "Although I am pretty full now."

It was time to set things straight with Carly. But when she got up and started making a pot of coffee, he decided to postpone it for a few more minutes. She made damned good coffee.

Instead of bringing the cups to the breakfast counter where they'd eaten dinner, she nodded at the doorway. "I thought we'd be more comfortable in the living room. There's something I wanted to talk to you about."

"There's something I'd like to talk to you about as well." He got to his feet and followed her into the living room. When she sat on the couch, he should've taken a chair. But he hated the damn spindly chairs and always felt like he was going to break them. So he sat on the couch and took the cup of coffee she offered him.

The couch was smaller than he'd thought. He was so close to her that he noticed things he hadn't noticed before. Like the different shades of gold in her hair. The length of her eyelashes. The sienna-colored rings around her pupils. The cute tilt of her nose. And the fact that her top lip was bowed and a little fuller than her bottom. On the very top of that bow was a flake of apple pie crust. That little piece of buttery pastry was distracting. So distracting that he had trouble looking away.

"Is something wrong?" she asked.

Trying to divert his attention, he took a sip of coffee and burned his tongue.

"Careful, it's hot," she warned, a little too late.

"Uh-huh." He nodded before he set the cup on the coffee table. When he turned to her, she was holding her mug just below her mouth and blowing to cool it. The pucker should've knocked the flake of crust off. It didn't. That itty bitty piece of flaky delight clung to that soft-looking upper lip like it was super glued. It was still there when she set her cup down on the end table and turned to him.

"I have a confession to make," she said. "I didn't cook you dinner to apologize for breaking into the diner to . . . get my cellphone."

He shouldn't have been surprised that she was getting ready to confess her real reasons for cooking him dinner. Carly wasn't the type of woman to beat around the bush. At first, he hadn't cared for her bluntness. But he'd started to admire it. A man would always know where he stood with her. She would never blindside him.

"In fact," she said, "I guess you could say I was

trying to butter you up."

Butter. His gaze returned to her upper lip. Was that buttery flake of piecrust never coming off? It clung there even as she bit her bottom lip and pulled it between her teeth, leaving behind a glistening streak of moisture. *Moisture.* That's what it would take to get that flake off. A sweep of moisture. Was it his imagination or was her mouth closer than it had been a second ago? Was she going to kiss him?

"I thought if I cooked you dinner," she continued, "that you would be more willing to give me what I want."

Want. Maybe he should give her what she wanted. And in return, he'd take what he wanted. That damn flake of piecrust.

But when their lips touched, he forgot about the piecrust amid the sweetness of her mouth. She tasted like all the flavors of the dinner put together—sweet wine sauce, fluffy potatoes, spicy apples, and rich coffee.

Suddenly he realized that one taste of Carly would never be enough.

"The man was insufferable! He had gotten her kicked out of the boardinghouse, and now Laura had nowhere to go but Duke Earhart's lair."

CHAPTER TEN

☾

CARLY HAD BEEN ABOUT TO broach the reason for her being there when Zane kissed her. She wasn't surprised. With the way he'd been studying her mouth, she'd seen it coming. He wasn't the first man who had wanted her after she fed him a great meal. It was the reason she wasn't a personal chef. Food was a major aphrodisiac. Especially for healthy eaters like Zane. She couldn't blame him for confusing his craving for her food with his craving for her.

And he did crave her.

His lips molded to hers and hungrily fed as if she was a feast he couldn't resist. Since she had always enjoyed feeding people, she had a hard time refusing him one little sip. But as soon as she parted her lips, she lost track of who was craving whom. He tasted like coffee—hot, rich, and addictive—and she wanted to drink an entire pot of Zane and plunge headfirst into a caffeine coma.

Unfortunately, the skinny couch wasn't made for kissing. As the kiss grew more desperate and frenzied, they somehow slipped off the couch and onto the floor. She landed on top, cracking her elbow on the coffee table. The pain brought her back to reality. She drew away, straddling him and rubbing her elbow while he lay there looking stunned.

She knew how he felt. If the couch had been big enough to accommodate his large body, there was little doubt that she would be well on her way to nirvana by now. Her nerve endings crackled and popped with desire, and she had a hard time not rubbing against the solid ridge beneath her butt. But sex with Zane wasn't part of her plan for the evening. She needed to get that straight. Before she could, he sat up, bringing his tempting lips much too close for comfort. The only thing that kept her from giving into temptation was the nonsense they were sprouting.

"Look, Carly," he said. "I know you can't help who you fall for, but I'm just not available."

She blinked. "Excuse me?"

His smile was sympathetic. "I figured out that you want me. Why else would a woman go to all the trouble to make such a spectacular dinner?"

The *spectacular* sidetracked her for only a second before she stared at him. "You think I want you? Like in bed?"

"Isn't that why you kissed me?"

"I didn't kiss you. You kissed me."

He held up his hands as if conceding a point. "Okay, maybe I kissed you back. But you kissed me first."

The arrogance of the man wiped out any residual desire. "You really do live in the land of denial, and someone needs to set you straight. Firstly," she held up a finger right in front of his nose, "you were the one who sat down next to me, stared at my mouth, then leaned in and kissed me. True, I didn't resist. But I certainly didn't initiate the kiss. Secondly," she held up another finger, "I didn't fix you a spectacular—thank you for the compliment—dinner to seduce you into bed. I fixed you dinner to butter you up for the question I was about to ask before YOU kissed me."

His forehead wrinkled. "You didn't come here to seduce me?"

"Of course not." She tried to ignore the strong desire to hump the still hard ridge of his fly like a dog in heat. "While you're not quite as annoying as I first thought, you're still not my type. I like my men far less controlling."

His forehead wrinkles deepened. "I'm not controlling. And I didn't kiss you."

"Uh-huh." She made sure to say it exactly like he did. She must've succeeded because his eyes filled with annoyance.

"Are you mocking me?"

"Yes. Now could we get to the real reason I'm here? I was wondering if you would lease the diner to me so I can open a restaurant."

Just that quickly, Zane's forehead smoothed out and he flashed his dimples. "You expect me to believe that an executive chef from a big city wants to move to Bliss, Texas, and lease a dusty old diner?" He winked at her. "That's a great cover story, but I'm not buying it, sweetheart. Now if you'll excuse me, I'm going to go check on my bull."

He lifted her off his lap like she was a rag doll and set her on the couch before he got to his feet. It was difficult not to look at his bulging fly when it was eye level. And of course, he caught her looking, which resulted in an "uh-huh" much more annoying than hers. With a grin, he turned on a boot heel and headed for the door, grabbing his cowboy hat on the way.

Carly should've let him go. The man was as arrogant as they come. But now that she'd decided to fix up the diner, she wasn't about to let anything stand in her way. She wasn't convinced that she'd make money opening a diner in such a small town, certainly not enough to open a nice restaurant in a metropolitan city. But money wasn't the only reason to open the diner. Opening her own restaurant would prove to the culinary world that she was more than a hot-tempered chef, and that given the opportunity she could run her own business. Although before she could prove anything, she had to get the diner.

She caught up with Zane as he was getting into his truck. "Okay, I get it. I thought it was a pretty crazy idea too when Emery first suggested it. But after mulling it over, it makes sense. I need a job, and Bliss needs a good restaurant. And the diner has the potential to be a good restaurant."

He ignored her and whistled. A black and white dog came racing out of the barn and hopped into the bed of the truck. She hurried around to the passenger side and got in.

"Yes, it will take a lot of elbow grease," she said, "but it's not like I have anything else to do." She grabbed her seatbelt and buckled it as he backed out. "Which brings us to the money part of things. I don't have a lot of money, and what I do have, I'll need to use for a new floor, upholstery, appliances, sign, etc. So I wouldn't be able to pay you anything right away to lease the building. I'd have to wait until after I start making money. But since you aren't making any money off it now anyway, I don't see how that would be a problem—"

Zane applied the brakes and stopped right in the middle of the road before he turned to her. "You're not kidding. You really want to rent the diner and fix it up."

"Wow," she breathed. "It takes a lot to get through your hard head, doesn't it? Yes, I really want to rent the diner from you and fix it up."

"So you don't want me?"

She glanced at his mouth, and the heat of his kiss came back like a bolt of lightning from the sky. She ignored her tingling female parts and shook her head. "No. Now what do you say? Will you lease me the diner or not?"

Instead of answering, he pushed on the accelerator, and the truck took off in a spray of gravel. She might've continued to push for an answer if the dirt road hadn't been so bumpy. It was hard to talk when being bounced around like the smallest kid in a blowup bouncer. When they stopped, he hopped out and strode across a pasture with the dog on his heels. She followed and found him leaning on a wooden fence, looking out at a group of cows. One of the cows she recognized.

"Hey, isn't that your hornless bull?" Zane shot her an irritated look, and she revised. "Not hornyless. Just a bull without horns." She leaned her arms on the fence next to his. "Although he doesn't look like he's very interested in those other cows. Or are those bulls too?"

He snorted. "You don't know a thing about cattle, and yet you want to run a diner in cattle country."

"The only thing I need to know about cattle is how to cook them. And I think my beef tenderloin tonight speaks for itself." Instead of replying, he looked at the cattle. Or maybe he was looking at the peacefulness of the setting.

Carly was about as far away from being a country girl as you could get, but she had to admit the Earhart Ranch was idyllically peaceful. The sun set over the green hills in muted rays of orange and yellow. The air carried the scent of rich earth and lush grass. From the cattle came the calming sound referred to as lowing. The dog raced around, nipping at wandering cows until they moved back to the herd. There was even something calming about that. She was so relaxed she jumped when Zane spoke.

"Horns don't always show the sex. These are Angus cattle. All purebred Angus are polled cattle—neither the males nor the females have horns."

She followed his gaze to the bull. He was huge and muscular, but also kind of cute. "So who named him?"

"The previous owners."

"And I guess you know the story of Ferdinand the bull."

He turned to her. "There's a story about him?"

"It's a children's book about a bull who wanted to smell flowers all day instead of fighting in the bull ring."

Zane rolled his eyes. "Great."

She laughed and studied the bull that was munching contently. "He does seem to like the flowers—eating more than smelling. So why don't you think he's interested in sex?"

"I wish I knew."

"Maybe he just needs to find the right woman."

He glanced over. "Bulls aren't like men. They go after whatever female is in heat."

"I don't know if I agree with that. There are a lot of men out there that go after any female in heat. My ex-husband is a perfect example."

His blue eyes registered surprise. "You were married?"

"When I was much younger and only for a brief time. Just long enough to clear the stars from my eyes and realize that not everyone believes in monogamy."

"I do." He looked away and cleared his throat. "I apologize for assuming you were . . . interested in me. But any man I know would've thought the same thing if a woman arrived at his house out of a clear blue sky and cooked him an amazing dinner."

Amazing. Spectacular. Zane Arrington was starting to grow on her. "You're right. I guess I should've gotten to the reason I was there during dessert and before the kiss."

He turned to her. "Damn straight, you should've." He pointed a finger. "And you kissed me."

Okay, maybe she didn't like him all that much. The man was beyond arrogant and stubborn. Still, she wasn't willing to lose an opportunity to be her own boss over such a trivial issue. "What can I say? You're a hard man to resist."

He squinted. "You're only agreeing so I'll lease you the diner."

"Okay, you got me there. But why does it matter who kissed who? It was a freak thing that will never happen again. Now what do you say? Will you lease me the diner or not?"

He looked back at the bull. "Not. At least not for the deal you offered. If I'm going to lease it to you, I expect to get paid."

Her shoulders wilted. "But I can't afford to pay you now. Especially if I want to get the diner fixed up and opened."

"I'm not talking about money."

Zane was too moral to be talking about something dirty, but she couldn't help teasing him. "So what kind of sex are we talking about?"

"I'm not talking about sex!" He spoke so loudly that the bull stopped eating and looked over. It was like the animal just realized they were there. His ears perked up, and he looked alert for the first time as Zane continued. "I'm talking about you cooking for me on a regular basis like you did tonight."

After what had happened with the kiss, it was a bad idea. "I can't be your personal chef."

"You won't be my personal chef. You'll be cooking for Becky too. And not all the meals. Just dinner." He glanced at the pasture. "What is that crazy bull doing?"

"I can't work in town at the diner every day, then drive out and cook for you every night, then drive back into town to sleep. That won't—" She cut off when Zane grabbed her around the waist and set her behind him. When she peeked around him, she saw the bull charging toward them. Ferdinand stopped inches from the fence, his hooves kicking up dust. But he didn't paw the ground like he had at the falls, and his eyes didn't look mean. Just kind of puppy dog sweet.

"Aww," she said, "I think he remembers me." She stepped around Zane and scratched the bull under the chin. Ferdinand closed his eyes and puffed out through his nostrils.

"He's not a dog." Zane moved behind her. With him towering over her, she felt small and . . . feminine. It was unnerving. "And why would you have to drive back to town? I thought you were staying with Cole and Emery."

She continued to scratch the bull and tried not to notice the heat that radiated off Zane like sun-scorched pavement. "It's past time for me to leave the newlyweds alone. I got a room at the motor lodge." She leaned in and kissed the bull right on his hornless head. "He's so precious. I don't know why you were worried about him the other night."

"Because nothing that weighs close to two thousand pounds is precious." He paused for a second. "Why don't you stay here?"

"Here?" She turned. With the fence behind her and Zane's muscled body in front, she felt even more claustrophobic—like she couldn't get enough air.

"Not here in the pasture," he said, "but here at the ranch. You can sleep in the guestroom for free. Which will give you more money to fix up the diner."

If she'd thought that cooking dinner for him was a bad idea, it would be nothing compared to living in the same house with him. Of course, it would give her a kitchen to try out different dishes for her menu. Once renovations started at the diner, she wouldn't be able to use the kitchen there. And she'd have someone to test her cooking on. What better test subject than a man who loved to eat. And if Becky was there, they wouldn't be alone.

"Come on," he pleaded, "you can't feed a man an awesome dinner like that and leave him high and dry."

The *awesome* cinched it. She'd always been a sucker for a compliment.

"Okay," she said. "I'll move in and be your personal chef. But only for dinner, and you have to help with the dishes."

"I don't do dishes, but I'm sure Becky will help." He flashed a dimple and held out a hand. "Shall we shake on it?"

He didn't shake her hand as much as cradle it. He had workman's hands. Big, callused, and strong. The kind of hands that a woman could count on to get any job done . . . including giving her an amazing orgasm. Her gaze collided with his, and the kiss they'd shared came flooding back, making Carly wonder if she'd made a big mistake by accepting his offer. But it was too late now. The deal had been struck. And she never went back on a deal.

He cleared his throat and released her hand. "Well, then, I guess—" He glanced over at the bull, and his eyes widened. "Uhh . . . maybe you shouldn't touch my bull."

"What do you mean?" She looked at the bull. At first, she didn't notice anything different. Then she glanced down. She wasn't the type to get embarrassed easily, but the enormous penis sticking out from between the bull's back legs made her face flush with heat. "Oh."

Her reaction had Zane tipping back his head and laughing. She had never seen him laugh before. It changed the entire look of his face from tough rancher to carefree cowboy. All the worry lines smoothed out of his forehead, and his eyes twinkled like the stars that had appeared above the last edges of sunset.

"Well, you helped me figure out one thing. My bull has no problem getting it up."

"'Welcome to the Earhart Ranch.' Duke grinned from ear to ear as he went to help Laura down from the buckboard. She ignored his hand and sent him a look that would have frozen Hell. 'I agreed to be your housekeeper. Nothing more. Do you understand, Mr. Earhart?' He understood. He understood that he had Miss Laura right where he wanted her."

CHAPTER ELEVEN

❧

IT WAS AMAZING WHAT A full stomach could do for a man. After only a week of Carly's cooking, Zane felt like things were finally looking up. Nothing had changed in his life. Rachel still hadn't come home. Ferdinand still wasn't doing his job of impregnating the herd. And the town was still gossiping about him. But as Zane finished off the last bite of his strawberry crepe and washed it down with a sip of perfectly brewed coffee, he felt a renewed optimism that everything would work out.

"Just wipe that satisfied look off your face." Carly pointed the knife she'd been using to cut up vegetables at him. The knife was one of hers. Apparently, all chefs carried a set of their own wickedly sharp knives. And he had to admit it was a little scary. "The only reason you got breakfast today was because I made too many crepes and you just happened to show up when you did." She paused. "What are you doing here? You never come back to the house before I leave for the diner."

He didn't know what he was doing there. One second he'd been standing in the barn talking to the vet about Cinnamon getting ready to foal, and the next minute he saw Carly's car still parked in front and he was headed inside. Maybe he had hoped that she would have some breakfast for him. Which wasn't good. He didn't need to get too attached to her cooking. Once Rachel came back, it might be awkward. Or maybe not. Rachel had never liked to cook, and he and Carly were just friends.

The thought surprised him, but once it settled into his mind, he realized it was the truth. He and Carly were friends. Since she'd moved in, things between them had become less volatile and more comfortable. He could talk about anything with Carly, and he knew he'd get her honest opinion. She was intelligent, quick-witted, and seemed genuinely interested in the ranch. The evening meals had become something he looked forward to all day. Even Becky had started staying home for dinner. She seemed to like Carly as much as Zane did.

A knife waved in front of his face. "Did you get up too early, Rancher Zane? Or are you daydreaming about your bull?"

He suddenly remembered she'd asked what he was doing there. "I was talking to the vet about Cinnamon foaling and noticed you were still here."

"So you were hoping to score some breakfast."

Her tone was light and teasing. He watched as she continued to cut the vegetables. The rapid slices she made with the sharp blade were fascinating. And also nerve-wracking.

"Do you have to chop so fast? If you're not careful, you'll cut off a finger."

"I'm always careful, but that doesn't mean I haven't cut myself a time or two."

"Well, I'd just as soon you didn't do it on my watch."

She glanced up. "Blood make you squeamish, does it?"

Not usually. But for some reason the thought of Carly bleeding did. Maybe because she was such a tiny thing and it wouldn't take much blood loss to drain her dry.

"Just be careful."

"Yes, sir, Boss." She went back to chopping and didn't slow down a bit. In fact, it looked like she sped up. The woman was the definition of obstinate. If he asked for pot roast, she made chicken. If he wanted mashed potatoes, she gave him rice. Although he had to admit she made the best chicken and rice he'd ever tasted.

He got up and carried his plate and cup to the sink. She had shared her crepes; the least he could do was clean the dishes. The entire time he rinsed them and put them in the dishwasher he kept an eye on the sharp knife and Carly's fingers. He wouldn't be able to stop her losing a digit, but he could get to her fast enough to apply a tourniquet. It was a relief when she stopped cutting and headed for the cupboards.

She opened one and stood up on her bare toes

to reach a high shelf. She hadn't been spiking her hair lately, and it curled naturally in the humidity. The curls were now long enough to fall into her eyes, and she'd taken to tying them back with a folded red bandanna. The ends stuck up like two little red rabbit ears. From what he could tell, her wardrobe consisted of t-shirts with weird logos and jean shorts that she'd cut off herself. The ones she wore today had lopsided, tattered hems that barely covered her butt cheeks. She had a nice butt. Just round enough to fill a man's hands—

Whoa. He pulled his mind back from the direction it was headed. Since she had kissed him, he'd been having trouble keeping the kiss out of his head. But that was to be expected. You couldn't share a kiss that hot and not have a few lingering thoughts about it. Or maybe more than a few. But he had things under control.

He pulled his gaze from her butt and reached for his hat. "I better get back to work. You headed to the diner?"

She closed the cupboard and turned. "Actually, I'm headed into Austin to pick up a second-hand deep fryer that I found online. Which is why I'm getting dinner ready now. Dirk and I might be a little late getting back."

Zane froze in the process of putting his hat on. "Dirk?"

"Yeah, I need a truck to haul the deep fryer, and Dirk volunteered to drive me in one of the ranch pickups." She must've sensed his displeasure. "Is that a problem? He said he got your okay."

Dirk had gotten his okay to take the afternoon off and to take one of the trucks into Austin. He hadn't gotten his okay to take his cook with him.

"I'm not forgoing the rent money on the diner so you can run off to Austin and party with Dirk," he said. "The deal was for dinner every night."

"And you'll get dinner. The pot roast you've been hinting for is in the Crock-Pot. Becky said she'll stop by at lunch and add the carrots and potatoes and I'm making a chopped salad to put in the fridge. And even though baking isn't my thing, I made a peach cobbler for dessert."

That pretty much left him without a leg to stand on. He was still trying to find one when the kitchen door opened and Dirk came strutting in like a peacock in full-feathered glory. His western shirt looked freshly ironed and his boots shone almost as brightly as his smile.

"Hey, good-lookin', whatcha got cookin'? You want to cook something up with me?"

Carly laughed. "I guess that depends on what you want to cook up, you sizzling hot cowboy." She reached out and, playfully, tapped the brim of his straw hat. Zane became even more annoyed. Women shouldn't touch a man's hat unless things were serious. "Let me finish putting this salad together, and I'll be ready to go."

"I'll drive you to Austin," the words just popped right out of Zane's mouth without any help from his brain. If his brain had been helping, it would've kept his mouth shut and let them go.

They both turned to him. Dirk looked surprised.

"Hey, Zane, I didn't see you there. I thought you were talking to the vet."

"I was, but we got finished a little early so I stopped by the house to . . . check on things."

Dirk looked at Carly, then back at him. His smile got bigger. "I bet you did. And there's no need to drive Carly to Austin. I think I got it covered."

That was exactly what Zane was worried about. Dirk covering Carly. For a second, he worried it was jealousy. But he quickly dismissed the thought. It had nothing to do with jealousy and everything to do with being a smart businessman. He hated to admit it, but Dirk had filled Jess's shoes very nicely. He was now Zane's right hand man. And Carly was the best damned cook this side of the Pecos. Zane didn't want an inter-ranch dalliance to force him to fire one or the other. Things were running too smoothly.

"That pickup is fine for ranch work, but it's too ancient to make the drive to Austin," he said. "I'd hate for you two to get stuck."

Dirk's grin hiked up even further. "It's only eight years old. I wouldn't call that ancient. And Austin is only an hour away."

"Anything can happen on the road." Which was exactly what he was worried about. "Besides, you'll need someone to help you lift the fryer into the back. Carly is too little of a thing to be doing that."

"Would you stop calling me a little thing," she jumped in. "I can lift a fryer."

Zane completely ignored her and headed for the door. "Let's get moving. I want to get back for that pot roast."

The trip into Austin wasn't that bad. In fact, it was kind of nice to get away from the ranch for a little bit. Dirk sat shotgun and told one humorous story after another about the many jobs he'd had in his life. And Carly sat in the back and mostly just laughed. Her entire face lit up when she laughed. Zane caught himself glancing in the rearview mirror a little too often. When he drifted over into the other lane and got honked at, he finally had to adjust the mirror so all he saw were the two bandanna rabbit ears.

The guy who had the deep fryer was a wheeler and dealer if ever there was one. He had an entire warehouse full of restaurant equipment, and Zane was doubtful that half of it worked. That's why he stepped in before the deal was finalized.

"So this fryer is in working condition?"

"Yes, sir," the guy said. "I guaran-damn-tee it."

"That's good to know," Zane said. "I'm Ms. Hanover's attorney and I'd hate to have to file a suit if it doesn't."

The guy's car-salesmen smile faded, and he shuffled his feet. "Well, now, I'm sure that wouldn't happen . . . but maybe there's a better fryer I can offer you for the same price."

The "better" fryer turned out to be newer and bigger. And for once, Carly didn't get after him for taking over. In fact, once they had it loaded, she gave him a big kiss right on the lips. The woman had no sense of propriety.

"There," she said with a twinkle in her eyes, "now I have given you a kiss. And for making such a great deal, I want to take you and Dirk to lunch. I heard about this new restaurant called The Pit that's supposed to have the best barbecue in Austin."

Zane was starving, so it sounded like a good idea to him. Although when they stepped in the door of the restaurant, it didn't look like any barbecue pit he'd ever been to. There were no long tables with wooden benches and plenty of napkins, and there were no slabs of meat cooking on a spit. The restaurant was much more upscale and chic. So much so that even Carly was surprised.

"I thought with a name like The Pit it would be a casual restaurant." She glanced around at all the businessmen and woman crowded in the glass and chrome lobby. "I'm not dressed for a place like this. I look like a hillbilly country girl who just rode in on her tractor."

Dirk grinned and reached out to tug on the bandanna ear. "You do look a little like a country bunny."

Her eyes widened, and she pulled off the bandanna just as the hostess walked up. Since there was over an hour wait, Zane would've just as soon headed back to the ranch and eaten there. Carly cooked better than any restaurant he'd ever eaten at. But then he realized that wasn't fair. She looked forward to trying the food here. Besides, she had spent the last week cooking for him and Becky. She deserved a nice meal that was cooked by someone else.

He asked for a table for three and slipped the hostess a twenty. A few moments later, they were directed to a table. Not that the corner table in the bar was worth an extra twenty. The chrome barstools were as uncomfortable as the ones Rachel had bought for the ranch kitchen and the wall of hanging glass that divided the bar from the restaurant looked more than a little dangerous.

"I hope you're not planning on making the diner look like this place," Dirk said as he took a seat on the other side of Carly. "I feel like I'm in a carnival's house of mirrors."

"No worries there," Carly said. "I want to keep the diner as original as possible. Emery had the idea to ask people in town if they had any old pictures of the diner so I could show them to my contractors. I've already had numerous people drop by with their old photos. Do you have any photos of the diner, Zane?"

"I might, but you'll have to ask Becky about where my mom would've put them. So the contractors I hooked you up with are working out?"

"Perfectly, thank you. From what they told me, I should have the diner ready to open in three weeks."

Zane lowered his menu. "Three weeks?"

"Or sooner if things go well." Her eyes lit up. "Wouldn't it be great if I could open it on the Fourth of July for the Chili Cook-off?"

The Fourth of July was only two weeks away. And two weeks of Carly's cooking didn't sound like nearly enough to Zane. Sure, he could go into town and eat at the diner. But then he wouldn't be able to sit in the kitchen and watch Carly cook. Or wake up in the morning to a cup of freshly ground coffee and her snarky remarks. Carly was the one responsible for keeping his stomach full and his mind on something other than Rachel leaving him. If she left too, he might not be able to hold things together.

A plan formed in his brain. A plan that was devious and underhanded. But a man had to do what a man had to do.

He closed his menu. "I wouldn't get my hopes

up. Contractors always over promise on the due date. You never know what kind of problems will crop up during a renovation. It could take months." He got up. "If you'll excuse me, I need to go to the bathroom."

It didn't take him long to step into the hallway by the bathroom and make the phone calls. When he returned Carly and Dirk were discussing a man on the other side of the glass wall.

"I don't think there's anything wrong with wearing yellow pants," Carly said.

"There is if they're as yellow as a canary and you're a man," Dirk retorted. "The guy looks like Big Bird's baby."

Zane took a seat and followed their gazes to the guy sitting at a table by the window. Dirk was right. He did look like Big Bird's baby. He also looked familiar. It only took a second to place him. He was the interior designer Rachel had hired to redecorate their house. Zane had only met Benny once. But it was hard to forget a man who wore Easter-egg–colored clothes and charged you a fortune to fill your house with uncomfortable furniture.

He watched as Benny leaned over and kissed the woman he was with. Zane was surprised. He'd thought Benny was gay. Obviously, he'd been wrong.

"Damn," Dirk said. "Maybe I should get some yellow pants. That woman is hot."

Zane finally paid attention to the woman. He couldn't tell much about her looks from where he sat, except that she had brown hair. But when Benny stopped kissing her and they got up to leave, he got a better look.

Dirk was right. She was pretty. She was tall with long legs that looked even longer in the blue high heels. There was something about those heels that struck a chord of recognition, and his gaze snapped up to the woman's face just as she turned.

Her name slipped out of his mouth on a whisper of surprise.

"Rachel?"

"Laura thought she'd be treated like a servant at the Earhart Ranch—like she'd been treated at her uncle's house. Instead, Duke's brothers treated her as a respected guest, while Duke treated her like his prize possession."

CHAPTER TWELVE

"IJUST CAN'T BELIEVE THAT YOU would move to Bliss, instead of moving to Atlanta and helping me with the wedding. And would you stop painting and look at me. Sweet Baby Jesus! I'm drowning in a quagmire of inept florists, bakers, and caterers, and you don't even care."

Carly stopped painting the diner wall and looked at her laptop, which sat on the nearest table of a booth. Savannah's face was almost completely obscured by her fat cat's furry body. All she could see were Savannah's eyes. Besides being a beautiful hazel, they were tear-filled and frantic. Of course, she was always frantic about something. Worrying was just part of Savannah's personality. But Carly couldn't ignore her friend's desperation.

She put the roller in the tray and sat down in the booth, turning the laptop on the table to give her friend undivided attention. "Stop being a pathological worrier. Your wedding is over two months away. I helped you plan the menu. I found you an amazing caterer. And I'll be there in plenty of time to make sure your reception dinner is flawless." Although how she was going to squeeze in the wedding in the midst of running a restaurant she had yet to figure out. Not that the diner would be even close to being finished in two months' time.

Zane had been right. Unexpected things had popped up during the renovation. The tile guy had called to say he was having trouble finding the right tile. The upholstery guy's grandmother died. And the plumber who was supposed to fix the leaky faucets and running toilet hadn't showed up due to a plumber's strike.

Carly had wanted to ask Zane if he knew any non-union plumbers, but he had enough to worry about after finding out that Rachel had left him for another man. Every time she thought of his face when he'd whispered his wife's name, her heart hurt. Maybe because that was the only reaction Zane had allowed himself. He didn't yell or jump up and hit the guy. He just whispered her name once, and then turned away and started talking to Dirk about getting in the rest of the hay before it rained.

Carly had opened her mouth to address the elephant sitting in the middle of the table, but Dirk stopped her by squeezing her knee hard. And maybe he was right. Maybe Zane didn't need her pointing out the obvious. She certainly hadn't needed her father to tell her what a big mistake she had made by marrying Sam.

Still, she hated to see Zane suffer in silence. He hadn't spoken a word on the way home from Austin. When they got home after dropping the fryer off at the diner, he'd gotten out of the truck and walked straight to the barn. She thought about taking him a plate of roast beef and potatoes, but then decided against it. Sometimes, a person just needed to be alone to lick his wounds.

"You're right," Savannah pulled Carly from her thoughts, "everything is going to be just fine." She grabbed Miss Pitty Pat and stroked the cat's head almost frantically. Miss Pitty didn't look like she was enjoying the attention. "I guess I'm just feeling a little left out now that you and Emery are living in the same town. I wish I could be there to help you with the diner and to help you search for the rest of the final book. Have you found any more chapters?"

"No, but Emery is convinced that there are more."

"And you're not?"

"From what I've read, Lucy was bedridden the last month of her life. I could see her finishing the last book, but I can't see her sneaking around and hiding it all over town."

"Maybe she had someone hide it for her?"

"Maybe, but why? It just doesn't make any sense."

"Lots of things in life don't make sense." Savannah sent her a pointed look. "Like you being Zane's personal chef for example. That makes no sense to me whatsoever. Especially when you swore you would never be anyone's personal chef. You're hot for his body, aren't you?"

When Carly's mouth dropped open, Savannah

pointed a finger. "Don't you dare try to act like you're offended by the question, Carly Sue. It's the same kind of question you would ask if I was living with a man whose wife just ran off with her designer."

Carly cringed. "I told Emery not to tell anyone about that!"

Savannah instantly looked hurt. "You wanted to keep a secret from me?"

"Only because you have the biggest mouth in the country."

"I do not. If you tell me to keep a secret, my lips are locked tighter than a Ziploc bag." She mimicked locking her lips and throwing away the key. Her silence lasted for all of two seconds. "Besides, what is the big deal about Zane's wife running off with another man? People have affairs all the time."

"That's easy to say if you haven't lived through an affair. I have, and I can tell you that infidelity is a big deal to the victim. It leaves you struggling with a boatload of insecurities that you don't get over easily."

"I don't think you have an insecure bone in your body, Carly Sue."

Savannah was wrong. Carly had more than a few insecurities. She was just good at hiding them. And so was Zane. Which was why she could sympathize with him. He was hurting. He just wasn't going to let anyone know it.

"So was this designer hot?" Savannah put Miss Pitty in her bed on the desk and picked up a king-sized Butterfinger. "He would have to be to lure a woman away from cutie-pie Zane."

"He was attractive, but not nearly as attractive as

Zane." She leaned closer to the screen. "What are you doing eating chocolate? I thought you were on a strict diet so you'd fit in your Dior wedding gown."

Savannah took another bite. "I am, but when I get stressed I crave chocolate. And I'm about as stressed as a girl—"

"Yoo-hoo! Anyone home?"

At the greeting, Carly glanced at the pass-through into the kitchen. A wide-brimmed hat appeared in the opening. Carly knew immediately who it was. Maybelline Marble's hats were easily recognizable. As was her small stature. It was nice for Carly to know she wasn't the shortest person in town.

She looked at the screen. "I've got to go, Savannah. I'll call you later. And stop worrying. Everything's going to work out." She closed her laptop just as Ms. Marble appeared in the doorway carrying a copy paper box.

"There you are."

Carly got up. "Come in, Ms. Marble. Please tell me you've brought some of your baked goodies."

The woman's aged eyes twinkled as she set the box down on the counter. "I might've brought a little something." She took the lid off and pulled a plastic-wrapped plate out of the box. "Cinnamon swirl muffins. It's my mother's recipe, although I decided to add a little sour cream to this batch." She took off the miles of plastic wrap and held out the plate to Carly. "With my diabetes, I couldn't taste them to see if it worked."

Carly took a muffin. "I'll be happy to be your taste tester." She took a bite. It was as delicious as everything else Ms. Marble baked. "Amazing," she said. "You could go up against any professional baker I know, Ms. Marble."

The old woman beamed. "Some folks think it's crazy that I still bake when I can't eat anything I make. But it's not about the eating. It's about the satisfaction I get when—"

"Someone enjoys what you baked," Carly finished the sentence for her. "I totally get it. I feel the same way when someone enjoys my cooking."

"Exactly right. Although from what I hear, you're a much better chef than I am a baker." When Carly shot her a curious look, she smiled. "A good-looking drifter has been filling my ears with what a great cook you are."

"Dirk? I didn't realize you were friends."

"When I found out he was a handy man, I hired him for a few odd jobs around my house. I didn't expect him to keep coming after he got the job with Zane, but that boy has a sweet tooth. He stops by every night to pilfer from my cookie jar and fix things he has no business fixing. The drippy faucet and broken back porch step could've waited until I got my pension check, but he says my cookies are payment enough."

Carly smiled. "He does have a kind heart."

Ms. Marble's eyes twinkled. "So you're gotten a glimpse of that too. Most folks in town think he's a no-account drifter, but I think there's a lot more to Dirk Hadley than he's letting on. And I'm not just talking about his kind heart. There's more to his story. I've just yet to figure out what." Carly had always thought so too, but before she could agree, Ms. Marble glanced around. "Do you mind if I look around? It's been a while since I've seen the place."

"Of course not." Carly followed behind her. "But I have to warn you, it's a mess."

"I'm not interested in the mess. Just the memories." She stood in the middle of the diner and looked around. She didn't seem to notice the paint-spattered tarp and painting supplies as she relived those memories.

Ms. Marble really was a tiny woman. Or maybe it was the large hat and loose-fitting dress that gave that illusion. With her double string of pearls and white gloves, she looked like a little girl playing dress up.

"My daddy brought me here after I lost my first front tooth," she said. "He told me that God had given me the perfect space for a drinking straw, and we probably should put it to good use." She pointed to the two barstools at the very end of the counter. "We sat right there and drank strawberry shakes through straws." She placed a hand on her droopy breasts. "Lord, that was the best milkshake I ever had in my life."

For some reason, tears welled in Carly's eyes. Maybe because her father had never been the kind of dad to celebrate her milestones and achievements. And he never would be.

Ms. Marble moved over to a booth and reverently touched the laminated tabletop. "And this was where I had my first date with my late husband. David was a good man. That's why I didn't hesitate to say yes when he asked me to marry him just a month later. I was more than ready for a man who would love only me."

"Were you married in the little white chapel?"

Carly asked.

Ms. Marble turned. "No. The Arringtons have always been a little possessive of that chapel. And I can't say that I blame them. It's a historical monument if ever there was one. It needs to be preserved and cherished." She glanced around. "As much as this diner does." She pointed to the corner booth where Carly's laptop sat. "Did you know that Lucy used to plot all her books right there in that booth?"

Carly moved closer to the booth and ran a hand over the laminate top. "I know. I saw a picture of her sitting here once."

Ms. Marble smiled. "But I bet you don't know what she ordered."

She glanced up. "Do you?"

"Of course I do. I knew Lucy better than most— or at least better than most anyone still living."

The information surprised Carly, then she realized it shouldn't. Lucy had died in the late 1960s and had only been thirty. It made sense that people were still living who had been her friends.

"What did she order?" she asked.

Ms. Marble hesitated for one dramatic second before she spoke. "A glass of water."

"A glass of water?"

"Yes." Ms. Marble laughed. "Lucy Arrington was the cheapest woman this side of the Mississippi. She would order water and five slices of lemon, then make herself a glass of lemonade, using half the container of sugar." She shook her head. "It never failed to amaze me that a woman so wealthy refused to buy a glass of lemonade."

Carly was thoroughly disappointed. She had

hoped for a relatively expensive menu item she could name after the great author. Now she was stuck with cheap Lucy's Lemonade.

"So why did the owner let her continue to come?"

"Because she was Lucy, a great author and an Arrington. The Arringtons are the reason this town is still here. Even if the last generation fell down on the job, I have high hopes for Cole, Zane, and even Raff—that bad boy. Reopening the diner could be the first step in our town's revitalization."

Carly instantly felt guilty. She wasn't interested in the town's revitalization. The diner was just a short-term plan. Something to erase the black marks beside her name and, hopefully, make her a little money. She had no plans to spend the rest of her life in Bliss.

Ms. Marble walked over and picked up the box from the counter and brought it over to the table. "That's why I'm here. I brought you all my old pictures. I was going to pick out the ones of the diner, but then I thought you might be interested in other old photographs too. I haven't looked through them in ages, but I'm sure you'll find lots from the late fifties and early sixties." She peeked in the box, and her eyes turned confused. "That's funny. I don't remember organizing them. Of course, I don't remember much of anything these days." She adjusted her hat. "I'd stay and help you, but I need to get going. I have a meeting about the Chili Cook-off."

"I heard about the Chili Cook-off. It sounds like a good time."

"It isn't really a cook-off as much as a potluck.

Last year, there were only three entries." Her eyes sharpened on Carly. "Although with a successful chef helping us out, things might be different."

Between the restaurant, cooking for Zane, and Savannah's wedding, Carly didn't have time to help with a cook-off. But since Ms. Marble had just brought her muffins and photos, she couldn't exactly decline. "I'd be happy to help. Just let me know what you need."

After Ms. Marble left, Carly went back to painting. Once she had finished two of the walls, she took a break and sat down in the booth to look at the photos. Ms. Marble was right. They appeared to be organized by the dates on the back of the pictures and who was in them. There was a stack of Ms. Marble with an intellectual-looking man. Another of her with a handsome cowboy. And others with various people Carly recognized from town. But it was the last stack of pictures that grabbed her attention. It appeared that Ms. Marble and Lucy had been more than just acquaintances. They had been friends. The pictures showed them as children picking flowers in front of the chapel, as teenagers on horseback, and as adults sitting on the porch of Cole's house and drinking lemonade in a booth at the diner. There was only one picture of Lucy by herself.

It was older than the other pictures. Lucy didn't look like she was much older than eighteen. She was sitting on a bunk bed and smiling. Carly could never remember seeing a picture of Lucy smiling. But she was smiling in this picture, not only with happiness, but also with sexual satisfaction. There was no other way to describe the sensual, droopy-lidded smile she was giving the camera. Or not the camera as much as the person taking it.

Most historians believed Lucy had been an old maid who spent all her time writing. Could they be wrong? Did Lucy have a lover? If she did, and if Carly and Emery could figure out who it was, they might be able to find the other chapters.

Wanting to call Emery, she searched for her cellphone. She found it under the picture of Ms. Marble and Lucy at the chapel. When she grabbed it, the picture slipped off the table and into a crack between the top and bottom cushions of the booth.

The crack wasn't big enough for Carly to get her fingers in. She couldn't lose Ms. Marble's picture, so she grabbed a crowbar the tile guy had left and pried the bottom cushion off. It would have to be removed when it was reupholstered anyway. If the upholstery guy ever showed up.

Once the seat was off, Carly looked down into the wooden base.

She found the picture.

She also found an envelope with another chapter of Tender Heart.

"Just like he'd thought, Laura was one hardworking woman. Now all he had to do was get her to stop thinking about housework and start thinking about him."

CHAPTER THIRTEEN

ZANE'S MARRIAGE WAS OVER. AFTER months of denial, seeing Rachel with another man had made him realize that she wasn't coming back. He should've felt hurt and angry. Instead, he just felt confused. He couldn't figure out where he'd gone wrong. He'd followed all the rules. He'd gotten her roses for her birthday and diamond jewelry for Christmas. He'd taken her to Austin for dinner and dancing on their anniversaries. He'd never complained about how much money she spent and told her she looked beautiful on a regular basis. He'd done everything his father had ever taught him, and still he'd failed.

Zane Arrington was a failure. And he wasn't sure how to deal with that.

A soft whinny had him glancing at the iPad on his nightstand. He reached out and tapped the screen. A picture of Cinnamon in her stall came up. The mare had been restless all day, a sign that her time was getting close, and now she was lying down in one corner. Not wanting to wake Carly and Becky, he dressed in the dark, then he grabbed his boots and softly walked down the hallway in his stocking feet. Once outside, he stopped on the porch to pull on his boots.

"So you couldn't sleep either?"

Carly's voice startled him and almost made him lose his balance. He hopped around on one foot until he could get his boot the rest of the way on. He turned to find her sitting in a rocker with the heels of her bare feet up on the chair and her chin resting on her knees. Shep was curled up next to the rocker.

He didn't know why the image soothed him, but it did. Some of the tension in his neck released, and he felt like he could finally take a breath.

"I hope you know you're spoiling my working dog." He tugged the other boot on and moved closer to the rocking chair. "He sleeps in the barn."

She reached down and scratched the dog's head. "He's just keeping me company. And don't act like you don't spoil him. I've seen you taking him food scraps after dinner."

He shrugged. "He's a good dog. So what are you doing out here?"

"After being a chef for so many years and not getting to sleep until the wee hours of the morning, my body clock is a little wacky. Of course, I'll never be like you and Becky, climbing into bed at eight-thirty and sleeping like the dead."

"How do you know we sleep like the dead?"

"You both snore. Becky a little louder than you."

She lowered her feet. "You didn't come home for dinner tonight. That makes two nights in a row you haven't eaten. Did you want me to make you something now?"

He shook his head. "Thanks, but I'm not hungry."

Her big brown eyes drilled through him like high-beam headlights. "Do you want to talk?"

Damn. Besides not being hungry, this was the other reason he hadn't stopped working until dark. He didn't want to be interrogated by Carly. Nor did he want her sympathy.

"I need to go check on Cinnamon." He turned and headed for the barn.

But he should've known an exit wouldn't be that simple. He'd just reached Cinnamon's stall when Carly came up behind him, Shep trailing in her wake. He steeled himself for a barrage of questions. Instead, she peeked in on the horse.

"You think she's going to give birth tonight?"

Relieved she wasn't going to force him to talk about Rachel, he rested his arms on the top edge of the stall door. A utility lamp had been placed in the stall for the camera. Its light was soft, but enough to clearly see Cinnamon lying down in one corner of the stall. "See how the muscles in her legs are twitching? And how swollen her vulva is?" Carly laughed, and he glanced over. "What?"

She bit back her grin. "Nothing. I guess I'm just not used to ranch talk. So a swollen . . . vulva means it's time. Shouldn't we call the vet?"

"Not yet. It could take a while. You can go to bed."

She continued to watch the horse. "I'd like to

stay if that's okay. I've never been present at a birth before."

He didn't want her to stay. He wanted to be alone. But he couldn't think of a good excuse to get her to leave so he only shrugged. "Suit yourself."

They stood there for a long time without saying a word, Carly standing so close that he could smell her. She usually smelled like a wide array of herbs and spices. But tonight she smelled like flowery soap. And since her hair looked damp, he figured it was her shampoo. She wore saggy boxers and a tiny white top that was low enough that he could see the top edge of her broken heart tattoo.

He looked away and concentrated on Cinnamon. Even from where he stood, he could see her large belly contract. He glanced at his watch and waited for the next contraction.

Carly leaned closer, her bare shoulder brushing the underside of his arm. "Is she in pain?"

"Probably. All childbirth is painful."

"Which is why I have no plans to experience it in the near future. I have a very low tolerance for pain."

He glanced at her. "You don't want kids?" He didn't know why he was surprised. Maybe because Carly had such a nurturing nature. *A nurturing nature?* He didn't know where that thought came from. But now that it was there, he realized it was an accurate description. Despite her outspokenness, she was nurturing. She nurtured people with food.

"I don't know that I'll never want kids," she said. "Just not now. I have too many things I want to achieve."

"Like opening a diner in a Podunk Texas town?"

She laughed. "Sometimes you have to start small and work your way up. Although I don't know if the diner is ever going to open when I can't get my contractors to show up and do any work."

He'd been so wrapped up in thinking about his failed marriage that he'd forgotten he had called the contractors and asked them to delay their work on the diner. It had been a childish thing to do. And tomorrow he intended to correct the situation. If he'd learned anything, he'd learned that you can't force a woman to stay if she wants to go.

Cinnamon whinnied, and he turned his attention to the stall. Her water had broken and he could see the whitish amniotic sac. He pulled out his phone and dialed the vet. When he didn't get an answer, he left a message and slipped his phone back into his pocket.

"Should we do something?" Carly asked.

"Not unless things go wrong." He glanced down and noticed she was standing on her tiptoes to get a better view. He grabbed a bale of hay and moved it next to the stall, then took her hand and helped her up.

It was a mistake. Now it was much easier to read the sympathy in the dark pools of her eyes.

"It's okay to let it out, Zane," she said in a low whisper. "I get it. You think that the only way to stop from shattering into a million pieces is to keep all the hurt, humiliation, and confusion buried deep down inside you. But believe me when I tell you it won't work. After I found Sam in bed with our neighbor, I was devastated. Like you, I thought that if I kept the pain buried and just kept going, everything would be okay. But burying hurtful things doesn't get rid of them. It just hides them from view. They're still there, rotting and decaying and poisoning you from the inside out. It's much better if you release them and let them go."

He ground his teeth and turned away. "I don't want to talk about this."

She grabbed his arm and forced him to look at her. "If you don't talk about it now, you never will. And if anyone needs to let it out, you do, Zane. You barely even flinched when you saw your wife with another man. That's just weird. Even I yelled and screamed and starting throwing things. You acted like nothing had happened and ordered barbecue ribs. Are you that cold or do you not even love her?"

"You think I don't love my own wife?" His voice shook with anger. "You think I only married her because that's what people expected? Because they expected Zane Arrington to marry the prettiest girl in town and live happily ever after like some fuckin' Tender Heart hero? Well, you're wrong. Only a fool would marry someone they didn't love. Well, I'm not a fool." He pointed a finger at her. "Do you hear me? I'm not a damn stupid fool!"

He yelled the last words so loudly that they echoed off the rafters of the barn and came right back at him. They sliced through him like Carly's wickedly sharp knives, taking off his skin and leaving his insides open and exposed. And without the façade of denial he'd been hiding behind, he was forced to accept the truth.

He was a damned, stupid fool.

He gripped his head in his hands as if to keep his

world from falling apart. But it was too late. It had already fallen apart. Now all he was left with were the pieces. "Why did you do that?" he asked. "Why do you always have to push me over the edge?"

Her answer was soft and low. "Because someone needs to. Someone needs to push you off the Great Arrington Pedestal that your father and the town has built for you and make you see that you're not a bigger-than-life fictional character. You're just a man. A man who needs to stop feeling responsible for everyone else and just take care of yourself."

He lowered his hands and looked at her. "Like you do? Tough Carly Hanover who tells everyone to go to hell and feels no responsibility to anyone. Funny, but it doesn't look like that has worked out so well for you." Before she could reply, a whinny of pain came from the stall. The foal was being born. The head and one front leg had appeared, but Zane couldn't see the other leg.

"Damn." He hurried to the sink.

Carly followed him. "What's wrong?"

"Foals should be born front legs first—both legs. There's only one leg showing." He scrubbed his hands. "I need to get the other one down."

"How?"

He grabbed a pair of rubber gloves. "By going in and getting it. If you don't have a weak stomach, you can wash your hands and help." He expected her to decline, or at least hesitate. He should've known better. Carly wasn't the type of woman to hesitate when something needed to be done. Even if that something was pushing him over the edge. She scrubbed up and grabbed a pair of gloves from the box.

"Stay," he ordered Shep as he opened the stall door.

Carly followed, but took a step back when she saw the mess on the straw. "Okay, maybe I do have a weak stomach."

"Too late now." He pulled on his gloves and knelt. "Hold her tail out of the way." She put on her gloves and knelt next to him, then grabbed the tail he'd wrapped earlier that day.

Since he'd done this before, he didn't waste any time pushing the foal's head back in to the birth canal and searching for the other leg. Once he found it, he made sure the head was nose down before he grabbed the other leg and pulled. With a little help from Mama, the foal slipped out in a wash of fluid. Zane finished tearing off the sack and was relieved to see the foal breathing and moving.

"It's spotted," Carly exclaimed with wonder.

Zane cleared the mucus from the foal's nostrils. "He sure is. But you will not call him Spot."

"I was thinking more of Muffin since he looks like Ms. Marble's cinnamon swirl muffins."

"I'm not having a male horse named Muffin."

She gave him a sassy look. "Why not? We could call him Stud Muffin." It was impossible to hold in his laughter. When he finally sobered, he discovered her watching him with a smile on her face. "I think you're going to survive, Zane Arrington."

She was right again. He would.

"Laura stepped into the room with a stack of clean, folded shirts. She dropped the entire stack when she saw Duke sitting in the brass tub as naked as the day he was born."

CHAPTER FOURTEEN

❦

CARLY HAD HEARD ABOUT PEOPLE being changed after witnessing a live birth, but she hadn't really believed it until she'd seen the foal being born. There was something about the miracle of birth that made you reassess what was important in life. As she watched the foal stagger to his feet and take his first steps, she had to wonder if Zane hadn't been right. She was a little too quick to tell people to go to hell. Her bosses. Her husband. Her father. When the little horse finally wobbled over to his mother and started to nurse, she left Zane and headed into the house.

It was still early in Washington, D.C. where her father was now stationed, but her parents had always been early risers. Especially her military dad. He answered the phone on the second ring, his voice as gruff and unbending as it always was.

"Colonel Bennett."

She swallowed the lump of longing that always formed whenever she talked with her father. "Hi, Dad."

There was a long pause. In the seconds that ticked by, she still held out hope that his reaction would be different. That he'd greet her, if not with love, then with concern for his only child. It was a futile hope.

"I'll get your mother."

"Wait, Dad." She took a deep breath and gathered her courage to continue. "I just wanted to tell you that I'm doing okay. And . . . I love you."

There was another long pause before he cleared his throat. "Okay then. I'll get your mother."

Even though he couldn't see her, Carly nodded as the phone was passed to her mom, who never acknowledged her husband's behavior. She chattered on about her knitting club, her hot flashes, and the trip they were planning to Italy. Finally, she asked how Carly was doing. She thought about telling her mom about moving and the new diner, but then decided against it. Her mother had never liked her choice of careers, just as her father hadn't liked her taste in men.

"I'm fine," she said. "I'm just fine."

After ending the call, the buoyant feeling of the birth was long gone. Now she just felt depressed. So she did what she always did after talking with her parents: She cooked.

She made boysenberry jam and cream cheese stuffed French toast, ham and asparagus quiche, homemade sage and maple sausage patties, fresh-squeezed orange juice, and fresh ground coffee. The smell of coffee always woke Becky up. She stumbled in wearing a high school football jersey with some guy's name on the back and grabbed a mug from the cupboard.

"You know you can never leave, right? Now that I've gotten used to waking up to your coffee, I won't be able to wake up without it." She poured herself a cup, then glanced at the clock on the way to the refrigerator to get her dairy creamer. She stopped in her tracks, sloshing coffee onto the floor. "Holy shit! It's only five o'clock."

Carly laughed. "Sorry. Cinnamon had her foal last night."

"Why didn't Zane wake me?"

She handed Becky a plate of French toast. "I guess he didn't want to ruin your sleep. I helped him." She didn't know why that made her feel so proud. All she'd done was hold the tail . . . and try not to gag.

"I knew I liked you." Becky sat down at the breakfast bar. "Rachel would never have been caught dead at a foaling." She cut into the French toast and took a bite. "Lord, this is good. It's better than my mom's. Just don't tell her I told you so. She's sensitive about her cooking. And about her kids." She took another bite. "She's going to be upset when she hears about Rachel leaving. Rachel is the perfect little lady as far as my mom is concerned. She tried out for all the girlie things I refused to. Homecoming queen. Cheerleader. Chili Cook-off queen."

"The perfect queen for a perfect Tender Heart hero," Carly added. Becky didn't seem to notice the sarcasm in her voice.

"Exactly. At least, that's what everyone thinks.

But not me. Zane doesn't need a prissy home-coming queen. He needs a woman who will be right there by his side through the messy times." She sent Carly a knowing look. "Like helping him deliver a foal."

Before Carly could dissuade Becky from any crazy ideas she was getting about her and Zane, the back door opened and Dirk peeked in. "I saw the light. Is everything okay?"

"Cinnamon had her foal," Becky said around a mouthful of French toast. "And Carly cooked a truckload of food to celebrate."

"Did she have it last night?" Dirk stepped inside and took off his hat. "I stopped by Cole and Emery's for dinner, and Emery seemed pretty giddy about something. But she refused to tell Cole and me what it was."

Becky perked up. "Maybe Emery's pregnant."

Emery wasn't pregnant. She was giddy over Carly finding the tenth chapter of the Tender Heart book. She'd been so excited after reading it that she'd danced around the diner like a crazy woman. It seemed that she was right. Lucy Arrington *had* hidden chapters of the book all over town. And now they had a clue as to where they'd find another chapter.

After seeing the picture of Lucy, Emery agreed with Carly. The heavy-lidded look was definitely sexual. Now they just needed to figure out who the man, or woman, was who had taken the picture and if that person still had the bed from the photo . Emery was convinced if they could find the bed, they'd find another chapter. Carly didn't think it would be that easy. The diner had stayed in the same place, but a bed could be anywhere.

"What's going on here?" Zane walked in. He looked exhausted, but his eyes held the same glow that Carly had felt earlier. "Are we hosting the entire town of Bliss for breakfast?" He sent her a smile.

There was a secretive sparkle in his deep blue eyes. A sparkle that acknowledged the fact they had shared something special in the barn. Beneath his gaze, a warm feeling settled in the pit of Carly's stomach. It was the feeling she had been searching for when she'd called her parents. The feeling of connection. That it came from Zane scared the hell out of her.

She grabbed a plate from the cupboard. "What do you want? Quiche, French toast, sausage?"

"How about a little bit of everything?"

She turned to find him standing right behind her. So close that she could smell his fresh hay scent and feel the heat that emanated from him like a pizza oven.

"I'm sorry I yelled at you in the barn," he said in a soft voice only she could hear.

She nodded. "I'm sorry I pushed you so hard."

It took him a while to answer, and when he did it wasn't what she expected. "Sometimes a person needs a push to get him moving in the right direction again." Their gazes locked, and Carly didn't know how long they stood there looking at each other before Becky spoke.

"What are we going to name the foal?"

"I haven't given it much thought." Zane took the plate from Carly and proceeded to fill it with more than a "little bit" of everything. Obviously his appetite was back. Which made her extremely happy. She filled a plate for Dirk, and then filled her own plate before taking a seat at the breakfast bar.

As soon as she was seated, Zane held out his hand. After eating numerous meals with them, she knew the Arringtons liked to say grace. But they usually only said it at dinnertime. Never at breakfast. But once her hand was nestled in Zane's and he started to pray, she understood why today was an exception.

"Dear Heavenly Father, we thank you for the new addition to the Arrington Ranch. The miracle of birth is a glorious reminder that life's a blessing and we should be thankful for each day you give us on this earth. And thank you for this bountiful feast." He paused and squeezed Carly's hand. "And for the woman who prepared it. She's been a true blessing to this household. Amen."

He released her hand and dug in, as did Dirk and Becky. Carly was the only one who didn't pick up her fork. No one had ever referred to her as a true blessing before. An outspoken pain in the butt, yes. A true blessing, never. It made her a little emotional. Or maybe it was just the effects of the birth and little sleep.

After breakfast, Zane took charge of cleanup. For a man who said he didn't do dishes, he had become quite the expert at loading the dishwasher. Once the dishwasher was running and the counters cleaned, Carly wanted to head to bed. But when everyone else went out to the barn to check on the foal, she couldn't help tagging along. The foal was curled up in a corner fast asleep. Cinnamon stood guard over him as any good mommy would.

"He's a paint," Becky said. "Why didn't you say something, Zane?"

"I figured you'd find out soon enough." He glanced at Carly, who was standing on tiptoe to peek into the stall. He shooed Shep off the hay bale where he was sitting and held out a hand to Carly. "Get up there, Shorty."

She sent him an annoyed look. "Don't you even think about giving me that nickname."

"I wouldn't dream of it . . . Carly Sue." He helped her up on the bale.

"Speaking of names," Becky stepped next to Carly, "we have to figure one out for this cute little guy."

"How about Apple Jacks?" Dirk said as he moved behind Becky. "I've always loved the name Apple Jacks for a horse."

"That sounds like a horse that should be put out to pasture. This little guy looks like he's going to have some speed. What about Thunder Bolt? Or something simple like Race? Yeah, let's call him Race."

"Nope." Zane moved behind Carly and rested a hand on the stall door. "You got to name the last foal. It's my turn. And he doesn't look like a Race. He looks like . . . one of Ms. Marble's Cinnamon Swirl Muffin. Which is why we're calling him Muffin."

"Muffin?" Dirk and Becky said together.

Zane glanced at Carly and winked. "Yeah, Muffin."

"'Have you ever been kissed, Miss Laura?' Duke backed her into the corner. 'And not a peck like your mama would give you, but an honest-to-good-ness, full-mouthed kiss that makes you feel like a woman?'"

CHAPTER FIFTEEN

☙

"HEY, ZANE!" EMMETT GREETED HIM as soon as Zane stepped out of his truck. "I heard about that new foal of yours. You better get ready to get into some major fights when you start riding a horse named Muffin."

Zane shook his head in disgust. What had he been thinking? No self-respecting rancher in the country would name a male horse Muffin. Or a female for that matter. And there was little doubt that Carly would call him Stud Muffin, which would be even worse. But it was too late now.

"Hey Zane," Stu Greenly, who was playing dominos with Emmett, greeted him. Stu was as deaf as a stone, but didn't realize it. "You brought us some muffins? Do you have bran? I've been a little con-stipated and could use the fiber."

"He didn't bring muffins, Stu!" Emmett yelled.

"He named his new foal Muffin."

Stu tipped back his head and laughed. Zane rolled his eyes before he nodded at the garage. "Is Cole around?"

"He's inside working on Joe Wheeler's truck," Emmett said. "Have you gotten things settled with Rachel yet? The Chili Cook-off is just around the corner. And seeing as how she was last year's queen, she'll need to be here to hand off her sash and chili queen crown."

Zane started to make up an excuse for why Rachel wouldn't be back in time, but then stopped. He was through with excuses. And with denial. The town would find out sooner or later, and Carly was right. It would be less pathetic if it came from him. "I don't think Rachel will be back for the cook-off, Emmett."

Emmett studied him for a moment before he nodded. "Fair enough. Sometimes you have to let things be what they'll be."

"You got bees?" Stu looked at Zane and shook his head. "Now that's one hell of a problem. They got into my attic one time and stung the hell out of me when I tried to extract the hive. Of course, it gave me and Martha some of the best honey I ever tasted."

Emmett huffed. "Just play, Stu!"

Zane laughed as he headed for the garage. He found Cole underneath a Chevy pickup. Cole was one hardworking son of a gun. He had to be since his late father hadn't been the best manager of their ranch. Zane had offered financial help time and time again, but Cole always refused. It seemed stubbornness was an Arrington trait.

Since the radio was blasting a country tune, Zane kicked the sole of Cole's boot to get his attention. He rolled out from under the truck, and his eyes sparkled with humor as soon as he saw Zane.

"Muffin?"

Zane sighed. "Yeah, well, that's what happens when you let good food go to your head."

Cole wiped his hands off with a rag before he got to his feet. "So you did let Carly name him. Emery said as much, but I didn't believe her."

Zane wasn't surprised that Carly had told her friend. She was pretty happy with the name, and maybe that was why he had no plans to change it.

"It's not that bad."

Cole squinted at him. "Looks like your brains did get scrambled because Carly is satisfying your bottomless pit of a stomach." He headed to the workbench and shut off the radio before turning back to Zane. "So what's up? Or did you just stop by to get razzed about Muffin? Speaking of which, that stud horse of yours has done his job—my two new mares are in foal."

It was nice to hear that one of his animals was producing. Ferdinand had yet to mount one heifer, and Zane had about given up on the impotent bull.

"Congratulations. Becky will be glad to get her stud back." He paused. "But I didn't stop by to talk livestock. I stopped by to tell you something."

Cole tossed down the rag and leaned back on the worktable. "Shoot."

Zane searched for the right way to broach the subject. And when he couldn't find one, he just blurted out the truth. "Rachel and I are getting a divorce. She left me for her interior designer."

Cole released his breath. "Well, shit." He placed his hands on his hips and studied his boots before glancing back up. "You want to go beat the crap out of him now? I can get off."

It was funny how much better that one question made Zane feel. Not that he wanted to kick the guy's ass, but it reminded him that his cousin had his back and always would.

He shook his head. "But believe me when I tell you that if I wanted to, I wouldn't need your help."

"I don't know about that. You lost a lot of wrestling matches between us cousins."

"That's only because you cheated, and Raff is as strong as an ox."

"Hey, it was Arrington rules—you know, do whatever it takes to win." Cole paused. "You could use the same rules in this situation if you want to. You can do whatever it takes to win Rachel back. I know that sounds weird coming from a man whose mother ran off and caused the family so much heartache. But after falling in love with Emery, I understand why my dad refused to give up. There's nothing I wouldn't do to keep Emery."

Zane wanted to say the same about Rachel, but after watching Muffin's birth, he'd felt something shift in his brain and he was able to see things for what they were. Or maybe it wasn't due to Muffin's birth as much as Carly's prodding. The woman could drive a man insane . . . or back to sanity.

He took off his hat and ran a hand through his hair. "Rachel and I never had the kind of relationship that you and Emery have. I've watched the two of you. The way you look at each other and are constantly touching."

"We haven't been together that long, Zane. You and Rachel have been together forever. I'm sure you were like that when you first started dating."

He released his breath in a long sigh. "We were never like that, Cole. Maybe it's because we've known each other for so long. Maybe we were too damned comfortable with each other to ever feel that spark of passion. And maybe that's why she left. Maybe she figured it out long before I did."

There was a somber silence before Cole spoke. "Are you going to sign the divorce papers?"

Zane gave a brief nod. "I already did. A divorce lawyer friend of mine from law school is stopping by later today to tie up any loose ends."

"So it's over?"

He rubbed his neck. "It looks like I'm the first Arrington to screw up a marriage. Even your dad stayed married to your mother."

"I don't know if that was a good thing. Sometimes you have to accept the truth and move on." Cole walked over and gave him a hard hug. "And Zane Arrington is the last person I'd call a screw-up."

Zane drew back. "Yeah? Have I told you about my half-million-dollar impotent bull?"

SINCE HE HAD A FEW hours to kill before he had to meet with his divorce lawyer at the ranch, Zane decided to stop by and check on Jess and see how his back was healing. But when he drove past the diner and saw the front door propped open, he altered his plans and pulled next to the curb.

He walked in to find Carly standing on a step-ladder peering into the vent close to the ceiling. Instead of wearing her usual cut-off shorts and t-shirt, she wore a dress. It wasn't close to being as short as her shorts, but it wasn't her legs that caught his attention as much as her bare back and shoulders. Since she didn't spend a lot of time outside, she wasn't as tanned as most women in Bliss. Her skin was pale as a peach and looked as soft as one. Suddenly, he felt extremely hot. Of course, the temperature inside the diner could've explained that.

It was scorching.

"Doesn't the air conditioning work?" he asked.

She whirled around so quickly that the ladder teetered. He had her in his arms before it could finish its first wobble. As usual, she didn't look happy about being saved. But she didn't look mad either. Just resigned.

"Do you always have to be the hero?" she asked.

"Do you always need to be saved?"

Her arms looped around his neck. "I don't need to be saved. You just jump in before I have a chance to save myself."

"Are you telling me you can save yourself? Even from spiders?"

"Okay, maybe not from spiders." She shivered, bringing his attention to the brush of her bare back against his forearm. She was as soft as a peach. A tempting peach just waiting to be tasted. At the thought, his arms tightened. Their gazes caught and held. It took a strong will to set her on her feet and look away.

"So what's wrong with the air conditioning?"

"I don't know. I'm supposed to meet Emery here.

We're having tea with Ms. Marble this afternoon. And when I got here, the place was like an oven. I have a call into my landlord, but he's ignoring me."

Zane pulled his phone out of his pocket, and sure enough, there was a missed call from her. "Sorry, I turned the ringer off when I met with the vet this morning and forgot to turn it back on."

She instantly looked concerned. "Is Stud Muffin okay?"

"Muffin. And he's fine."

She visibly relaxed. "I'll stop calling him Stud Muffin if you stop calling me Carly Sue."

He thought for only a second. "No can do, Carly Sue. Now if you'll excuse me, I need to fix the air conditioning so my tenant doesn't turn me in for running a sweat shop."

"You can actually fix things? I thought you just ordered other people to do that."

He didn't reply as he grabbed the ladder and headed toward the back door.

"Hey, I was using that!" she called after him.

"Accident-prone people are not allowed on ladders. Especially on my watch." He heard her mutter "control freak" before he walked out.

Once he was up on the sweltering hot roof, he realized how little he knew about refrigerated air conditioner units. But Carly's comment stung his ego just enough that he refused to call for help. It took a trip to the hardware store, about five gallons of sweat, and every stitch of patience he had to get the job done. But when he and Carly stood beneath the blast of cold air, he was more than a little proud.

"So you can fix things." Carly held up a hand

and high fived him. "Good job, Mr. Landlord. While you were up there did you notice if the roof needs repair? I would hate to have a leak ruin all the work that's not getting done."

Zane had forgotten to call the contractors and get them back to work. He was going to do it. Soon.

"That will have to wait for another day. I need to stop by and see Jess before I head to the ranch."

Since he couldn't stop by Jess's looking like a sweat-soaked rat, he walked to the sink and turned on the faucet. Once he'd stripped off his shirt, he dunked his head under. When he came up for air, Carly was there holding out a kitchen towel. He dried his hair over the sink, then straightened and turned.

"Man, it's hot out—" He cut off mid-sentence.

She stood only inches away, her gaze sweeping over his body like it was a road map and she a stranded traveler. As soon as she raised those hot, passion-filled eyes, something broke loose in Zane. Something wild and all-consuming. Before his logical brain could kick in, he pulled her into his arms.

He wasn't gentle. But neither was she. Their mouths met in a tangle of wet heat and aggressive tongues. Her fingers scraped through his hair, her nails scratching his scalp, as his hands slipped beneath the skirt of her dress and grasped her bare butt cheeks. He lifted her completely off the floor and stepped forward, pinning her between the counter and the hard bulge beneath his fly. She wrapped her legs around his waist, her hips riding him with mind-blowing undulations.

He gripped her ass and thrust back as he sucked in her bottom lip and bit down. She groaned and grabbed handfuls of his hair, tugging to angle his head so she could deepen the kiss. With their lips still locked, he set her on the counter and reached for the button of his fly.

But before he could get it open, Emery came in the back door.

"Sorry I'm late, but I stopped to talk with Cole—"

Zane released Carly, but couldn't turn unless he wanted his cousin-in-law to get an eyeful of just how close he'd been to having sex with her friend. Not that Emery couldn't figure that out. Carly sat on the counter looking like she'd been thoroughly kissed. Her hair was wildly mussed and her lips swollen. And it took everything Zane had not to pull her into his arms and kiss her all over again.

"Oh," Emery said. "I didn't realize you had company. Umm . . . I'll just wait outside."

Once the door closed, Zane grabbed his shirt and pulled it on. It took a second to find his voice. "Look, Carly, I'm sorry. I don't know—"

She held up a hand. "There's only one thing I want from you, Zane Arrington. And it's not an apology." When he looked confused, she sent him a saucy smile. "Admit it. You kissed me."

He couldn't deny it.

He'd kissed her.

And he wanted to kiss her again.

"If Duke Earhart thought that after one little kiss Laura would be putty in his hands, he had another think coming. She hadn't grown up with an overbearing uncle and not learned a few things about how to cut an arrogant giant down to size."

CHAPTER SIXTEEN

"OH. MY. GOD." EMERY BREATHED as soon as Carly stepped out the back door of the diner. "Why didn't you tell me that you and Zane were having sex?"

Carly handed Emery the box of pictures Ms. Marble had loaned her and turned to lock the back door . . . and to get a grip on her body. Her hands shook. Her heart beat in double time. And the spot between her legs felt all needy and desperate. She hated feeling needy and desperate.

She took a deep breath and slowly released it before turning around. "We are not having sex. That was just a kiss."

Emery's eyes widened. "Just a kiss? I think my eyeballs are scorched."

Carly felt scorched too. She had kissed numerous guys, but she had never experienced a kiss like that one. Zane had taken lust from zero to a hundred and ten in only seconds, and she had no one to blame but herself. When he'd turned from the sink, she couldn't take her eyes off his naked chest. She'd had the overwhelming desire to lick off each droplet of water and trace each hard ridge of muscle with her tongue.

It was crazy. She had no business lusting after Zane. And it had nothing to do with him being married. After their discussion in the barn, she'd come to the conclusion that Rachel had done him a favor by leaving. Their marriage hadn't been a love match as much as a recipe for disaster. That's exactly what an affair between Carly and Zane would be. He wasn't the type of man to have a casual sexual romp. He was too responsible and too moral. Sex without a commitment wasn't part of his playbook, and Carly didn't want a commitment. She'd made a commitment once. Never again.

Wanting to get off the subject of the kiss, she took back the box of pictures. "We need to hurry if we want to get to Ms. Marble's on time." As she had hoped, the mention of Ms. Marble distracted Emery, and she followed Carly down the alley.

"I'm so glad she invited us to tea. It will give us a chance to ask her about the Laughing Lucy picture. If we can figure out who her lover was, I bet we'll find another chapter of the book."

"I've been thinking about that. Maybe we're wrong about the picture. If her lover took it, why does Ms. Marble have it? Why wouldn't Lucy's boyfriend have it? Or the Arringtons after Lucy died?"

"You're right. That doesn't make sense." Emery

paused. "Unless Ms. Marble and Lucy were so close that Lucy gave her the picture to keep her secret."

They stopped at the corner and waited for the light to change. It was a city girl thing to do. In Bliss, there was little traffic. There was only one truck on Main Street, and the driver stopped when he saw them and rolled down his window. Carly didn't recognize the man, but he seemed to know her.

"When is the diner opening? My wife and I are celebrating our fortieth wedding anniversary at the end of July and I was hoping we won't have to travel to Austin for a nice dinner."

A woman pushing a double stroller walked up. "I was wondering the same thing," she said. "I would love to have a place to eat lunch with my mommy's day out group. And are you going to do takeout?" She looked at her kids. "Some nights, I just don't feel like cooking."

Before Carly could answer, another car pulled up and a woman leaned out the window and started asking questions about the diner. Carly politely answered all the questions, but finally had to make her excuses so they wouldn't be late for Ms. Marble's.

When they finally made it across the street, Emery flashed her a smile. "I told you people would be excited about the diner opening. It almost feels like fate brought you here to feed the people of Bliss." Her smile got even bigger and a lot slyer. "And maybe even fate that landed you at Zane's."

Carly sent her a hard look. "Don't go there."

"Fine. But I think you should know that Zane signed the divorce papers. Cole told me today."

She wasn't surprised. She had seen a difference in Zane since the night in the barn. He was happier and much less tense. It was like watching Muffin being born had helped him to see that life was too precious to waste a second of it.

"I'm glad," she said. "Zane deserves to be happy, and it sounds like he wasn't with Rachel. But that has nothing to do with me. You can get any match-making ideas out of your head right now." She stopped and turned to her friend. "I'm not staying more than a year, Em. Do you hear me? You might be okay living in a small town, but I'm not. I like to have more things to do than sit on a porch and watch the corn grow. I need movie theaters, muse-ums, and great restaurants."

Emery studied her for a moment before she nodded. "I know. I guess I'm just looking for any reason to keep you here. But you're right. If you're not going to stay, it's probably best if you don't start something up with Zane. He's been through enough. In fact, maybe you should move back in with me and Cole."

Carly wasn't going to move in with Emery and Cole, but she did need to move out of Zane's. Now that he was no longer married, it would be best not to play with fire. And Zane's kisses certainly set her on fire.

Ms. Marble lived in a house that looked like she'd baked it herself. It was a one-story with a steeply pitched roof and scrolled Victorian-style corbels that gave it the look of a Christmas gingerbread house. The inside was filled with antique furniture, lace doilies, and more figurines than Carly had ever seen in her life. Talk about feeling like a bear in a china shop. She was afraid to move for fear of knocking into something and breaking it.

"I'm so glad you two could stop by." Ms. Marble glanced at the box Carly carried. "But you didn't need to bring the pictures back so soon. You can hang on to them for as long as you like."

"Actually, there are a few I kept to have enlarged and framed for the diner," Carly said. "And the others, I was hoping you'd tell us more about. Since Emery and I aren't from Bliss, we don't know a lot of the history and people."

Ms. Marble smiled. "Come on into the kitchen and I'll try to tell you as many stories as I can remember."

She led them through the array of figurines to the kitchen and pointed to the table in the breakfast nook. "Set the box on the table and make yourself comfortable while I brew the tea. I'm sorry it's not ready. Emmett's wife, Joanna, stopped by earlier and we got to reminiscing about our teaching days and chatting about chili recipes—not that I'm about to share my recipe. I want that blue ribbon all for myself."

She put an old kettle on the stove. "Are you still willing to help out with the cook-off, Carly? Professional chefs can't enter, but you'd make the perfect judge. As a chef, you have a refined palate. So you'll know the best chili when you taste mine." She winked.

Carly couldn't help smiling. "If your chili tastes anything like your baked goods, the other contestants won't stand a chance."

"Speaking of baking"—Ms. Marble pulled a plate from a cupboard—"you have a choice of lemon bars or oatmeal cookies."

"Lemon bars for me," Emery said.

Carly didn't hesitate to indulge. "I'll try both."

"Atta girl." Ms. Marble opened a Tupperware container and started placing cookies on the plate. "Now's the time to eat your fill of sweets before they start clinging to your hips and thighs . . . or screwing up your blood sugar. And I hope you'll take some home. I was in a baking fever this week and have an overabundance."

Carly glanced around at the Tupperware containers that cluttered the counters. That was an understatement. Obviously, Ms. Marble had a baking obsession as bad as her own cooking one. A thought struck her.

"Have you ever thought about selling your baked goods?"

Ms. Marble opened another container. "I sell them at church bake sales all the time."

"I was thinking of selling them at the diner. I've never enjoyed baking as much as I do cooking, and I'll have my hands full with the regular menu. It would be a great help if I didn't have to worry about desserts too."

Ms. Marble looked startled at first, then almost embarrassed. "I don't know if I bake well enough to sell to the public."

Carly laughed. "I think you underestimate your ability. The entire town loves your baking."

"She's right," Emery said. "Your desserts are just as good as the finest bakeries in New York City."

Ms. Marble blushed and pressed a hand to her chest. "Oh, goodness, you girls certainly know how to make an old woman feel proud." She paused for a moment before a gleam came in her eyes. "And if it would help you out, Carly, I certainly couldn't say no."

"Great! Now all I need to find is a short-order cook."

"What about Dirk?" Emery asked. "I bet somewhere along the line he's been a cook. He's done everything else."

"I tried getting him to be my sous chef already, and he turned me down. Besides, Zane has come to rely on his help out on the ranch. In fact, I wouldn't be surprised if he doesn't keep him on even after his foreman comes back."

"And you think Dirk will stay? You know he doesn't like to be tied down to one job."

Ms. Marble brought over a tray with tea and desserts and set it in the middle of the table. "Oh, I don't know about that. I think that young man is looking for something to tie him down."

Carly reached for an oatmeal cookie. "What makes you say that?"

Ms. Marble sat down. "Just an old woman's theory. The times he's stopped by to help me, I've gotten the feeling that his bright smile is hiding a very lonely heart."

"What I wonder is how he ended up in Bliss." Emery grabbed a lemon bar. She took a bite and sighed. Carly knew how she felt. The cookies were definitely going on the menu. "I mean why would a young, good looking guy want to live here when he could live anywhere?"

"I haven't figured that one out." Ms. Marble poured the tea. "Nor have I figured out why he won't take any money for helping me. Especially when I know he needs it."

"I don't think he needs it anymore," Carly said. "Zane pays him pretty well, I feed him, and he doesn't have to pay rent for sleeping in the bunkhouse."

Ms. Marble paused in the process of handing Carly her teacup. "He sleeps in the bunkhouse?" Before Carly could answer, she quickly went on. "Well, of course, that makes sense now that he's working at the ranch. And it's certainly good to know he has a place to sleep. I've gotten plenty attached to that young man. He's the only person in town, besides you girls, who hasn't come snooping around asking questions about Lucy Arrington."

Carly and Emery exchanged looks. "People have been asking you questions about Lucy?" Emery asked.

Ms. Marble snorted. "Almost everyone in town has dropped by to see if they can get clues about where Lucy hid more chapters of the last book in the series." She casually blew on her tea and took a sip. "It's pure silliness if you ask me. If Lucy had wanted that book to get into just anyone's hands, she would've published it. Which is why I refuse to answer their questions." Her gaze shifted from Emery to Carly, and she smiled. "So what pictures were you interested in knowing about?"

Since now there was no way they could ask her about Lucy's picture without seeming like fortune hunters, Carly cleared her throat. "The ones with you in them. I was wondering if the handsome cowboy in the pictures was your husband."

"Yes, that's Justin."

Carly was confused. "I thought your husband's name was David."

"David Marble was my second husband. Justin Bonner was my first." She hesitated, and a far-off look entered her eyes. "I had a crush on him ever since I was knee high to a grasshopper. Of course, all the girls in town did. He was a drifter much like Dirk. He worked for the Arringtons for a short period of time, then left and didn't return until he was older." She smiled. "And I like to think wiser because that was when we started dating. Of course, we only had a few years together before he died of a heart attack. I never thought I'd get over him. But then I met David."

She spent the next hour talking about her life with David and the places they'd traveled once they both retired from teaching. She didn't talk about any children, but Carly didn't find that curious. Lots of women chose careers over having kids, and it sounded like Ms. Marble had loved teaching.

Finally, Carly noticed the time and brought an end to the afternoon. "Thank you so much for the tea, Ms. Marble, but I'd better get back to the ranch. I need to get Zane's dinner ready."

"Goodness," Ms. Marble scooted her chair back, then used the edge of the table to help her stand, "I didn't mean to monopolize the conversation like I did. You girls must think I'm just a talkative old magpie. Let me get you a plate of goodies to take with you."

While she got the plates ready, Emery sent Carly a defeated look. There was little doubt that she was as disappointed as Carly that they hadn't learned anything about Lucy's lover. But there was no help for it now. They each accepted their plates, and Ms. Marble guided them to the room off the kitchen.

"You can go out this way," she said. "Then you won't have to deal with the front gate when you have your hands full." She led them to the back door where she gave them each a big hug. Carly had never been much of a hugger, but there was something comforting about being squeezed by a loving woman who smelled like cinnamon and vanilla.

"Thank you again, Ms. Marble," she said. "And I'll let you know when I'll start needing baked goods." She turned to leave when her gaze caught on the row of hooks by the back door. She expected to see an array of wide-brimmed hats and grocery totes. What she didn't expect to see was a backpack.

A navy-blue backpack with green stitching.

"First, his stomach ached like a sore tooth, and now he was itching like a dog with fleas. If he didn't know better, Duke would think that someone was out to get him."

CHAPTER SEVENTEEN

ALL THE WAY TO THE ranch, Zane thought about the kiss. Not that a kiss was the best way to describe what had happened in the diner. At the first touch of Carly's lips, something had been unleashed inside him. Something wild and primal that he didn't even know existed. It scared him, and at the same time, made him feel exhilarated and alive for the first time in years . . . maybe ever.

Of course, he couldn't kiss Carly again. He had just gotten out of one relationship. He certainly didn't need to get into another. Especially when he didn't trust his instincts anymore. He'd thought Rachel was the perfect match for him, and he'd been dead wrong. Before he got into another serious relationship, he would spend a lot more time making sure he and the woman were compatible.

And he and Carly were about as compatible as fire and gasoline.

A brand-new Range Rover was parked in front of the house when Zane pulled up. Obviously, Mason Granger had gotten here before him. Zane and Mason had gone to law school together, and Mason was a good friend and a successful divorce attorney. He was the first person Zane had thought to call when he'd made his decision to sign.

Since he didn't see Mason sitting in his SUV, he figured Becky had invited his friend into the house. But as he climbed out of his truck, his sister walked out of the barn, or rather stomped. She looked fit to be tied. Her face was red with anger and her fists clenched. Straw stuck out of her mussed hair like she'd taken a tumble. He immediately became concerned.

"What happened?" he asked.

She didn't slow down on her way to her truck. "Why don't you ask your friend?"

Zane glanced at the barn. Mason appeared, his sedate stroll the complete opposite of Becky's hurried stomp. Of course, the man had always been sedate. In law school, he'd been nicknamed the Iceman because he never lost his cool. Which is why he made such a good divorce lawyer. Nothing ruffled his feathers. Not even a firebrand like Zane's sister. He didn't even blink when she backed up the truck and held her hand out the window, flipping him the bird.

Zane headed over to his friend. "Sorry, about that. My sister is a little volatile at times."

Mason watched Becky's truck head down the road in a plume of dust. "That's an understatement." He turned to Zane and smiled. "It's good to see you, man." He gave Zane a hard thump on the back. "How have you been? Although I guess that's a stupid question, considering you're getting a divorce. Or I should say you are divorced."

Zane was surprised. "Divorced? It's final?"

Mason nodded. "It seems Rachel was in a hurry to finalize, and since you waited so long to sign . . ." He paused. "If you have a problem with that, we can contest."

He didn't hesitate to answer. "No, I don't have a problem with it. I was just surprised." He shook Mason's hand. "Thank you. I appreciate you taking care of things. But you didn't have to drive all the way out here to tell me."

"To be honest, I used the excuse of bringing the finalized papers so I could see the famous Earhart Ranch." He glanced around. "It's a nice spread, Zane."

He couldn't help feeling prideful. "Thank you. It's home. Although it's not nearly as exciting as Austin. How is city life?"

Mason stared down at his cowboy boots for a long moment as if contemplating how to answer the question. "A little too exciting. In fact, I was thinking about buying a weekend place where I could get away from the rat race and maybe do some hunting and fishing. You wouldn't know of any properties around here, would you?"

"The Reed place is for sale, but it comes with a lot of land and a hefty price tag."

Mason lifted his head, and it was easy to read the flicker of interest in his eyes. "After living in an apartment, I wouldn't mind having a little land. How about if we check it out and then I'll take you to dinner?"

"I'd agree if Bliss was known for its great restaurants. Why don't we eat here after we check out the Reed property?"

Mason got a wary look. "Here? Are we talking your cooking? Because I still haven't gotten rid of the taste of that burnt macaroni and cheese you made when we were in law school."

Zane laughed. "It wasn't that bad. But I won't be doing the cooking. I have a chef." A sexy chef that made him crave her body much more than he craved her food.

"In that case," Mason said. "I accept."

It didn't take long to drive out to the Reed property. Zane could've called the Realtor, but there was no need to bother Tom Steward unless Mason decided he liked it. The house wasn't much. It was old and needed a lot of work. But it was on a good chunk of land with water rights, which was why it wasn't cheap. Mason must've been doing well, because he didn't even blink when Zane told him the asking price. He took down the name and number on the Realtor's sign before they headed back to the ranch.

They were in Zane's study enjoying a beer when Carly poked her head in. At the sight of her big brown eyes and blond curls, the exhilarating feeling returned. And even though he knew they weren't compatible, Zane had a hard time not getting up and kissing her all over again. But she didn't look like she was in the kissing mood. She looked all business.

"I think we need to have a talk—" she stopped when she noticed Mason. "Oh, I'm sorry. I didn't know you had company."

Both Zane and Mason got to their feet. "This is Mason Granger, Carly," Zane said. "I went to law school with him. Mason, this is Carly Hanover, my chef."

She walked in and held out her hand. "It's nice to meet you, Mr. Granger."

"Just Mason." He took her hand. "And the pleasure is all mine. When Zane said he had a chef, I pictured an old cowboy on a chuck wagon. I did not picture a beautiful woman. He found you in Bliss?"

Two things annoyed Zane: The fact that Mason still held Carly's hand. And the fact that she didn't seem to be in any hurry to pull away.

"Thank you." She gave him one of her rare smiles. "And no, I'm not from Bliss. I was living in San Francisco until a few weeks ago."

"I travel to San Francisco on business occasionally. Where did you live?"

Before she could answer, Zane came around the desk. "My Carly was an executive chef at a restaurant there."

He didn't know where the "my" came from. It sounded stupid as hell. And Mason and Carly must've thought so too. Carly looked at him like he'd lost his mind while Mason studied him for a moment before a smile spread over his face. The same crocodilian smile he used when he'd gotten a reaction out of a classmate he was interrogating in one of their mock trials. Zane had to wonder if he hadn't just been manipulated by his friend. It seemed likely when Mason immediately released Carly's hand.

"Well, I don't know why she'd choose to work

for an ornery cowboy like you when she could be a chef at a restaurant in San Francisco."

Feeling perturbed about being manipulated, Zane's reply was short. "Maybe she likes ornery cowboys."

"Or maybe I'm just stupid." Carly shot him a hard look. "Now, if you'll excuse me. I need to get dinner started." It was obvious by the slamming door that she was pissed. It didn't take a genius to figure out why. He had acted like a dog marking his territory. Even Mason realized it.

He laughed. "Now I understand why you weren't upset about your divorce being finalized so quickly."

❧

DINNER WAS NOT A PLEASANT affair. Carly refused to even look at Zane and spent the entire time talking to Mason. They were annoyingly compatible. They both had moved a lot as kids—Carly because of her military father and Mason because of his mother's many marriages. They both were only children. And they both loved food and had been to restaurants all over the world. They spent a solid hour talking about French cuisine. Since the only French cuisine Zane knew happened to be fried potatoes, he had nothing to contribute to the conversation, so he sat there and sulked.

It was a relief when Mason declined dessert.

"I need to get back to Austin," he said as he got to his feet. "But thank you so much for dinner, Carly. I'll have to wrangle an invitation out of Zane more often."

Carly pushed back her chair. "Actually, I won't be working for Zane after tonight. But I'm opening up the old diner in Bliss. So whenever you're in town, be sure to stop by. I'll give you the friends and family discount." Without one glance at Zane, she turned and walked out of the room.

It was a struggle to remain cordial as he walked Mason out. After his friend drove away, Zane stood on the porch staring sightlessly out at his land, trying to digest the fact that Carly was leaving. His brain knew it was for the best. He didn't need to get involved with another woman so soon after Rachel. But his body felt gutted. Sort of like he was losing his best friend. There would be no more stopping in for homemade crepes with a bandanna-eared bunny whose sassy remarks kept him smiling all day? No more walking in after a hard day at work to an aroma-filled kitchen and a petite chef with black-painted toes? No more late-night barn conversations with a blunt, honest woman who didn't pull punches?

He turned and walked inside. The kitchen was a mess, which proved how angry she was with him. She wasn't a messy cook. And she never left her knives out on the cutting boards. She always cleaned and rinsed them as soon as she finished using them and put them back in their case. He walked around collecting the knives, then cleaned them like he'd seen her do. Once they were clean, he pulled out the nylon case she kept in a drawer and carefully placed each knife in its own sleeve before rolling the case up and tying it closed. He carried it to the guestroom where he found her packing. He tried to keep his voice steady and even, but it was a struggle when his emotions were all over the place.

"I thought we made a deal," he said.

She whirled on him, her brown eyes snapping with anger. "We did. We made a deal for me to cook dinner for you. We did not make a deal for you to treat me like a piece of property." She rammed a finger at him. "I am not yours."

She went back to packing, leaving Zane nothing to do but watch. As each pair of cut-off jeans and every logo t-shirt went into the suitcase, the fist that squeezed his chest tightened more and more. By the time she zipped the suitcase closed and turned for the door, he swore he was having a heart attack.

"You're right," he said. "It was a stupid thing to say. I guess I just didn't like Mason being so possessive of my . . . friend."

She seemed startled by the word. "Your friend?"

He swallowed hard and nodded. "It's hard to believe that an arrogant country boy and a blunt city girl could become friends. But sometimes things just happen." He held out the knife case. "I cleaned them for you, but I didn't know exactly what knife went in what sleeve."

She stared at the case for a long moment before she set down her suitcase. Just the simple act lessened the pain in his chest. "It would've been so easy to leave if you'd continued to be an arrogant jerk. But then you had to go and clean my knives." She took the knives and set them on the dresser before turning to him and releasing a sigh. "We have become friends. That's exactly why I think it's a good idea if I leave."

"You're leaving because we're friends?"

"No. I'm leaving because we're friends who are sexually attracted to each other."

That took all the wind out of his sails. Leave it to Carly to cut to the chase. He wanted to deny it, but damned if he could. Especially after the kiss in the diner . . . and how just the mention of her being sexually attracted to him made lust pound through his veins like a charging cavalry brigade.

"Oh," he said. That was it. That was all he had.

She continued as if she were talking to one of her girlfriends instead of the man she was sexually attracted to. "If you were any other man, I would have sex with you and go on about my business. But you're not any other guy. You have become a friend. And I don't want to hurt you. I like you too much."

It was nice to hear that she liked him, but the rest of what she'd said made him feel like a kicked puppy that needed coddling.

"Let me get this straight," he said. "You're leaving me now, so you won't hurt me later when I can't control myself and fall head over heels in love with you?"

She gave a brief nod. "Exactly."

It never failed to amaze him just how quickly Carly could deflate his ego. And he didn't know why that made him smile. He sidestepped the suit-case and moved closer. "And what about if it's the other way around? What about if you can't keep from falling in love with me and I hurt you?"

"Won't happen. I'm not as vulnerable as you are."

Vulnerable? That did it. He was not vulnerable. Nor was he a man to back down from a challenge. "Well, it's real sweet of you to watch out for me. But I'm a big boy who knows the difference between lust and love. It doesn't matter if we had sex a hundred times, I'm not going to fall in love with you."

His bruised ego was talking. But now that the words were out, they made sense. He wasn't going to fall in love with Carly. They were too different. And it certainly sounded like she wasn't going to fall in love with him. So why shouldn't they give into their sexual attraction? People gave into their carnal desires every day. Not responsible people. But Zane was tired of being responsible. He was tired of being the guy who walked the straight and narrow path. For once, he wanted to walk on the wild side. Be the bad boy. And Carly's stunned expression made it even more appealing.

He smiled. "You said if I were any other guy, you would have sex with me and be done with it. So what do you say, Carly Sue? You want to have wild, raunchy sex and get it out of our systems so we can go back to being friends?"

"Putting castor oil in his stew and rubbing his shirts and sheets with poison ivy had seemed like great fun, but there was nothing funny about seeing Duke's handsome face covered in red welts. Her concern made her wonder if she was starting to care for Duke Earhart."

CHAPTER EIGHTEEN

THE *WILD, RAUNCHY SEX* PART stunned Carly so much that she didn't resist when Zane lowered his head and kissed her. The warmth of his mouth and the hot slide of his tongue made his proposal tempting. So tempting that she might've stripped off his clothes right there and pushed him back on the bed if her cellphone hadn't started to ring. She pulled away from his arms and moved around him to grab her phone from the nightstand. Before she could even say hello, Savannah started in.

"You have to catch the first flight to Atlanta." Her hysterical voice came through the receiver. "If you are truly my friend, you wouldn't care about the diner or the last book as much as you care about my wedding being the biggest flop of the century."

She turned to Zane who stood there with heat in his eyes, his lips still wet and delicious looking from their kiss. She cleared the lust from her throat. "I need to take this."

"Just think about it," he said before he flashed her a sexy, dimpled smile and walked out of the room. When he was gone, she closed the door, fell back on the bed, and released her breath.

"Carly?" Savannah said. "Are you okay?"

She wasn't okay. She was stunned that her responsible rancher had turned into a naughty cowboy. Stunned and a little turned on. But she wasn't going down that road. He might act like he could handle a one-night stand, but she didn't believe him. He was just feeling a little froggy after the divorce. Once he had some time to think it over, he'd realize he wasn't the kind of guy who could have no-strings-attached sex.

"I'm fine," she said. "Tell me what's going on."

"It's the caterer you talked me into. I wanted those cute little skewers of chicken for appetizers, but he refuses to make them. He says that chicken dries out easily. So he's insisting on the bacon-wrapped scallops instead. Just what kind of tyrant did you saddle me with, Carly Sue?"

Carly rolled her eyes. "An excellent chef who knows his business. He's right. Chicken will dry out while it's waiting on trays to be served. Not only that, but people never know what to do with those wooden skewers after they finish eating. Bacon-wrapped scallops will stay moist and delicious. And they are easy to eat in one bite."

There was a long stretch of silence before Savannah conceded. "You're right. The last wedding I went to I was stuck holding five of those little skewers while people looked at me like I was some kind of pig. I hadn't eaten lunch, for goodness sake, and I was starving. The chicken seemed delicious at the time, but now that I think about it, it was pretty dry." She took a deep breath, then continued in a much cheerier voice. "So now that we've got that settled, why didn't you call and tell me about finding the tenth chapter? I always have to hear everything from Emery."

"Between cooking for the Arringtons and dealing with contractors who never show up, I've been a little busy. Did Emery tell you about us seeing the backpack at Ms. Marble's today?"

"What backpack?"

"The one I found at the diner the night of the fire."

Savannah's shocked silence was understandable. Carly had been pretty shocked herself when she saw the backpack hanging on a hook by Ms. Marble's door.

"Sweet Baby Jesus," Savannah said. "I wouldn't have guessed that in a million years. Ms. Marble was in the diner the night of the fire? She's the one who found the sixth chapter at the cemetery?"

"I don't know. When I asked where she got the backpack, she said that her friend Joanna must've left it when she came to talk about the Chili Cook-off. But I've met Emmett's wife, and she carries a little shoulder purse, not a backpack."

"Do you think Ms. Marble is lying?"

"It's possible. Occasionally, I get the feeling that she knows more than she's letting on about Lucy and the book. Or maybe the backpack is Joanna's. It seems everyone in town is in on the search for the chapters."

Savannah sighed. "I wish I was there to help you and Emery search, instead of stuck here in wedding hell."

"You don't have to be in wedding hell. You could call it off."

There was a long silence, and Carly had to wonder if Savannah was getting closer to realizing that Miles was a bad choice. She should've known better. Once Savannah made her mind up about something, there was no going back. "Of course I'm not going to cancel the wedding, Carly Sue. I made a commitment and I'm sticking with it. And speaking of commitments, did Zane's wife ever come back?"

"They're divorced. Which is why I'm considering not working for Zane anymore." Considering? How had she gone from leaving to considering leaving?

"He tempts you that much, does he?" Leave it to Savannah to hit the nail on the head. When Carly didn't say anything, she laughed. "I'm not sure how leaving his house will help lessen the temptation. In a town that small, you're bound to run into each other." She had a good point. Especially when he owned the building where Carly would be working every day. With the way the man ate, there was little doubt he'd come into the diner often.

"And why are you avoiding the temptation now that he's single?" Savannah asked. "Take it from me. When you deny a craving, it only gets worse. I tried to deny myself chocolate, and all I could think about was chocolate. So yesterday I went to the bakery and bought a dozen chocolate-covered donuts and ate seven of them. After I threw up, I swore I'd never eat chocolate again. I say go for it. I say screw that man's brains out until you can't stand to look at each other."

Carly was about to comment on Savannah's crazy advice when the sound of boot heels had her sitting up. A slip of paper slid under the door. It was from the lined grocery notepad she kept on the refrigerator, but Zane hadn't stayed in the lines. The bold black words covered the entire paper.

Whispering Falls.

The boot clicks continued down the hallway, and a second later the front door slammed, making her jump. An image popped into her head of Zane swimming naked . . . with his lightsaber. Suddenly, she wasn't just considering staying. She was considering his offer of a one-night stand.

"You think sex will take care of the craving?" she voiced her thoughts.

"Of course," Savannah said. "True love isn't about craving a man sexually. It's about common personality traits, morals, and beliefs. You and Zane are complete opposites. He's stable and controlled. You're unstable and volatile. This is just a fling that will burn out quickly. Unlike Miles and I who are similar in every way and will last forever."

That's not how Carly saw it, but she kept her opinion to herself. Once she hung up, she picked up the note and read it again. She should've crumpled the paper and tossed it in the trash then grabbed her suitcase and headed into town. But the motor lodge office would already be closed by now.

And she couldn't bother Emery and Cole so late. Besides, maybe Savannah was right. They couldn't avoid each other in a town so small. Maybe all they needed was one night to get over their craving and see how incompatible they were.

She stared down at the paper for only a second more before she folded it and placed it in the drawer of her nightstand. Then she grabbed a couple of towels from the bathroom and headed for the door. On the way past the kitchen, she stopped. The mess she'd left after dinner was completely cleaned up. The dishwasher was running and the pots and pans were clean and neatly stacked on the counter.

It seemed that Zane had figured out how to seduce a chef.

By the time she reached the falls, he was already in the water. The moon wasn't as full and bright as it had been the first night she'd seen him skinny-dipping. But it was bright enough to reflect off his wheat-colored hair and the hard edge of each defined muscle as he swam.

She watched him for only a moment before she dropped the towels and slipped out of her clothes. The coldness of the water took her breath away, and she gasped just as Zane came up for a breath. His head turned in her direction.

"Carly?" He spoke her name in a low, hushed voice that sent shivers through her body.

She swam toward him. She stopped a few feet away, treading water. The moon reflected in his eyes and off the droplets of water that dripped from his wet hair.

"Just for the record, I think this is a stupid idea,"

she said. "Once sex is introduced, it screws up everything—pardon the pun."

One corner of his mouth quirked up, and a dimple appeared. "But that's why we're doing this. So our sexual attraction won't screw up our friendship and you can continue to stay without worrying about breaking my heart. Which means we need some ground rules." Obviously, the responsible Zane wasn't completely gone. "This is a one-shot deal. No emotions. No strings. When we leave, we put what happens here behind us and don't mention it again. Agreed?"

She didn't think it would be that easy, but she nodded. "Fine."

He laughed. "You sound like you're getting ready to face a firing squad. Are you worried that sex with stick-in-the-mud Zane won't be any fun?" Before she could answer, he disappeared beneath the water. A second later, Carly felt him grab her foot and pull her under.

Water filled her nose and burned like heck. She came up coughing and sputtering. She looked around for Zane, but he was nowhere to be found. The silky wisp of hair against her calf alerted her before she was tugged under again. But this time, Zane brought her flush against his hard body as he kicked to the surface.

When they broke through, she was gasping while he was laughing.

"It's not funny." She slapped at his shoulder. "You could've drowned me."

He grinned down at her, his eyes sparkling with humor beneath his long, water-droplet-lined lashes. It was hard to stay angry at such a devastatingly good-looking man. Especially when that man held her so close she could feel the thump of his heartbeat against her breasts, the rippled muscles of his stomach, and the enticing brush of his legs as he treaded water.

Something else enticing brushed her thigh. Something long and hard and needy. She glanced up to see the humor fade from his eyes. Just that quickly desire flowed through her like the waterfall that splashed behind them. Her hand was still tangled in his hair, and she tightened her grip and tugged until his lips moved closer.

"One night," she whispered before she kissed him.

It wasn't as hungry as the kiss they'd experienced in the diner or as brief as the one in the guest bedroom. This kiss was slow and thorough as they learned the tastes and textures of each other. His lips molded against hers in a deep slide and pull as his tongue entered her mouth in a gentle sweep. She brushed her tongue against his, and they tangled in a sultry dance that left her dazed and wanting more. She wrapped her legs around his waist and pulled him closer until her needy center was flush against the hard ripples of his stomach.

Groaning, he pulled away from the kiss and kicked to shore. Once he could reach the bottom, he kissed her again, his tongue delving as his hands slid down to her butt. His hands were so large that his middle fingers pressed into the deep crevice between her cheeks. Tingling heat ricocheting through her body. She tightened her legs and wiggled against him.

His hands tightened as he drew his teeth along

her bottom lip. "Jesus, Carly, I want you so damn bad." He carried her out of the water to where they'd dropped their clothes, then glanced around. "Maybe we should go back to the house."

She nuzzled his neck, sucking on a spot behind his ear. "I can't wait that long."

He growled deep in his chest as he unhooked her legs and set her on her feet. He wasted no time getting the towels and spread them over the thick grass that grew along the bank. Before he came back to her, he pulled a condom out of the back pocket of his jeans. It showed how ditzy he made her. She hadn't even thought about protection.

"You were pretty confident I was going to follow you," she said.

He slipped his arms around her waist and smiled down at her. "I hoped that you would follow me. And it's always best to be prepared."

She stood on her tiptoes and kissed him. "I like a man who's prepared."

He deepened the kiss as he swept her up in his arms and laid her down on the towels. She expected him to put on the condom and get straight to the sex. It was obvious he was more than ready. Instead, he stretched out next to her and looked his fill. It was a little embarrassing to be so thoroughly examined. She wasn't ashamed of her body, but she wasn't exactly proud of it either. And she couldn't help wondering if he was making comparisons between her short, average body and his ex-wife's tall, lithe one.

"If you use the word little, I'm out of here."

His smile flashed. "You are a petite woman, Carly Sue." He gently ran his callused fingertips back and forth over her stomach, causing her abdominal muscles to twitch. "But I've always believed that good things come in small packages."

His hand moved lower, one finger slowly tracing the scrolled letters of her tattoo. "Do you know how sexy your tattoos are? I can't stop thinking about them at night. This one." His fingers trailed heat up to the broken heart on her left breast. "And especially this one."

She thought he would question her about the tattoo, but instead he leaned over and kissed it as if trying to heal the two broken halves. And surprisingly, his warm, moist lips did make her feel healed. She felt as if all the pieces of her heart suddenly came back together and thumped wildly against Zane's lips. It almost jumped out of her chest when he gently tugged her nipple into his hot mouth. He suckled until it ached with the same need that throbbed between her legs.

"Zane," she gasped in a half groan and half plea.

He brushed her nipple one more time with his tongue before he kissed his way over to her other breast. When it was beaded into a tight nub of tingling sensation, he kissed and nibbled his way down her body. He stopped when he reached her belly button, then shifted until he was between her legs with her thighs propped over each of his broad shoulders. His hands scooped beneath her hips and lifted as his mouth hit its mark. Between the hot sips and experienced tongue flicks, it didn't take her long to topple over the edge of a muscle-tightening, nerve-exploding orgasm.

She had just relaxed back to earth when he moved over her. His warm fingers searched out her wet heat, and she drew in her breath as his hard length entered her. The sweet stretch on her still-quivering internal muscles sent her right back to the edge. She lifted her hips to meet his hard thrust, but the thrust never came. She glanced up to find his eyes clamped shut and his jaw clenched.

"You're so damn tight," he said through gritted teeth, "I'm worried I'll hurt you."

Since she had seen his penis, she couldn't deny being a little worried about the fit herself. But there was only one way to find out. "You aren't that big, Arrington."

The tension on his face released as he sent her a startled look. When he noticed her smile, he laughed. "Then I guess we're a perfect match." He slowly eased in.

The small amount of discomfort was quickly flooded with a whole lot of delicious heat. The heat swelled and then ebbed as he settled into a gentle rhythm that wasn't close to being enough. Obviously, he was still worried about hurting her. She couldn't have that.

Pressing her heels against the ground, she met his next trust with a hard trust of her own. Once he was deeply embedded, Zane lost all control. He began thrusting so hard and so deep that he inched Carly right off the towels. She didn't care. When he came with a tense of muscles and deep groan, she followed right after him. He pumped until she was finished, then brushed a kiss on her shoulder and rolled onto his back.

He took her hand, his fingers interlocking with hers. They lay side by side, looking up at the multitude of glittering stars and the gibbous moon that hung amid them. The night blanketed them in a soothing cacophony of insect chirps, the splash of the falls, and the uneven puffs of their breathing. There was something about the simple act of holding hands after such an intense experience that seemed almost too intimate. And Carly finally pulled away.

Zane glanced over. "You okay, friend?"

The question took away all her fear. She turned to look into his moonlit eyes. "Yes. Are you?"

A huge smile split his face. "Better than I've ever been in my life." He glanced at the sky. "And I was thinking. Since the night is still young, maybe we could . . ." He let the sentence drift off.

She bit back a smile. "You mean you aren't finished proving you can have sex without falling head over—" A rustling in the bushes cut her off, and she sat up and covered her breasts with her hands. "What's that?"

"Probably just some cows." Zane reached for his jeans. "But I'll go check to be sure. The last thing I need is Becky showing up after I've given her more than one lecture on behaving appropriately in public."

She smirked at him. "I like you misbehaving."

He leaned over and kissed her deeply. "You're going to get more of it when I get back." He got up and slipped on his jeans.

She rolled to her stomach and watched as he made his way to the bushes where the rustling was coming from. Whatever he saw on the other side made him laugh. Not a chuckle, but a deep belly laugh that had her grabbing his shirt and pulling it on.

When she reached the bushes and looked over, she couldn't figure out what was so funny. All she saw were two cows going at it hot and heavy. Or at least, the cow on top was going at it hot and heavy. She took a good look at the rutting cow and finally understood why Zane was laughing.

It seemed that she and Zane weren't the only ones who had gotten lucky that night.

Ferdinand had finally proven he was a real stud bull.

"Duke had the ring bought and the chapel reserved. He whistled 'Here Comes the Bride' as he pulled a shirt out of his dresser drawer. He stopped whistling when he saw the twig of poison ivy."

CHAPTER NINETEEN

T HE BEDROOM DOOR FLYING OPEN woke Zane from a deep sleep, the first deep sleep he'd had in months. He was reminded of what had caused him to sleep so soundly when the warm body next to him emitted a startled gasp and ducked beneath the sheets just as Becky strode to the foot of his bed.

"How could you do it, Zane?" she asked.

The better question was how could he not. Even now, with all of Carly's soft curves pressed against his side, he was struggling to keep desire at bay. The woman tempted him beyond all reason. He had made a deal with her for one night. But after a night spent in her arms, he knew it was impossible not to want more. He wanted to be her friend, but he also wanted to be able to touch her whenever he wanted. He didn't care if it would confuse their relationship. And he didn't care if he was setting a bad example for his sister. Becky had been a wild child all her life. Now it was his turn to walk on the wild side.

He cleared his throat. "I'm not going to discuss my sex life with you."

Becky looked completely baffled. "What are you talking about? I'm not here to talk about Rachel. I'm here to talk about why you took that asshole of a lawyer to see my house."

Zane glanced down and realized that Carly was such a little bit of a thing that his sister had no clue there was someone in bed with him. He smiled. She had a petite body, but it seemed to fit his perfectly.

Becky released an angry snort like a bull getting ready to charge. "You're smiling about it?" She threw up her hands. "I don't know why I expected a different reaction. You don't care what I want. You just care about being a controlling big brother who tells me what to do."

"And right now, I'm telling you to leave." Zane slipped a hand under the covers and curved his fingers over one smooth butt cheek. Carly's muscles tensed, but she didn't utter a peep.

Becky crossed her arms and gave him a stubborn look. "I'm not leaving until you explain why you would show that jerk Mason Granger my house."

"Your house? You bought the Reed Property?"

"Not yet, but as soon as I turn twenty-five and get my trust fund, I plan on buying it."

"Don't be stupid, Becky. You don't need the Reed place. You already have a ranch. This one. And Mason isn't a jerk. He's a nice guy—something you seem to steer clear of. Instead, you collect bad boys."

She placed her hands on her hips. "Well, for your information, that nice guy accosted me in the barn."

That got his attention in a hurry. He sat up so quickly that he uncovered Carly. "What do you mean he accosted you? He attacked you?"

Becky blinked. "Carly?"

Carly gave him an annoyed look before she jerked the sheet back and covered her naked breasts. "Good morning, Becky. Would you like me to make you some coffee? Or how about break-fast?"

A sly, all-knowing smile spread across Becky's face. "No, thank you. I already made coffee and had some cereal." She looked as Zane. "Speaking of bad boys . . ."

At the moment, he wasn't worried about being caught in bed with Carly. He was worried about his sister. "Just answer the question. Did Mason attack you?"

The smile faded. "Not attacked exactly."

"Then what exactly?"

She thought for a few seconds before she answered. "He overpowered me. I was putting Ghost Rider in his stall after I brought him back from Cole's when Shep came running in and spooked him. I totally had control, but your friend didn't think so. He shoved me away from the horse, knocked me down in the hay, and then covered me with his big suffocating body."

The tension in Zane's shoulders eased. He should've known that Mason would never harm his sister. The man was as moral and upstanding as Zane. He felt Carly's leg brush against his and instantly grew hard. Maybe more so.

"He was protecting you from getting beaten to death by your horse's hooves," he said.

His sister glared at him. "Didn't you hear me? Ghost wasn't going to hurt me. I had complete control."

Carly stifled a laugh behind her hand. Zane knew exactly what she thought was funny. She had been on him about being controlling, and it looked like his sister had the same trait. Not that Zane was even close to being as controlling as Becky. But he had learned a thing or two in the last few months that he didn't mind sharing with his sister.

"No one has complete control over anything, Becky. Especially a wild stallion that needs more training. You're lucky Mason was there to save you." He pointed a finger. "Now stay off that damn horse until I've had a chance to teach him some manners."

It took a minute for his sister to react. By the fire in her eyes, he figured she wasn't going to thank him for his words of wisdom. "That's all you have to say? You're trying to sell my ranch and now you want to take away my horse? Well, I'm tired of you telling me what I can and cannot do, Zane Duke Arrington. To hell with you. And to hell with Mason Granger!" She whirled and strode out of the room, slamming the door behind her.

When she was gone, he heaved an exasperated sigh and flopped back on the pillows. "As you probably know by now, my sister has no problems sharing her true feelings."

There was a pause. "Something you need to do

more often . . . Duke."

He lifted his head and cocked a brow. "Are you making fun of my name?"

"Yes. Although Duke Earhart happens to be my second favorite character in the Tender Heart series."

"And who is your first? Don't tell me it's the villain Dax Davenport."

"Of course not. It's Laura for being strong enough to cut Duke down to size when he was being overbearing. And you're being overbearing, Duke. I get that Becky is your little sister and you feel protective of her, but you need to tone it down a little. Instead of yelling at her all the time, you need to let her know you love her."

"She knows I love her."

"Does she? How? From what I can tell, you never give her any attention."

He sat up. "I give her plenty of attention. I've spent the last few years watching over her like a parent."

"Except you're not her parent. You're her brother."

Feeling a little perturbed, he punched a pillow and stuffed it behind his back. "As her brother, it's my job to keep her safe."

Carly's eyes turned soft. "That might've been your job when she was younger, but she's an adult now. She gets to make her own decisions—even if they're stupid. As her brother, you shouldn't be ordering her around as much as giving her sound advice."

The joy of waking up with Carly was quickly dissipating. If she was going to give him lectures every morning, it might be better if she went back to her own bed. "And I guess your big brother gave you sound advice? Funny, but if he's such a great guy, why haven't you ever mentioned him?"

"I don't have any siblings. But I wish I did. I wish I had a big brother who loves me like you love Becky. Instead, I had a tough military dad who viewed me as one of his troops that he had to keep in line. For most of my life, he ordered me around. He tried to act like he did it out of love. But if someone loves you, they shouldn't want to control you. They should let you make mistakes and forgive you when you do."

The aching need in her voice made Zane realize the importance of what she was sharing. "What didn't your father forgive you for?"

"I was a bit of hellion when I was a teenager. Whatever I thought would tick my dad off, I did. Including marrying a bad boy loser."

"Sam?"

She nodded. "After I caught him with the other woman, I called my father. Looking back, I guess I hoped he would come and rescue me. Instead, he completely disowned me." She lifted her eyes. There were no tears, and for some reason, that was even more heartbreaking. "I don't want that happening to you and Becky."

Unable to stop himself, he reached out and pulled her into his arms. When she was nestled against his chest, he smoothed back her hair and kissed her forehead. "That would never happen to me and Becky. There's nothing I couldn't forgive her for. But you're right. I should spend more time just being her brother, instead of her parent." He brushed his fingertips up and down the soft skin of her arm. "I bet your dad feels bad about how he treated you."

There was a long pause before she spoke. "If he does, I wouldn't know. We still don't talk."

His heart tightened as he searched for something to say. But he couldn't find anything that would ease her pain. He didn't always look forward to his dad's phone calls, but he didn't know what he'd do if his dad suddenly stopped speaking to him. What kind of an asshole would do that to his only daughter? If the man were there right now, Zane would kick his ass into the middle of next month. But the man wasn't there. Just his scarred daughter. Zane wished like hell he could heal those scars as easily as he killed a spider.

"Stop it," Carly spoke against his chest.

"Stop what?" He continued to caress her arm.

"Stop trying to figure out how you can fix it."

He reached down and tipped up her chin. Her eyes still looked sad, but there was a sparkle of mischief that made him smile. "You're right, I can't fix it. But I wish I could do something to make you feel better."

Her gaze lowered to his mouth. "I could probably think of something."

He leaned in and kissed her. "Better?"

She blinked those big brown eyes and nodded hesitantly.

"You don't seem so sure." He slid the back of his finger across her wet bottom lip. "Maybe I kissed the wrong spot." He slowly pushed down the sheet to reveal her rose-tipped breasts. Right before his eyes, the centers tightened. The sight made him happy. It was nice to know that he wasn't the only one about ready to combust from desire, and it was a struggle not to head straight for those sweet buds. Instead, he brushed a kiss over one creamy shoulder. "What about here? Does that make you feel better?" He worked his way down, sipping at her soft skin. "Here?" He shifted her to the side and kissed the swell of one breast. "What about here?"

She hummed deep in the back of her throat and pressed her head into the pillow.

"Ahh, I must be getting warmer." He circled her nipple with kisses before he sucked it into his mouth. She groaned and her hips lifted off the mattress. "Easy there," he spoke against her chill-bumped breast. "If I'm going to find the perfect spot to make you feel better, then I need you to be very still."

He slipped a hand between her legs, and just the feel of her wet heat surrounding his fingers almost made him lose it. But he ignored his own need and concentrated on Carly's. He stroked her clitoris with his thumb as he drew her nipple into his mouth. When she grew even more moist and started bucking against his hand, he kissed his way down her stomach to the spot that throbbed beneath his fingers.

But before he reached it, she tugged on his hair and stopped him. He lifted his head to find her eyes sex-dazed but also fearful. She glanced at the window where sunlight poured in. "It's no longer night, Zane."

He knew immediately what she was saying. If they continued, they would break the pact they'd made the night before. The realization made him a little scared too. Scared that maybe Carly had been right. Maybe he was vulnerable. He certainly felt vulnerable to the pair of uncertain brown eyes that turned back to him. As much as he knew he should stop, he couldn't.

"Just one more time," he said as he lowered his head. But as he took her heat into his mouth, he knew it was a lie. One more time wouldn't be enough. Or two more. Or even a thousand.

They didn't leave the bed until close to noon, and even then he didn't want to. It was Carly who ignored his coaxing kisses and left to shower. And since he needed to get some work done, it was probably for the best. Still, he didn't waste any time showering and shaving in hopes that he'd get to see her before she headed to the diner. Unfortunately, she was already gone by the time he got to the kitchen. His disappointment evaporated when he found the note on the breakfast bar with an egg and sausage sandwich.

Thanks for making me feel better, Duke. Have a good day.

After carefully folding the note and tucking it in his shirt pocket, he grabbed the sandwich and headed to his truck. He wanted to check on Ferdinand. A horny bull could do some serious damage to himself and other cows if he wasn't monitored. But when he saw his sister's truck still parked in the garage, he figured Ferdinand could survive on his own for a little longer.

He found Becky in the stall with Muffin. It was a Kodak moment if ever he'd seen one. His pretty sister sat on a hay bale petting the foal. Becky's long cinnamon-colored hair matched the horse's spots.

And her Arrington blue eyes sparkled with laughter when the horse nudged her hand for more attention. She had always been a happy, fun-loving kid. And maybe that's why Zane had so little patience with her. He'd felt so burdened with being the only son and having to live up to the Arrington name that he resented her lack of responsibility. But that was a false perception. Becky was responsible. She worked the ranch as hard as he did. She just didn't let it consume every second of her life. She worked hard, and she played hard. Obviously, she was a lot smarter than he was.

He enjoyed watching her and Muffin for a few more minutes before he opened the stall door and stepped in. Startled, the foal danced away. Becky glanced up, but then completely ignored him. He took a seat on the hay bale next to her.

"Where's Cinnamon?"

"She's in the paddock. I thought she could stand a little time away from this greedy one constantly wanting to nurse."

"I don't think mamas mind."

She shot a glance over at him. "Then you haven't talked to very many mamas. Jennifer Farrell about went insane when little Daryl kept screaming for food. She said her nipples were so sore she had to switch him to a bottle."

Not wanting to get into a conversation about nipples with his little sister, he nodded at Muffin, who had cautiously come back for more petting. "He's a good-lookin' horse, isn't he?"

"He sure is." She stroked the foal's forehead. "What are your plans for him?"

"I haven't really thought about it." He paused.

"Do you want him?"

Her jaw tightened as she grumbled her reply. "What if he's ill-tempered like Ghost Rider? I would hate to fall in love with him just to have him taken away."

Zane took off his hat and ran a hand through his hair. "I didn't take Ghost Rider away. I just want to make sure he spends more time with an experienced rider—" He paused, remembering what Carly had said about treating Becky like an adult. "I'm sorry. That's just arrogance talking. Especially since you've been riding horses just as long as I have."

She turned to him, her eyes wide. "Did you just say you were arrogant?"

"No. I said it was arrogance talking."

"Which is the same thing."

He heaved a sigh and rested his elbows on his knees, twirling his hat in his hands. "Okay, I'm arrogant. It's not like you didn't already know that. You've had to live with it all your life." He cast her a sideways glance. "And that couldn't have been easy."

She stared at him as if he was an alien from another planet. This was confirmed with her next words. "Who are you? And what have you done with my big brother?"

"Don't be a smartass. I've conceded things to you before."

"Like never. At least not without a fight." She cocked her head. "Did you fall and get a concussion? Or did sex with Carly act like a truth serum?"

It was probably the sex. But like nipples, sex was not a subject he would be discussing with his sister. "Maybe I just figured out that I'd been acting like more of a parent to you than a brother. And I figured it's time to start treating you like the adult you are."

Becky stared for one second more before she lifted her hands in the air. "Hallelujah, it's a miracle." She lowered her hands and grinned. "Does this mean you're going to stop intimidating my boyfriends?"

"No. That's part of a big brother's job."

She rolled her eyes. "Okay, then does it mean that you're going to keep your friend from buying my house?"

"Sorry, but if he's already struck a deal, there's not much I can do." He reached out and ruffled her hair. "Besides, I kinda like you living with me now that you aren't constantly bickering with Rachel."

She slapped his hand away. "I like Carly. Which brings up a good question. Just how are you going to explain your live-in girlfriend to Mama and Daddy when they get back from Hawaii?"

Zane hadn't really thought about that. But now that he did, it seemed simple enough. "There's nothing to explain. She's our cook."

Becky laughed. "Daddy might fall for that, but Mama will see right through you. Just like I see right through you. You haven't conceded one thing to me. So I don't believe you've changed at all."

Since she had a point, he had to do some fast thinking to come up with proof. The mud on her boots gave him an idea. "How about if we take the dirt bikes out?"

She perked up. "Are you serious? But what about the ranch? We still have hay that needs to be loaded in the storehouse."

"It can wait." He got to his feet. "Besides, I think you need a little lesson on who's the best rider in the family."

She gave Muffin one last pat before she stood and flashed Zane a smug smile. "No lesson needed, big brother. I know exactly who she is."

"Laura took a step back. 'Don't you dare lay a hand on me, Duke Earhart.' He took a step closer. 'After all the things you've done to me, I'm going to lay more than a hand on you, honey.'"

CHAPTER TWENTY

❧

IT SEEMED LIKE MOST OF the town was at the Chili Cook-off meeting. At least fifty people sat in folding chairs in the Sunday school room of the Baptist church. Carly included. She wondered why she had let Emery talk her into coming when she had an entire list of things she should be doing. She should be on the phone yelling at the tile guy who kept coming up with excuses why he couldn't do his job. Or searching the Internet for a plumber who wasn't on strike. Or back at the ranch making love to Zane.

Their experiment had completely failed. The one-time sex had turned into too many to count. From the time they finished the dinner dishes until they fell into an exhausted sleep in each other's arms, they went at it like rabbits on spring break. Savannah's theory was wrong. Carly had gorged herself on chocolate donuts, and she didn't feel the least bit sick. In fact, she felt the opposite. She felt energized and alive. Contentment swirled in her stomach and a effervescent warmth filled her chest. She could explain the contentment. Five days of great sex could make you content. But what she couldn't seem to explain was the buoyant feeling in her chest, which caused her to giggle at inappropriate times.

"Just what's so funny?"

Carly stopped daydreaming and turned to find Mrs. Crawley looking at her with lowered eyebrows. And the woman had some thick, scary-looking brows. Before Carly could find an excuse for her giggles, Emery leaned around her and intervened. "Carly wasn't laughing about you nominating Winnie for Chili Bowl queen, Mrs. Crawley. She just gets nervous in crowds. I'm sure she thinks Winnie would make a perfect queen."

On the other side of Emery, Ms. Marble snorted. "Perfectly awful."

Mrs. Crawley leaned over to glare at Ms. Marble. "What did you say, Maybelline?"

Thankfully, Emmett's wife, Joanna Daily, interrupted. "I second the nomination for Winnie. Now, if that's all Chili Bowl queen business, we can move onto the next order of business."

Ms. Marble lifted her white-gloved hand. "I nominate Carly Sue Hanover."

It was a sweet gesture, but Carly had no intention of being queen of anything. She would feel guilty enough leaving them without a chef for the diner. She refused to leave them without a chili queen. "I appreciate the gesture, Ms. Marble, but I'm not really queen material."

"Any member of this community is queen material," Ms. Marble said. "And seeing as how you're reopening a historical landmark, you're a part of this town."

Carly didn't know why the statement made her feel so happy. Maybe because she had never been a part of anything—let alone an entire town. But she couldn't accept the nomination.

Unfortunately, before she could decline, Emmett, who sat in front of her, lifted his hand. "I second the nomination." He turned in his chair and gave her a wink and a wide grin. "I'm looking forward to the diner opening again. The thought of a big juicy burger and crispy fries was what got me through the war." He turned back to his wife. "And of course, your kissable lips, Jojo."

Joanna blushed as she wrote on her notepad. "Carly Sue Hanover. Now let's move on to the t-shirt design." She pulled a t-shirt out of a bag that sat on the table next to her. Not the navy backpack with green stitching but a floral tote bag with a coffee stain. Carly exchanged looks with Emery, but they didn't get a chance to talk until the meeting had adjourned. Once it did, Emery quickly pulled Carly over to one corner of the room.

"You noticed too," she said in a hushed voice. "She didn't bring the backpack."

"I noticed, but that doesn't mean anything. Maybe Ms. Marble didn't give it back to her. Or maybe she just wanted to use her tote today." She glanced over to where Joanna was folding the t-shirt samples she'd brought. "But I guess there's only one way to find out."

"Fine, but let me do the talking," Emery said.

"You don't know how to be subtle."

As they approached, Joanna stopped folding t-shirts and smiled. "I'm so glad you girls are on the committee. We need fresh, young ideas to liven things up. I loved your idea about having a music festival in conjunction with the cook-off, Emery."

Emery couldn't seem to pull her gaze away from the tote to answer. Talk about subtle. Carly pinched her arm to snap her out of it. "Oh! Yes, the bands. With Austin being so close, I got some great country groups to perform. And the bandstand will be in the Watering Hole parking lot alongside the beer stand."

"Good idea. Although I don't think Hank should serve food." She looked at Carly. "I was hoping that the diner would be open, but I hear that the renovations aren't going well."

"That's an understatement," Carly said. "The only thing that I've gotten fixed so far is the air conditioning. I can't seem to get any work out of the contractors I've hired. So it doesn't look like I'll be open in a month, let alone a couple of weeks."

A determined look came over Joanna's face. "Well, that's ridiculous. It sounds like people are taking advantage of you and that's just not right." She pulled the notepad from her tote bag and started writing, then tore off the paper and handed it to Carly. "This is my nephew's number. He's a contractor in Austin and he'll be able to recommend some people for the bigger jobs. As for cleaning and painting, I'm sure the entire town won't mind chipping in. Including me. I think we should set up a schedule."

Carly understood why Joanna had been voted

Chili Cook-off chairperson. She knew how to take charge and get things done.

She patted Carly's arm. "Don't you worry, dear. We'll get that diner opened if it's the last thing I do. Like the rest of the town, I'm excited to see it reopen. Before I started teaching school, I was a waitress at the diner. I even got to wait on Lucy Arrington when she came in." She laughed. "Not that the woman ordered anything but water and lemons."

At the mention of Lucy, Emery couldn't hold herself back any longer. "I love your tote," she said. "You have the cutest bags. In fact, I've been meaning to ask you where you got your navy backpack."

Joanna looked confused. "My navy backpack?"

"The one you left at Ms. Marble's."

The confusion remained. "I didn't leave a backpack. I don't even own a backpack." Her eyes narrowed in thought, and she pointed a finger. "Although I remember seeing that backpack at Maybelline's. I just assumed it was hers. She said it was mine?"

Both Carly and Emery glanced over at Ms. Marble, who was opening Tupperware containers and filling plates with cookies. In her gardening hat and white gloves, she looked sweet and innocent. But it seemed that looks were deceiving. Of course, until they knew for sure, they needed to keep their cards close to the vest.

"We must've misunderstood," Carly said. "Well, if we want the diner open, I'd better get back to it." She glanced at Emery. "Since I walked, do you want to give me a ride?"

Once outside the church, Emery released her

shock. "It's Ms. Marble! She's the one who found the sixth chapter in the cemetery. Which makes perfect sense because she was there long before my wedding started. Remember, she had to deliver the wedding cake she made for us. She could've easily slipped out to the cemetery when no one was looking."

"But why would she choose that time to be in the cemetery looking for the book? Why wouldn't she look for it when no one was at the chapel?"

Emery thought for a moment before she spoke. "Maybe she wasn't looking for it. Maybe she had just stopped by to place the pink roses that were on Lucy's grave and found it by accident. She was Lucy's friend."

It did make sense. But other things didn't. "And you think she was there at the diner the night of the fire looking for more chapters? I realize she's light on her feet for an old woman, but I don't think she could've slipped out without Zane or me noticing."

"Of course she could've. When you and Zane are together, you don't notice anything *but* each other." Emery gave her a pointed look. "And when were you going to tell me that you are having sex with him?"

"Who told you? Becky?"

Emery rolled her eyes. "No one had to tell me. All I had to do was take one look at your face to know. You have sex glow."

Since it was a pretty accurate description of how she felt, Carly couldn't very well deny it. "Fine. We had sex. I know I said I wasn't going to. But sometimes the best laid plans fall completely apart."

"That's called destiny," Emery said smugly.

Carly sighed in exasperation. "It's not destiny. It's called being horny. Zane and I are just sexually attracted to each other." That was an understatement if ever there was one.

"What happened to you being worried about hurting him?"

People started coming out of the church, and since Carly didn't want anyone else knowing about her sex life, she pulled Emery into the dirt parking lot.

"I *was* worried about hurting him. But after talking to him, I realize he's not interested in getting serious either. Right now, he just wants to have a little fun. That's exactly how I felt after my divorce. I wanted to experience life to the fullest without commitment. It will take time before Zane's ready for a serious relationship. Hopefully, he'll find a good woman. One who will keep him from taking life too seriously, and one who understands that beneath the tough façade is a man who cares deeply."

Emery's eyes filled with awe. "Oh. My. God. You love him. You love Zane." Carly stared in open-mouthed shock as Emery continued. "Here, I was thinking it was Zane who would fall head over heels. I never thought you would. I guess because you always act so tough, like you're immune to love." A smile bloomed on her face. "But you were just waiting for the right man to trust your heart to. You were just waiting for Zane."

Carly stepped back and shook her head. "No. Zane is the last person I would trust my heart to. He's too controlling, he lives in a state of denial half the time, and he has trouble letting his feelings out. Not to mention that he's a country boy who couldn't live anywhere but a small town and I'm definitely a city girl who couldn't live anywhere but a bustling city. So it would be really stupid of me to fall in love with a man like that. Like totally and utterly—"

She cut off when a movement over Emery's shoulder caught her attention. A cowboy on an ebony black horse came galloping across the open fields behind the church. A cowboy she recognized immediately. She recognized the broad chest and knotted biceps that flexed as he jumped the huge horse over a deep gully. Recognized the muscular thighs that tightened when he urged the magnificent animal back into a gallop. And recognized the sensual smile that tipped his mouth as he drew nearer.

Lust swirled through her body in heavy, sweet waves. But eclipsing the lust was the light and airy feeling that expanded in her chest. And not just her chest, but her heart. It felt like it was filled with helium, and if it could escape her body it would float right up into the sky and touch the sun.

And if her heart could hold helium, it was no longer broken.

The realization struck her like a bolt of lightning from the clear Texas sky. All she could so was stand there in stunned disbelief as the man who had mended her heart galloped closer.

With his hat pulled low she couldn't see his eyes, but she didn't need to see them to know they were pinned on her. She thought he would slow down when he reached the parking lot. He didn't. If she hadn't been so stunned by her realization, she would've moved out of the way like Emery. But she didn't move. She just stood there like a love-struck heroine straight from the pages of a Tender Heart novel.

And like a fictional hero, Zane leaned out of the saddle and swept her off her feet.

*"After almost being poisoned, Duke wanted noth-
ing to do with Laura or any of the mail-order brides.
He was plenty content to live out his life on the
ranch with his brothers. Yes sir, plenty content."*

CHAPTER TWENTY-ONE

"I GOTTA TELL YOU THAT I'M a little worried," Dirk said. "That bull has been going
after those heifers non-stop for the last four days.
It's like someone put Viagra in his drinking water
and he's got a permanent boner."

Zane knew exactly how the bull felt. No matter
how many times he and Carly had sex, it was never
enough. Just the thought of being deep inside her
warm, loving body made him as hard as the fence
railing he leaned on. He had the strong desire to
head into Bliss and take her on the diner counter.

Down, boy. He couldn't leave the ranch. He had
work to do. And Carly was busy with the diner.
Tonight would be soon enough to strip her naked
and kiss every square inch of her delectable body—

"You okay?" Dirk cut into his fantasy. "You look
a little flushed. Is the heat getting to you?" He took
off his hat and ran his arm across his forehead. "It's

sure as hell getting to me. I can't remember a summer this hot in Texas."

Zane glanced at him. As close as he'd gotten to Dirk in the last few weeks, he realized he didn't know that much about him. "Where in Texas are you from again?"

Dirk looked at the bull. Ferdinand was still going at it with one of the heifers. "Just north of Dallas. You think I should corral him when he's finished?"

The change of subject was obvious. But Zane was a firm believer that a man had a right to his own secrets. And it looked like Dirk had more than a few. "That might not be a bad idea. He could probably use a rest."

Dirk smirked. "He's not the only one."

"What does that mean?"

"Just that you don't look like you're getting a lot of sleep." The smirk turned into a big smile. "After that sappy stunt you pulled in town the other day, I figure I know why."

Zane knew exactly what stunt he was talking about. The entire town was abuzz about him riding into town and sweeping Carly right off her feet like Duke Earhart. And he didn't doubt that more than a few people were wondering if his affair with Carly was the reason for the divorce. He should be working to squelch the gossip. But after spending most of his life worried about what other people thought, he'd didn't care anymore. All he cared about was what Carly thought. She hadn't acted mad. Just a little stunned.

"Yeah, well, sometimes a man needs to make a fool of himself," he said. "It keeps him humble."

Dirk's hat shifted as he cocked an eyebrow.

"Humble? You?" He shook his head and chuckled. "Becky said Carly has changed you, but I didn't believe it until now."

Zane's spine stiffened. "No one has changed me. Especially not Carly. Just because I've been hanging out with my sister more and showing a little horsemanship in town, that doesn't mean I've changed."

Dirk held up his hands. "Don't go all postal. There's nothing wrong with a little change. I think you and Carly are good for each other. She ruffles your smooth feathers and you soften her rough edges. Although just so you know, she might be tough on the outside, but she's a marshmallow on the inside. And if you hurt her, I'll have to hurt you."

Zane knew exactly what Dirk was talking about. Carly wanted everyone to think she was as tough as nails. But underneath her blunt talk and strong will was a soft heart. It showed through her desire to feed everyone, the love she gave Shep and Muffin, and the friendship she'd offered Becky. She was a good woman. A damn good woman. And the last thing he wanted to do was hurt her.

"I'm not going to hurt Carly."

Dirk nodded. "I figured as much, but I couldn't leave without making sure."

Zane straightened. "Leave? Now hold up there. I realized that Jess comes back on Monday, but he still can't do any heavy lifting. And even when he's back to full steam, I could use you. In a few weeks, if things keep going the way they're going, I'll give you a raise."

Dirk smiled. "I sure appreciate the offer, but when Jess gets back, I think I'll be on my way."

It was hard not to push the issue. Especially when Zane had gotten to know and like Dirk. The man wasn't just an employee. He had become a friend, which was why Zane knew it wouldn't do any good to push. Dirk was the type of man who when he made up his mind about something, he stuck with it.

"Fair enough," he said. "If you need a place to stay, you can still stay in the bunkhouse."

"I appreciate that. But if I'm going to help Carly get that diner open before the Chili Cook-off, I figure I'll need to stay in town."

Okay, so maybe Dirk wasn't such a good friend.

"You're going to help Carly with the diner?" With Dirk's help, the diner could open in a couple of weeks and Carly would move into town.

"She claims she doesn't need my help," Dirk said. "I think she doesn't want to add to my ranch work. But after her tile guy quit on her and the plumber didn't show up, I figure she needs my help more than you do."

Zane cleared his throat. He knew keeping the contractors from working on the diner was dishonest and lowdown, but he just wanted to keep Carly at the ranch for a little while longer. "I agree, but I think you helping her is a bad idea. What do you know about tile and plumbing? Those are jobs for professionals."

"Actually, I did a little tile work in El Paso. And I was a plumber's apprentice during high school."

Damn, Dirk of all trades was starting to piss him off. "Well, being an apprentice isn't being a plumber. And how do you know that Carly is going to pick the kind of tile you've laid before?"

He shook his head. "No, I think it's best if she has professionals. I'll call a couple friends of mine and have them stop by."

Dirk's eyes squinted. "But weren't the tile guy and the plumber your friends? And not showing up doesn't sound very professional to me."

"Well, I'm sure they had a good reason." Like being paid double not to work. "You need to be patient when you renovate."

Dirk studied him for a long, uncomfortable moment before he spoke. "Funny, but I've never taken you for a patient man. When you want something, you go after it. Which has me wondering if you aren't responsible for—"

Thankfully, Zane's phone rang and cut Dirk off. He looked at the number and cringed. He had been dodging his dad's calls for the last few days in an effort to postpone telling him about the divorce. But his parents were due back from Hawaii next week, and Zane knew he would have to face his father's wrath eventually. And it might be best if his father was thousands of miles away when he got the news.

He tapped the accept button. "Hey, Daddy."

By the tone of his voice, it didn't sound like his father was enjoying his Hawaiian vacation. "Don't you dare 'hey, Daddy' me. Get your ass back to the house. Now!" He hung up.

Zane lowered the phone. It appeared that his father was no longer in Hawaii. It also appeared that the shit was about to hit the fan.

He realized what an understatement that was when he walked into his study fifteen minutes later and found his father sitting behind the desk with a glass of whiskey in one hand and Zane's divorce papers in the other.

"Just what the hell is this?" He shook the papers. "I thought you had everything under control? This doesn't look like control to me. It looks like you have given away half of my ranch while I've been out of the country."

Zane took off his hat and hung it on the hook by the door before looking back at his father. "Hawaii is part of the United States. And hi to you too, Daddy."

If the red that suffused his father's face was any indication, that wasn't the response he wanted. Of course, Zane knew what he wanted. He wanted his son to cower like he always had and tell him that he would make things right. But Zane couldn't. For once in his life, everything *was* right.

"Are you being a smartass?" his father asked.

Instead of answering, he moved to the liquor cabinet and poured two fingers of his father's favorite whiskey. As he poured, he wondered why he still had his father's whiskey in his study. Probably because he still thought of the room as his dad's. Which explained why his father was comfortable sitting in the chair behind the desk. Zane had never laid claim to the room—or to the ranch.

Maybe it was time he did.

After pouring his drink, he turned. "I don't mean to be disrespectful. But this is my study, Daddy. And those papers in your hand are my personal documents. You have no right to touch them."

His father came up from the chair. "No right? This is still my ranch and I don't want to see it handed over to someone who doesn't have a drop of Arrington blood!"

Zane could feel his temper rising. And this time he didn't try to hold it back. This time he let his father see that he wasn't the only Arrington who could get loud and overbearing.

He tossed back the drink, and then slammed the glass on the liquor cabinet so hard that the other glasses rattled. "It's not just your ranch. It's mine, and Becky's, and Mama's. We've all put blood, sweat, and tears into it. We've all earned a share. Even Rachel has earned her share by putting up with my arrogant ass."

"Like hell! I should've never retired and left you in charge."

"But you did. Legally, I'm CEO of the company and Becky and I own the majority of the ranch."

His father's eyes narrowed. "Are you saying I have no say?"

"No, you have a say in how I run the ranch. You just don't have a say in how I run my life."

"I do when your stupid mistakes affect the ranch." He pointed his finger. "Now you're going to do whatever it takes to get Rachel back. I don't care if you have to kiss her ass every second of every day for the rest of your life."

Zane crossed his arms. "Not happening."

There was a moment when he thought his father's eyes were going to pop right out of his head. But he should've known better. His father hadn't built an empire by being a hot head. He'd built it by being levelheaded . . . and ruthless.

He studied Zane for a moment before he sat back down. "This has to do with your little cook, doesn't it?"

He wasn't surprised that his father had heard about Carly. Not only did he have friends in town, but Zane didn't doubt for a second that his dad had informants on the ranch as well. That probably explained why his parents had come back from Hawaii early.

"She's not little. She's petite," he said. "And she's not a cook, she's an executive chef."

His father snorted. "I don't care what size she is or what title she uses. She's still just a piece of tail. And you need to remember that, son."

Talk about hotheaded. Zane felt like his head was filled with steam. The only thing he needed to remember at the moment was that killing your father isn't a good idea. But punching wasn't so bad. He strode over to the desk with clenched fists. In the end, all he did was slam his fist down on the wood surface.

"Don't you ever say anything like that about the woman I love again. Do you hear me? Never again!"

At first, he thought the startled look on his father's face had to do with him finally standing up for himself, but then Zane realized what had slipped out. Anger died to be replaced with disbelief and shock.

"You love her?" His father spoke the exact words that were circling around in Zane's brain.

"No," he spoke more to himself than his father. "I can't love her. I mean I like her. I like her a lot. She's sassy." He pictured her fighting him when he pulled her out of the diner after she almost burned it down. "And she's outspoken and truthful." He pictured her standing in the kitchen in her baggy boxers confronting him with the truth about Rachel leaving. "And she's dedicated and hard-working." He pictured her standing at the stove cooking and working in the diner. "And she's loving." He pictured her after they made love—with her smile soft and dreamy eyes twinkling with contentment. A contentment that made him feel like the virile bull of the herd. Except there was only one woman he wanted to satisfy. Only one woman he wanted to spend the rest of his life satisfying.

As the truth dawned, it felt like his heart cracked wide open. He had spent a lifetime denying his own feelings. He refused to waste a second more. Not when his happiness was at stake.

"I love her." He laughed. "I love Carly Sue Hanover!"

He expected some kind of response from his father, but instead his dad just sat there staring. Not at him, but at the doorway. When he glanced over his shoulder and saw the woman standing there, he understood why.

"Rachel?"

"Duke's brother Rory was the one who drove Laura back into town. As they left the ranch, Duke came out of the barn with Elsa at his side. The goat bleated a goodbye, but Duke didn't even lift a hand."

CHAPTER TWENTY-TWO

CARLY HAD BEEN WORKING LIKE a demon at the diner. Her contractors still hadn't shown up, and Joanna's nephew couldn't start until the following week. So after she'd finished painting, she started ripping up the tile. The work was physically hard, but unfortunately not mentally demanding. It gave her plenty of time to think about Zane. And to beat herself up for falling in love with him.

She couldn't deny it any longer. She loved him. But that didn't make it any less stupid. Loving Zane was a dead-end street. She had no plans to live in Bliss forever. She was a big-city girl with a dream of owning a five-star restaurant. Although she had to admit that owning an exclusive restaurant in a big city didn't hold the same excitement as it once had. Now she was more excited about picking out gingham fabric for the diner curtains. Or getting pictures of Lucy enlarged and framed. The diner was only supposed to be a jumping-off point for bigger and better things, but lately it had started to feel like . . . her destiny.

She blamed Emery for putting the thought in her head. Carly had never believed in destiny. She believed that freak things just happened. There was no master plan. Probably because she had always felt like her life was a boat in a storm—tossed first one way and then the other as if at any second it could capsize. But since she'd moved to Bliss, her life boat hadn't been tossed and turned. It felt like it had found a safe harbor.

"Excuse me?"

Carly was startled out of her daydreams. She dropped the scraper she'd been using to pop up the tile in the kitchen and turned to see a man with a clipboard standing just inside the back door.

She brushed her dirty hands on her paint-stained shorts. "Please tell me you're the tile guy."

"I'm afraid not." He smiled and held out a hand. "Kyle Meade, plumber."

She was so excited that she clasped his hand in both of hers and shook it vigorously. "Thank God. I thought the plumber's strike was going to go on forever."

Kyle looked confused. "Strike? I wasn't on strike."

She dropped his hand. "But I thought that's why you haven't shown up to work."

He shook his head. "I didn't show up because Zane told me to hold off because you hadn't decided what fixtures you wanted yet." He unclipped a catalog from his clipboard and held it out. "When I didn't hear from you, I thought I'd drop this catalog by to help you decide."

It took only a second for the truth to sink in. When it did, she wasn't worried about falling in love with Zane as much as strangling him.

"Thank you so much, Kyle." She spoke through her teeth as she took the catalog. "I'll be sure to look this over and call you as soon as I decide. Right now, I have an appointment I need to go to."

As soon as Kyle left, she locked up the diner and headed to her car. It didn't take her long to get to the ranch. In her anger, she exceeded the speed limit. She thought she would have to drive all over the ranch looking for Zane, but his black truck was parked in front. There was also a truck and SUV she didn't recognize, but she didn't care who they belonged to. The only person she cared about was an arrogant rancher who thought he could hold her hostage.

She slammed through the front door and would've stomped right back to his study if a man hadn't been sitting in the living room. Even if Carly hadn't seen pictures, she would've known who he was immediately. Zane's father looked like an older version of his son, from the thick blond hair with only a hint of silver to the intense Arrington blue eyes. Becky had mentioned that her parents were in Hawaii. Obviously they were back, and Zane had not given Carly fair warning: another reason to be mad at him.

"Excuse me," she said, "I was looking for Zane."

Mr. Arrington got to his feet. "I'm Dale Arrington, Zane's father. You must be Carly. I've heard a lot about you."

His tone reminded her of her own father's—stiff and unyielding. That probably explained her sudden defensive stance. "I hope it wasn't all bad."

His sharp gaze ran over her from head to toe, and it was a struggle not to smooth her hair out of her face or cover the paint on her shorts. But if this man was anything like her father, weakness was not something he respected. She stiffened her spine and held out a hand.

"It's nice to meet you."

He shook her hand, then nodded at the chair across from the couch. "Won't you sit down, Ms. Hanover?"

She didn't want to sit down. She wanted to have it out with Zane. "I'm afraid I don't have time. I need to talk to Zane and then get dinner ready." She shouldn't cook dinner for him after what he'd done. But since his parents were here, she couldn't leave him in the lurch. "Is there anything you and your wife would like? Any food allergies?" she asked.

"My wife didn't make the trip with me. It was something I wanted to handle on my own." He nodded at the chair again. "Please sit down. Zane is tied up right now, and dinner can wait."

It wasn't a request. It was an order. And as much as she loved to buck authority, she couldn't bring herself to be disrespectful to Zane's father. She sat.

"How was Hawaii?" she asked.

A look of distaste entered his eyes. "Tropical." He leaned back and openly studied her. She had thought that his eyes were like Zane's. But on closer examination, she realized that she had been wrong. Zane's eyes held a friendliness that this man's lacked. Or maybe he just wasn't feeling friendly toward her. This was confirmed when he spoke.

"From what I've heard, cooking isn't all you do for my son."

Few things shocked Carly. But Mr. Arrington's bluntness did. Was he referring to her sleeping with Zane? When he lifted an eyebrow, she realized that was exactly what he was insinuating. Since he wasn't being respectful to her, she figured she didn't have to be respectful to him.

"I don't think it's any of your business what I do for Zane."

His other eyebrow joined the first. "You don't think my son is my business?"

"I didn't say that. I don't think his personal life is your business."

"And you've become part of his personal life, haven't you, Ms. Hanover?" He didn't give her a chance to reply before he went on. "I understand why. His wife ran off, and his ego was bruised. Then a beautiful woman shows up and starts cooking for him." He cocked his head. "Did you know how much Zane loves food? He almost ate us out of house and home when he was a kid. And Rachel never did like to cook. So Zane probably thought he'd died and gone to heaven when you showed up."

Carly didn't like where this story was going. "Get to your point, Mr. Arrington."

"My point is that Zane has a wife. He doesn't need another one. Nor does he need a . . . cook."

Anger rose inside her, and she couldn't contain it a second longer. "You don't know what Zane needs. Only Zane knows that. And Rachel isn't his wife anymore."

Mr. Arrington didn't look surprised. "Yes, I know all about the divorce. And it's a mistake." He paused. "You see, Zane and Rachel have known each other all their lives. They learned how to swim in Whispering Falls, they learned to ride horses in the corral right outside, and they have their initials carved in an oak tree in the south pasture. They're what you would call childhood sweethearts."

Carly had known they were childhood sweet-hearts, but it was hard to hear about it in such detail. Especially the initials in the tree. That piece of information hurt. And when she was hurt, she became a bit of a smartass. "Being his childhood sweetheart didn't stop her from leaving him. Or shacking up with her decorator."

Mr. Arrington was one cool customer. He didn't even flinch. She understood now why Zane worked so hard to hide his emotions. He had been trying to emulate his statue of a father. But as it turned out, Mr. Arrington wasn't a statue, he was only a man who had more information than Carly did.

"Things happen in a marriage," he said. "But I'm sure Zane will be able to forgive her." He paused. "In fact, he's probably forgiving her as we speak."

Carly felt like she had in third grade when she fell out of a swing and got the wind knocked out of her. There was an empty void in her chest where air should be, but she couldn't seem to draw in a breath. All she could get out were three words.

"Rachel is here?"

RACHEL WAS USUALLY GROOMED TO perfection, her makeup flawless and not a hair out of place. But today, tears had left long trails of black on her cheeks and her hair was mussed. Zane should feel at least some concern for her tears. He hated to see a woman cry. But at the moment, he was too elated.

He loved Carly.

He wanted to shout the words from the highest mountain. Then he wanted to go find Carly and whisper them softly in her ear. Of course, that would be stupid. Carly wasn't ready to hear his words of love when she was still desperately trying to keep things on a friendship level. But she felt more than friendship for him. He knew she did. All he needed was a little time to make her realize it.

But first he needed to talk with Rachel. He guided her over to a chair, and then pulled a tissue from the box on the desk and handed it to her. She took the tissue and blotted beneath her eyes before looking up at him.

"I'm sorry, Zane."

A few weeks ago, the simple apology wouldn't have been nearly enough. Now it was more than enough. He leaned on the desk. "Why didn't you tell me you were unhappy? Why did you leave without a word?"

"Because I knew you'd try to fix things or talk me out of it." She smiled weakly. "You could talk a bear out of hibernation if you set your mind to it." He laughed, and she looked surprised. "I haven't heard that in a long while. You lost all your smiles after we got married."

Now that he thought about it, he realized she

was right. He'd thought his unhappiness had to do with all the stress of becoming a lawyer, followed by all the stress of taking over the ranch. But now he knew that his unhappiness had more to do with the stress of keeping up a pretense.

"I'm sorry too," he said. "I'm sorry I didn't . . ." He searched for the right words, but Rachel found them first.

"Love me like a husband should love his wife?" She gave a soft laugh. "Don't look so surprised, Zane. I'm not an idiot. I knew you didn't love me when you asked me to marry you. I knew you only asked because you thought it was the right thing to do." She paused and stared down at her tissue. "And I thought it was the right thing too. It took a long time for me to figure out that we'd made a mistake. Which is why I left. I knew you'd never do it. Once you make a decision, you stick with it. You hate change."

He had hated change. But a few weeks ago, a tornado named Carly had whirled into his life and turned everything upside down. Now he knew that change wasn't always bad. In fact, once you got over the initial shock, it could be wonderful.

"So I guess my daddy talked you into coming here today," he said.

She glanced up and nodded. "He wanted me to try to fix things. But I think we both know that things are already fixed. I came because I didn't want us to end on a bad note."

A bittersweet pang of sadness tightened his heart for his childhood friend. "I don't want us to end like that either." He took her hand and pulled her into his arms. She felt familiar, but far from perfect.

There was only one woman who fit in his arms perfectly.

"I thought we were Duke and Laura," Rachel said in a choked voice. "I thought we'd ride off into the sunset together."

At one time, he had fed into the entire town's obsession with Tender Heart. Not anymore. "We're not Duke and Laura. We're Zane and Rachel, two people who make better friends than we did a married couple. I'm sorry I didn't realize it sooner. But I can't make you happy, Rach." He drew away and smoothed her hair back. "And you deserve to be happy . . . we both do."

She blinked back the tears. "I guess this is good-bye."

He smiled. "I hope not. I hope we can still be friends."

She leaned up and kissed him. It was a goodbye kiss, filled with sadness and a wish for things to be different. He allowed it because he felt bad, but he didn't participate. The woman he wanted to kiss had expressive brown eyes and held his heart in the palm of her hand.

"Laura had done it! She'd finally gotten rid of Duke Earhart. And she was happy . . . or she would be as soon as she stopped crying."

CHAPTER TWENTY-THREE

SEEING ZANE KISS RACHEL HURT much worse than when Carly had seen Sam in bed with another woman. Then she'd felt wounded, but not mortally. Now she felt as if she could die from the gaping hole in her heart. The irrational part of her wanted to race into the study and yell at him for making her fall in love with him—for making her believe that he was a man she could trust with her heart. The logical part knew that he hadn't asked for her love and trust. He had followed the rules of their no-strings relationship. It was Carly who had broken the rules. Carly who needed to realize that there was no such thing as destiny.

She softly closed the door and headed to her room to pack.

Tears threatened, but she refused to let them fall. She was stronger than that. She would get through this just like she got through everything else: one miserable step at a time.

After packing, she slipped out the back door. It was better if she left without a goodbye. She didn't want Zane feeling guilty. Nor did she want to look like the pathetic loser she was. As she put her suitcase in the trunk, she heard Shep barking in the barn. She couldn't leave without saying goodbye to the dog—or to Muffin.

Shep was whining at Muffin's stall when Carly entered the barn. He raced over with his tail wagging. She knelt to scratch him behind the ears, and he gave her a soulful look as if he knew she was leaving. She pressed her nose into his soft fur.

"You need to take care of him," she said. "You need to make sure he doesn't work too hard. And that he doesn't take himself too seriously. And that he eats more than just cheese sandwiches—"

Becky popped up from Muffin's stall, causing Carly to lose her balance and fall back on her butt. "You're leaving?" She stepped out of the stall. "But you can't leave. Not when I've finally gotten a brother."

Carly stood. "Rachel's back."

The look on Becky's face could only be described as horror. "No-o-o." She shook her head. "Cruella can't come back." She glanced at the open doorway, and her eyes narrowed. "My daddy is responsible, isn't he? He just had to stick his nose in." She started for the door. "Well, I'm not going to let him get away with it. And I'm certainly not going to let Zane choose Rachel over you."

Carly stepped in front of her. "I told Zane that he needed to start treating you like an adult instead of his kid sister. Now I'm going to tell you the same thing. Zane is a big boy. He makes his own choices. You can't do that for him. He chose Rachel. You need to accept that." She needed to accept that.

Becky stared at her. "So you're just going to leave?"

"It's for the best. Tell Zane . . ." She paused because she didn't know how to finish. She didn't know how to end something she didn't want to end. She just left the sentence hanging and turned to Muffin's stall. The foal came over to the door to greet her, and she stroked his velvety soft nose. "Bye, Stud Muffin, I'm going to miss—" Before she could finish, a lasso slipped over her head and her arms were tugged almost painfully to her sides. When she turned, Becky was holding the other end of the rope and smiling.

"Sorry, but here in Texas we fight for our own happiness. I won't be happy if you leave. And neither will Zane."

Carly had always thought she was pretty strong for her size, but she was no match for a determined woman who spent her days wrangling cattle. Within seconds of lassoing her, Becky had her roped, tied, and tossed in a wheelbarrow.

"You are crazy, Becky Arrington!" Carly struggled against the rope. "You can't hold me hostage."

Becky pulled a bandanna out of her back pocket and tied it around Carly's mouth. "I can't hold you forever, but I figure I can hold you long enough to make sure my brother doesn't make the biggest mistake of his life." She covered her with a tarp.

Carly couldn't see anything but dots of sunlight as Becky wheeled her out of the barn. A few minutes later, she was pushed inside a building and the tarp was pulled off. The room was large with exposed log walls and scarred oak floors. There was a long harvest table and a potbelly stove at one end and rows of bunks at the other.

"It's the bunkhouse," Becky explained as she rolled her over to one of the beds and dumped her out like a sack of grain. With her arms tied down, Carly would've rolled right off the other side if Becky hadn't grabbed her.

"At one time, this place was used by all the ranch hands." She rolled Carly onto her back and completely ignored her glare as she continued. "Now all of them live in town. Well, except for Dirk. He's been living here." She leaned over Carly and checked the ropes. "You stay put. I'm going to go and talk with my brother. I'll be back shortly."

Shortly? What did shortly mean?

Carly muttered a few cuss words against the bandanna, but Becky waltzed right out the door without a backward glance. She did leave Shep for company. Although she could've done nicely without her face being licked clean. She turned her head to avoid the dog's kisses and worked on getting herself untied. But Becky was as good at knots as she was at lassoing. And after a few frustrating moments, Carly gave up and relaxed.

The bed wasn't exactly comfortable. The mattress was thin and the pillow hard. But the wood frame was pretty. The thick posts were stained a deep, rich walnut and they looked handmade and . . . familiar. It only took a second to remember where she'd seen the bunk bed before.

Laughing Lucy's picture.

Carly glanced over at the bunk bed next to her,

and her breath whooshed out against the bandanna. Lucy had sat on that bed. The quilt was the same. The window next to it the same. Even the angle the photo had been taken from was the same. Which meant that whoever had taken the picture had been lying where Carly was. And since Becky had said that only ranch hands stayed in the bunkhouse, maybe Lucy's lover had been a ranch hand. It also made sense that another chapter was hidden somewhere here.

Shep jumped up from where he'd been lying on the floor and started barking. The door opened, and Dirk walked in whistling. He stopped when Shep raced over to him.

"How did you get in here, boy?" He scratched the dog's ears. "You haven't gotten into my cookies, have—" He cut off when he noticed Carly trussed up on the bed. A seductive smile creased his face, and she knew exactly what the rascally man was thinking even before he spoke.

"Well, now, I never mind finding a beautiful woman all tied up on my bed." He took off his hat and tossed it at the hooks on the wall. It caught on the first one and swung back and forth as he walked toward her. "And while I've never been much into bondage, since you've gone to all the trouble, I wouldn't want to disappoint."

She narrowed her eyes and mumbled against the bandanna. "Mmm. Mmm. Mmm."

With his gray eyes dancing with delight, Dirk sat down on the bunk across from her. "I'm sorry, honey, but could you repeat that? I didn't quite get it." She glared at him, and he laughed as he pushed down the bandanna.

"Becky!" she yelled the name so loudly that Dirk cringed and Shep cowered under the bunk. "That brat tied me up and brought me here. I used to think that Zane was being too hard on her, but I was wrong. She's spoiled rotten and needs her butt paddled."

Dirk grinned. "I offered once, but she didn't take me up on it. And I agree that she's spoiled and pretty hardheaded." He paused and squinted his eyes. "But she usually doesn't do things without good reason."

"She doesn't have a good reason this time. She just doesn't want me to leave. Now would you please untie me?"

His smile dropped. "You're leaving? Are we talking about moving to the diner? Or leaving town altogether?"

A lump formed in her throat, and it was hard to get the words out. "Leaving town altogether. Now would you please untie me?"

He studied her for a moment before he shook his head. "I'm afraid I can't do that."

"What do you mean? This isn't funny, Dirk." She wiggled like a worm. "Now untie me."

"Nope. I have to agree with Becky. I don't think you should run off half-cocked like you always do."

"What is that supposed to mean?"

He sent her a pointed look. "I hate to say it, honey, but you're a runner. And believe me, I know a runner when I see one."

He coaxed Shep out from under the bed with a click of his tongue. Once the dog was sitting between his boots and receiving an ear scratching that made his tongue loll out, Dirk continued.

"You see, my daddy was a runner. When things got to be too much for him to deal with he just packed up and moved to another place, leaving his wife and four kids. I won't let you leave and ignore your responsibilities."

It was the most information Dirk had ever given her about his past, and it struck her a little speechless. She had always known there was more to Dirk's story. She just hadn't thought it would be so sad. He acted like he didn't have a care in the world. But now she knew that wasn't true.

"That's why you never have any money," she said. "You send everything you make home to your mother."

He went back to scratching Shep's ears. "My mama died soon after my daddy left. My grandma raised my three sisters and me. I send money to her."

Carly had never been much of a crier, but it was hard to keep the tears from her eyes. When he noticed them, he looked more than a little scared. "Don't you do it, Carly Sue. Women's tears make me crazy."

She sniffed. "You're a good man, Dirk Hadley. Even if you won't untie me."

"I can't. I meant it when I said you had responsibilities here. You have a responsibility to the townsfolk to give them a good place to eat. A responsibility to Becky to be the big sister she desperately needs. And a responsibility to Zane." He paused. "That man loves you."

She wanted him to be right more than anything in the world. But even if he was, she knew it wasn't enough to hold Zane. "He might love me, but he feels as strongly as you about responsibility. Which is why he'll take Rachel back."

Dirk eyebrows lifted. "And what makes you think Rachel wants to come back?"

"His father told me, and I saw her and Zane kissing in the study."

Dirk stopped scratching Shep. "There are all kinds of kisses, Carly Sue. Some are passionate and some are just friendly. Until we hear that Zane's getting back with Rachel straight from the horse's mouth, you're not going anywhere. You hungry? I got some of Ms. Marble's oatmeal cookies." He reached under Carly's bunk and pulled out a backpack.

A navy backpack with green stitching.

Carly's eyes widened. "Where did you get that?" When he froze in the process of pulling out a plastic baggie of cookies, she drew her own conclusions. "That's your backpack. You're the one who left it at Ms. Marble's house."

He shrugged. "What if I did? Everyone knows that I do odd jobs for Ms. Marble." He opened the bag. "You sure you don't want one?"

"What I want is to know where the sixth chapter of the Tender Heart book is. And don't tell me you don't have it. You were there the same night that I was. You were the one that made the noise in the diner that made me knock over the candle and start the fire."

He took a bite of cookie and chewed before he answered. "I'm surprised you didn't figure it out sooner. You know I sleep at the diner when I don't have other accommodations. Which is exactly what I was doing when you woke me up by banging around in the kitchen. I was in the process of putting on some clothes and greeting you when the fire started. Then Zane rushed in and all hell broke loose."

"So you put out the fire and slunk out without saying a word? Why would you do that?"

"I wouldn't say slunk. I walked right out the back door. You and Zane were too busy sparking to notice."

More like fighting, but she didn't argue the point. "You could've mentioned you were there later. Just like you could've mentioned that you found the sixth chapter in the cemetery."

He finished off the cookie. "I could've. But you and Emery were having so much fun playing detectives, I didn't want to ruin it for you."

If all the pieces of the puzzle hadn't started falling into place, she might've believed him. But things were becoming clear, and the picture that emerged wasn't of an innocent country boy.

"You want to find the rest of the chapters your-self," she breathed. "That's why you stayed at the diner. Why you help Ms. Marble." She glanced around. "And why you took a job with Zane and stayed here. I wouldn't even be surprised if that's why you came to Bliss."

He placed a hand over his heart. "You wound me, Carly Sue. I'm not that devious. I can assure you that I didn't come to Bliss for any book. I was helping Ms. Marble long before I found the chapter in the cemetery. And I didn't discover the picture of Lucy sitting right here on this very bed until after I started working for Zane. But like I said before, it does seem like fate wants me to have that book." He winked at her. "Especially when I keep finding chapters."

"Chapters? You found another chapter?" She glanced at the bunk.

He smiled. "No wonder Zane loves you. You're smart as a whip." He stretched out on the bed and stuffed a pillow under his head. "Now if you're done with your interrogation, Nancy Drew, I think I'm going to take a little nap." He crossed his arms and his boots and closed his eyes.

But he wasn't going to shut Carly up that easily. "What are you going to do with the chapters?"

He shrugged. "I'm not sure. Maybe I'll sell them. Even a couple chapters should be enough to keep my grandma in yarn for years to come."

If the book didn't mean so much to her, Carly wouldn't have minded Dirk selling the chapters and helping his grandma. But Carly loved the Tender Heart series, and she agreed with Emery that it should be published as a complete work. Not as separate chapters. Lucy's characters deserved that. And so did her readers.

"You can't, Dirk," she pleaded. "The last book of Tender Heart needs to be published as a complete story. Now that we know there are more chapters, we need to keep looking until we find them all. That's what Lucy would've wanted."

He cracked open one eye and looked at her. "I don't really give a rat's behind what Lucy Arrington would want. And what do you mean 'we'? I thought you were leaving."

"I am, but that doesn't mean you and Emery shouldn't keep looking. Between her knowledge of Tender Heart and your ability to charm the townsfolk, I know you'll find the other chapters."

He closed his eyes, and for a second she thought he'd gone to sleep. But before she could wake him, he spoke. "I'll make you a deal. You stay, and I won't sell the chapters."

"But that's blackmail!"

The smile that spread across his face was pure devilish Dirk. "Just like I said before, you're smart as a whip, Carly Sue."

"The news was all over town. Laura had set her sights on marrying the shopkeeper, while Duke had set his sights on a bottle of whiskey. Once he'd finished the bottle, he came to two realizations: He was going to have one hell of a hangover. And as ornery as she was, he couldn't live without Miss Laura."

CHAPTER TWENTY-FOUR

Z ANE STOOD ON THE PORCH and watched Rachel drive away. There was sadness, but it was balanced with a feeling of rightness. For the first time in a long time, he felt like this was his life. It wasn't his father life. Or the townsfolk's. Or Rachel's. It was his. He got to make the choice on how he wanted to live it . . . and with whom.

He glanced at the Subaru parked out front and overwhelming joy filled his heart. With a beaming smile, he headed inside to the kitchen. Unfortunately, the only person there was his father, sitting at the breakfast bar eating some of Carly's leftovers. When he saw Zane, he lowered his fork.

"Rachel's gone?"

Zane should've been mad at him for butting into his business. But he was too happy to be mad.

"I know how much you and Mama love Rachel and want us to get back together. But believe me when I tell you that we'll both be much happier divorced, and once you get to know Carly, you're going to love her just as much as I do."

Surprisingly, his father didn't argue. Maybe the discussion they'd had in the study had sunk in. "And I guess she loves you?"

"I think so. If not, I'm sure going to work hard at getting her to."

A look came to his father's eyes that Zane hadn't seen often. Regret was not something his dad wasted time on. "Then I'm sorry. Your mother has gotten onto me about treating you and your sister like kids instead of adults. She's right. I shouldn't have butted my nose in and asked Rachel to come here. I was just convinced that if you two had a chance to talk things out, you'd get back together." He paused. "I convinced Carly of that too. That's why she left."

There was a moment when he was consumed with fear, but it quickly dissipated. "Carly didn't leave. Her car is right out front. She's probably in her room."

He left his father sitting there and strode down the hallway to the guestroom. On the way, he thought about how to tell her that he loved her. He should wait until he could plan a nice dinner in Austin with good food, champagne, and flowers. But he was too excited to wait. That excitement fizzled when he got to her room.

She wasn't there. She wasn't sitting on her bed scrolling through recipes on her laptop or talking on the phone to Savannah or Emery. Nor was she in the bathroom. The fear came back as he pulled open a drawer and found it empty. No cut-off shorts. No weird logo t-shirts. No sexy panties. He pulled open another drawer. And then another. But all of them were empty. As empty as he suddenly felt.

With panic welling, he headed for the front door and was relieved when he stepped outside and saw Carly's car still sitting there. But the empty dresser drawers proved that she planned on leaving. Obviously, she was upset about Rachel showing up. Now all Zane needed to do was tell her that they weren't reconciling, and then Carly would put all her clothes back in the dresser. Or better yet, in his dresser.

He headed to the barn and found his sister trying to calm an agitated horse while a ranch hand wrapped the tendon on his back leg.

"Have you seen Carly?" he asked.

Becky glanced over her shoulder and smiled. "As a matter of fact, I have. I was coming to get you when Billy needed my help." She waited until Billy had finished wrapping the horse's leg before she stepped out of the stall. "Please tell me that Cruella's not coming back."

"She's not coming back. Now where is Carly?"

She threw her arms around his neck and gave him a tight hug. "I knew you would figure things out. All you needed was some time." She drew back and the smile reappeared. "Carly's in the bunkhouse and fit to be tied—pun intended."

Zane didn't know what pun his sister was talking about, and he didn't care. All he cared about was explaining things to Carly. He left the barn through the side door and skirted around the back of the bunkhouse. As he passed an open window, he heard Dirk's voice.

"...I wondered why you wanted to remodel that old place. Now I get it. You wanted to tear it apart looking for another lost Tender Heart chapter. Did you just find the one, or were there more?"

The mention of a lost Tender Heart chapter had Zane stopping in his tracks and wondering whom Dirk was talking to. He had his answer only a second later when Carly spoke.

"Just the one, and believe me, I've looked beneath every booth seat and square of tile."

It took a moment for Zane to make sense of the conversation. Then all the pieces fell into place. Like Dirk, he had wondered why an executive chef would be interested in an old diner. Now he had his answer. Carly didn't want to remodel the diner. She wanted to find the last Tender Heart book. That's why she'd been in such a hurry to get back into the diner the night of the fire. Why she and Emery broke in. Why she had agreed to cook for him.

While he stood there feeling stunned and hurt, Dirk continued. "I wish you'd reconsider leaving, Carly. I think you could be happy here in Bliss."

There was a long pause before Carly answered. "I could never be happy here. I'm a big-city girl, remember?"

Just that quickly, Zane's entire world fell apart. He leaned against the side of the building as his legs buckled. He had been so convinced that Carly was starting to care for him like he cared for her. How could he be so stupid? She didn't care about him. She'd used him. Used him to get the last Tender Heart book so she would have enough money to open an exclusive restaurant in a big city far, far away from a small Texas town and an ignorant cowboy who couldn't stop choosing the wrong women.

Anger joined the pain of betrayal that clawed at his chest, and he didn't try to repress it as he headed for the door of the bunkhouse. As soon as he stepped inside, he understood Becky's pun. Carly was hogtied and lying on a bunk.

"Hey, Boss," Dirk flashed a bright smile. Zane wanted to wipe if off with his fist. Dirk had been in cahoots with Carly all along. They'd made a fool of him together.

"Get out." He fired off the order.

Dirk studied him for a moment before he got up and walked over to get his hat from the hook. He whistled for Shep, and the dog loped out the door after him.

Once the door clicked closed, there was nothing but silence. A silence so thick that Zane's boot heels rang out against the hardwood floor like a hammer on an anvil. He stood over the bed and looked down at her. She looked guilty as hell. Her cheeks were flushed, and she refused to look him in the eyes. She also looked helpless all tied up. Even as hurt and angry as he was, he couldn't stand the thought of Carly being helpless. He knelt next to the bed and untied her.

He ignored the feel of her soft skin against his calloused fingers. Ignored the spill of her golden hair across her forehead. Ignored the spicy, flowery scent that filled his lungs with each breath. What he couldn't ignore were the big brown eyes that locked with his. They tore a hole in his soul. Or maybe her lies had done that. And she had lied.

She had made him believe. Believe in her smiles and her laughter. Believe in her sweet kisses and the breathy moans she made when he was deep inside her. But mostly she had made him believe in the man reflected in her eyes. A man who was more than just the Arrington name. A man who had a right to be happy. But now that man was gone, and there was nothing left to believe in.

"You're leaving." It wasn't a question, and yet, he wanted an answer.

She held his gaze. "Yes."

The single emotionless word sliced him open as if she'd cut him with one of her knives. He wanted to hurt her back. He wanted to throw all her lies like darts at a board, in rapid succession and with deadly aim. Or maybe it had nothing to do with hurting her. Maybe he hoped that she would deny the lies and everything would go back to the way it was. But he knew better. Carly didn't live in denial. That was what he did. And it was time that he stopped.

He stood. "Goodbye, Carly."

CARLY KNEW AS SOON AS Zane stepped inside the bunkhouse that he was there to say goodbye. The hurt in his eyes said it all. It was obvious that it wasn't easy for him. He cared enough about her that he didn't want her to go. And she cared enough about him not to make it harder than it was. She didn't let one tear fall when she answered him.

"Goodbye, Zane."

As he turned and headed for the door, she felt like all the life was being sucked out of her. When the door slammed behind him, her heart shattered like sculptured sugar. She didn't know how she made it to her car. Or how she made it to Emery and Cole's house. She tried to pull herself together before she knocked on the door, but she must've failed miserably. Emery knew something was wrong immediately.

"What happened?"

Carly tried to sound nonchalant. Instead, she sounded as hurt as she felt. "Zane got back together with Rachel."

Emery looked shocked. "Oh my God. You're kidding."

Cole came to the door. "What's wrong?"

"Your stupid cousin took his wife back," Emery told him.

"But that doesn't make any sense. In the last few days, he's been happier than I've seen him . . . well, ever."

Carly blinked back her tears. "It was the food and the sex, that's all. Good food and sex make all men happy."

"There's some truth to that," Cole said.

Emery reached out and swatted him. "You're not helping matters."

"What do you want me to do?"

"Go yell at Zane."

Carly shook her head. "Zane never made any promises to me. And I didn't make any promises to him." She swallowed hard. "In fact, I was wondering how I was going to end things between us. Him getting back with Rachel worked out perfectly."

Emery and Cole might've believed her if her voice hadn't cracked on the word *perfectly*. They exchanged looks before Emery placed an arm around her shoulders. "Come on inside, sweetie. I have a container of chocolate ice cream with your name on it."

But Carly didn't need ice cream. She needed to cook. Once she got in the kitchen, she cooked like a woman possessed. She made comfort foods because more than anything she needed comfort. She whipped up meatloaf, mashed potatoes, green bean casserole, and biscuits for Emery and Cole's dinner, then she made chicken noodle soup, chicken pot pie, mac and cheese, lasagna, and three different kinds of cookies that weren't nearly as good as Ms. Marble's. It was close to midnight when she finally ran out of ingredients.

Emery who had stayed with her the entire time, washing pots and pans so she could fill them again, wrapped an arm around her shoulders and led her to Gracie's room. "You need some sleep, Carly. I promise everything will look brighter in the morning."

She thought there was no way she would be able to sleep, but she was so mentally and emotionally exhausted, she fell asleep within minutes. The sun was hot and high in the sky when Emery woke her up. "Come on, sleepyhead. It's after ten, and we've got work to do."

She blinked. "What work are you talking about?"

Emery unzipped Carly's suitcase and pulled out

shorts and a t-shirt. "We need to get to the diner."

The mention of the diner brought back every-thing that had happened the day before. Tears welled in Carly's eyes, but she refused to give in to them. She needed to pull herself together and move on just like she always did. "I'm not going to the diner. I'm leaving for Atlanta this morning. Savannah needs my help with the wedding, and I've started to rethink asking Miles for a loan for a restaurant."

Emery tossed her the shirt and shorts. "You already have a restaurant, and Savannah doesn't need your help. Right now, you're the one who needs help. Which is why Savannah is on her way here."

Carly stared at her. "Please tell me you didn't call her, Em."

Emery shrugged. "Sorry, but that's what friends are for. I get that you like to be the tough one in the group, the one who never needs any help. But you need help now, and you're going to get it whether you want it or not. Now get dressed so we can get to the diner. Then if you still want to leave, I won't stop you."

Since Emery had on her stubborn face, Carly got up and dressed. She didn't know what to expect when Emery parked in front of the diner, but it wasn't a swarm of people. She got out of the car and watched as men she recognized from town hauled loads of old tile to a dumpster and carried barstools and booth benches to a truck with an upholstery company logo on the side. Emmett winked at her as he limped through the door, carrying a box of new fixtures. Mrs. Crawley, who held what looked like gingham curtains draped over her arm, followed him. In the midst of the chaos, Joanna Daily stood on the curb directing the workers with a loud, stern voice.

Carly turned to Emery. "I don't understand."

Emery smiled. "It's called being part of a community. And regardless of what happens with Zane, you're part of this one."

"Of course she is." Ms. Marble appeared out of nowhere and pulled Carly into her arms for a hug. "Welcome home, Carly Sue."

Right there in front of the entire town of Bliss, Carly finally lost control of her emotions. After holding back her tears for so long, she felt them rush out like water over a dam, and she sobbed like the heartbroken girl she was.

"Oh, Carly," Emery said as she hugged her from the other side. "I didn't mean to make you cry."

"Don't be silly," Ms. Marble said. "Sometimes a good cry is exactly what a person needs. Now why don't you go get Carly one of those cinnamon swirl muffins I brought?" Once Emery was gone, Ms. Marble drew back and pulled an embroidered handkerchief from her cleavage and handed it to Carly. It smelled of lilacs and vanilla extract, a combination that soothed Carly as much as the little old woman's hug had.

Once Carly had her tears under control, she handed the hankie back. "I'm sorry. The town's generosity took me by surprise. I traveled a lot as a kid, and even more as an adult, so I've never had a place to call home."

Ms. Marble smiled. "You do now."

"Thank you." Tears welled again, and she didn't

try to stop them. She let them slide down her cheeks as she spoke in a quavering voice. "But I can't stay." She tried to think of a good excuse, but she couldn't. So she told the truth. "I'm in love with Zane Arrington. And now that he's back with Rachel, it would hurt too much to live in the same town with him."

She expected Ms. Marble to be surprised by the news. She wasn't. "Yes, I heard about that. Rachel stopped by on her way out of town to drop off the chili queen crown." When Carly stared at her with surprise, she smiled. "It seems she won't be able to present the crown to the queen this year because she's headed to the Turks and Caicos with her new interior decorator boyfriend."

"Duke was prepared to stride right into the chapel and steal back his bride. But as luck would have it, Laura came running out just as he was riding up. All he needed to do was sweep her off her feet and straight into his arms where she belonged."

CHAPTER TWENTY-FIVE

ZANE NOW UNDERSTOOD THE PURPOSE of alcohol. It didn't take away the pain, but it had numbed it enough to get him through the first twenty-four hours. He'd woken up with a bitch of a headache and the realization that he needed to get a grip. He had a ranch to run, and he couldn't run it drunk. So he learned to deal with the pain. He learned to deal with the ache in his chest and the knot in his gut. He learned to deal with the restless nights when he couldn't get her out of his brain.

What he couldn't deal with was hearing her name. The first time his sister brought her up, he'd exploded and scared Shep so badly it was days before the dog would come to him. When Cole mentioned her, Zane had sent him packing and told him not to come back to the ranch. And when Dirk stopped by and called him all kinds of a fool, he'd hauled off and punched him right in the mouth.

That's why Zane had stayed away from Bliss. He didn't want to lose it in front of the entire town. It was bad enough that Becky tiptoed around him. He didn't need the people of Bliss doing it too. Nor did he want them to know that Carly had been right. He was vulnerable. He had fallen head over heels in love and it hurt like hell.

"Are you sure you don't want to come to the Chili Cook-off?" Becky stood in the doorway of the kitchen, her Arrington blue eyes studying him with a mixture of wariness and concern.

He attempted a smile. "Yeah, I'm sure. But you go and have fun." He cracked another egg into the bowl, and then beat the eggs for the omelet he was making. When he glanced up, Becky was smiling.

"I never thought I'd see the day my brother cooked." He knew who she wanted to bring up, but, thankfully, she didn't. Instead, she gestured at her dress. "What do you think? Do you think I'm pretty enough to win chili queen?"

"You're trying for chili queen?" He was surprised. Not that she had been nominated—Becky was nominated every year—but that she'd actually decided to show up. She didn't usually go for anything girlie, and she flat-out hated the chili queen crown.

She shrugged. "I was talked into going by one of the other nominees."

He couldn't think of one person besides Gracie who could talk Becky into anything. And Gracie was still in Dallas. He continued to beat the eggs.

"Who talked you into it?"

"Carly." When he froze and shot her a glance, she held up her hands. "Before you lose it, I'd like to point out that you asked."

He set the fork down and tried to ignore the ache in his heart. "I apologize for losing it. It's just that now that she's gone, I'd like to forget her." Something that was turning out to be much more difficult than he'd thought.

"About that . . ." Becky paused. "She's not exactly gone. And she's opening the diner today, so I don't think she plans on leaving any time soon."

He didn't think anything could eclipse the ache in his chest. He was wrong. Disbelief and anger overshadowed his pain. "My diner? She's opening my diner?"

Becky looked relieved. She smiled and nodded. "Yes, and I think it's pretty ballsy of her to open a diner in a building you own. I think you should go and tell her so." She paused and gave him an innocent look. "Unless you're afraid of her."

He knew his sister was trying to manipulate him, but he also knew that she was right. He had been acting like he was scared of Carly. So scared that he couldn't even hear her name. That stopped now. He wasn't scared of Carly Hanover. He was pissed. She couldn't take over his diner. And she certainly couldn't live in his town.

He left the eggs and grabbed his hat. "Come on. We're going to the Chili Cook-off."

The cook-off was much bigger than in previous years. The streets were jam packed with cars and hordes of people walked between the tents where the contestants cooked their chili and the Watering

Hole parking lot where a band played.

He dropped Becky off at the Watering Hole and set off for the diner. A line of people wound out the front door and halfway around the block. The crowd didn't surprise him. Carly was a damn good cook. But the new sign that hung over the front windows was a surprise.

Lucy's Place.

The name made Zane even more ticked off. Carly had said she could never be happy here. So why was she still here? In his town? In his diner? Using his great-aunt's name?

Not wanting to deal with the crowd, he parked in the alley and entered the diner through the back. The kitchen was a beehive of activity. Dirk flipped hamburgers on the flat top, Ms. Marble took brownies out of the oven, and teenage boys hustled in with tubs of dirty dishes.

He peeked into the diner and was stunned by the transformation. How had Carly gotten it finished so quickly? The chipped floor had been replaced with new black and white checkered tile. The torn booths and barstools had been reupholstered in bright red. Framed pictures of Lucy Arrington and her book covers hung on the freshly painted walls and blue-and-white gingham curtains hung from the sparkling clean windows. He had to admit that she had done a good job. It looked exactly like Zane remembered it, but newer.

"Hey, Zane," Emery moved out from behind the counter. She was dressed in a crisp fifties-style waitress uniform, complete with saddle shoes. "Did you want a burger? We ran out of chili an—"

There was a loud crash, followed by "Sweet Baby

Jesus." Zane glanced over to see Carly's friend Savannah dressed in the same waitress uniform as Emery and staring down at the tray of drinks she'd just dropped.

"I'd better go help her before she has a meltdown," Emery said. "Waitressing is not really Savannah's forte."

When she hurried off, Zane returned to the kitchen and walked over to Dirk. "Where's Carly?"

Dirk glanced over his shoulder and flashed a grin. Obviously, he wasn't holding a grudge about the bruise on his chin, but the sight of it made Zane feel guilty as hell. "Hey, Boss," he said. "I hope you're not here to hit me again."

"I'm sorry about that," Zane said. "Do you know where Carly is?"

Before he could answer, Ms. Marble stepped up. "She's at the bandstand getting ready for the chili queen crowning." She pointed to the blue ribbon pinned on her dress with the knife she'd been using to cut the brownies. "My chili won first place. Of course, I wouldn't have won if Carly had entered." She nodded at the oven. "Will you be a dear and get the other pan of brownies out of the oven while I finish cutting these? We need to hurry if we don't want to miss the crowning."

Since he was programmed to follow his teacher's instructions, he got the brownies out of the oven. Then he impatiently waited while she got on her bonnet and gloves before escorting her out the door. They had just turned the corner onto Main Street when she started lecturing him like he was a six-year-old who had just failed his spelling test.

"I always thought you were a bright young man,

but you certainly haven't been acting very bright. You've been acting like a stubborn mule. And if you hadn't come today, I'd have personally driven out to the ranch to box your ears."

When they reached the bandstand in the Watering Hole's parking lot, and she released his arm and poked him in the chest with her finger. "And if you don't pull your head out, I still might do it." She turned and walked off in a huff.

He watched her bonnet bounce through the crowd until a crackle from the microphone drew his attention to the stage. The country band had stopped playing. and Joanna was adjusting the microphone stand. Once she had it where she wanted it, she leaned close to the microphone.

"Could I have all the chili queen contestants up on stage, please?"

Women moved out of the crowd and climbed the stairs that lead to the stage. Carly was the last one. She looked even prettier than he remembered. Her hair surrounded her face in fluffy curls that reflected the sun like spun gold. She wore the backless sundress she'd worn the day he kissed her in the diner and high-heeled sandals that made her legs look a mile long. When she got on stage, she turned to the crowd, and it was as if her gaze immediately found him. A hesitant smile tipped the corners of her mouth.

It was that smile that brought him back to earth in a hurry. She shouldn't be smiling at him as if nothing had happened. Maybe she hadn't lied about wanting to open the diner. But she had lied about searching for the Tender Heart book. And he had little doubt that the book was the only reason she was staying. As soon as she grew tired of the search, she'd be gone. She could never be happy in Bliss. Which meant she had no business acting like she was part of the town. No damned business at all.

He intended to tell her all of that right after his sister was crowned chili queen. Not only did he refuse to ruin his sister's big moment, he also wanted Carly to learn the lesson that you never go up against an Arrington and expect to win.

He gave her a smug smile when Joanna opened the sealed envelope, leaned into the microphone, and said, "And the winner of this year's chili crown is . . . Carly Sue Hanover." Zane watched in confusion as Joanna placed the plastic chili pepper crown on Carly's head. She glowed with happiness like she had the right to wear it. The right to the applause and accolades.

"No!" He yelled the word so loudly that everyone in the crowd turned to look at him. They seemed shocked that Zane Arrington would cause a scene. But he was going to do more than cause a scene. He was going to right this injustice.

With long strides, he made his way through the crowd to the stage. He leaped up the stairs in two bounds and took the crown right off of Carly's head. "I refuse to let a liar who is only using this town for her own personal gain be our next chili queen." With the microphone so close, his voice resonated from the speakers.

The joy in Carly's eyes died a quick death and was replaced with the same anger that filled him. And he was glad. He didn't feel joyous. Why should she?

"Let's talk about liars, shall we?" she snapped. "Let's talk about a liar who lied through his teeth about a plumber's strike and a contractor's dead grandma just so he could continue to get his big fat belly filled." Her words rang through the speakers even louder than his had. A ripple of muffled laughter went through the crowd. Zane wondered if calling her out on stage had been such a good idea.

She stepped closer, and it was hard to ignore her spicy scent or the way the dress hugged her breasts. "Let's talk about a liar who said he got a divorce, but then I caught him kissing his ex-wife in his study. Let's talk about that liar!"

She grabbed the crown away from him and plopped it back on her head at a lopsided angle. "And I'm the chili queen!" She turned to leave, but he caught her arm and whirled her back around.

"And what about what you made me believe? You made me believe that you cared about me— that you were happy." He leaned so close their noses almost touched. "Then I heard you tell Dirk that you could never be happy with me. And you proved it when you were going to leave without one word. Not one damn word."

"What did you want me to say after I saw you and Rachel kissing? Did you want me to congratulate you on getting back together and make you a big dinner to celebrate?"

"We're not back together!"

"I know that now, but I didn't know that then. And you could've told me instead of just letting me go."

"Just like you could've told me why you really

wanted the diner. You acted like you wanted to start your own restaurant, but the real reason you wanted to lease the diner was to find another chapter in the Tender Heart series."

A murmur went through the crowd, but he ignored it as Carly crossed her arms and glared at him. "If that's true, then why am I still here?"

He crossed his arms. "I don't have a clue. Why don't you tell me?"

He thought she would come up with some smartass reply. Instead, all the anger seemed to drain right out of her, and she stared back at him with eyes that held something in their dark brown depths he was afraid to define. Her voice was strong and unfaltering as she spoke.

"When I first came to Bliss, I didn't believe in love or family or community. I was this island who thought I could survive on my own." Tears collected in her eyes. While Rachel's tears hadn't affected him, Carly's tore out his soul. "Then I started working for this arrogant rancher who believed in everything I didn't. He believed in the sanctity of marriage, respecting his parents, and making the people of his town proud—even at the expense of his own happiness."

"We're damn proud of you, Zane!" someone in the crowd yelled.

Carly took a breath and continued. "This man taught me that there are still good men in the world. Men who might get off the straight-and-narrow occasionally, but will never lose sight of what is right. I love that about him." At the words, Zane's heart seemed to stop beating altogether. He struggled to catch his breath as she went on. "I guess I love everything about him. Even his hard-headedness and controlling nature. And while I'm terrified that he doesn't love me, I will not pack up and run off like I always do." Her chin tipped up. "This is my town, and I'm here to stay."

The crowd broke out in hoots, whistles, and applause. But Zane could barely hear it over the sound of his own heart, which had starting beating again. It took a moment for it to pump life back into his veins, and that moment was too long for Carly to wait. Before he could begin to express his emotions, she hauled off and socked him in the arm.

"You jerk, Zane Arrington!" She whirled and headed for the stairs, and he was forced to jump from the stage and head her off. He got to the stairs just as she stumbled in her high heels and fell. He caught her before she could hit the ground. When he had her tucked close to his chest, he said the words he'd planned to say in the bunkhouse.

"You once asked me what I wanted. At the time, I didn't have a clue. But I have a clue now. I want you, Carly Sue Hanover. I want you in the morning and I want you during the day and I want you every night." He smiled down at her. "Until you stepped into my life with your spunk and sass, I didn't know what love was. But I know now. I love you, and I have no intention of ever letting you go again."

He kissed her. Amid the cheers of the towns-folk, she kissed him back so enthusiastically that she knocked his cowboy hat to the ground.

The chili crown stayed right where it belonged.

"If someone had told Laura Thatcher she would one day marry a big, loud Texan and live happily ever after, she would've laughed herself silly. But that's exactly what she did."

CHAPTER TWENTY-SIX

"YOU JUST HAD TO BE married before me, didn't you, Carly Sue?" Savannah, who looked stunning in a teal bridesmaid's dress, fussed with Carly's hair.

Carly batted her hands away. "Would you leave my hair alone? You already have me looking like Shirley Temple on the Good Ship Lollipop. And it wasn't my idea to get married so quickly. I wanted to wait until next summer, and I almost had Zane talked into it before his mother showed up. Talk about a control freak. She flat-out refused to let us live in sin a second longer."

"Which is why I have no intention of getting married," Dirk said. "I like living in sin." He lounged in a chair in one corner of the room, unconcerned with wrinkling his tux. His matching tan cowboy hat was tipped back, and his gray eyes twinkled with mischief.

Carly laughed. "And just what sin is that? The only woman I've seen you with is Ms. Marble when you escort her to church. You're not as bad a boy as you want people to think."

He grinned. "So I guess you're no longer mad at me for keeping the chapters I found a secret."

"She might not be, but I am," Emery said as she fluffed out Carly's floor-length veil. "I can't believe you kept that a secret from me. You know how much I want to find that book."

"Now didn't I let you look at the chapters I found, honey?"

Emery lifted an eyebrow. "After I signed your handwritten contract stating they were yours. Thanks for trusting me."

"I never trust anyone when it comes to money." He glanced at Carly. "Which reminds me. I think it's about time you gave me a raise, Boss. I've been working my tail off in the diner."

Carly couldn't argue. So far, the diner had been busy for breakfast, lunch, and dinner. And since she liked fixing breakfast for Zane—and cuddling in bed—Dirk had taken over the morning shift. The man had proven to be quite adapt at following her recipes.

"We've all been working our tails off." Savannah took Carly's chin none too gently and held her as she applied lipstick. "And some of us without pay."

Carly pulled away. "I would pay you, but I've had to cover the cost of all the glasses you keep breaking."

"What do you expect? I'm an interior decorator, not a waitress. And I shouldn't even be here. I should be back in Atlanta taking care of my last-minute wedding arrangements." Savannah leaned closer to the mirror and applied the lipstick to her full lips, then pursed. "Although I can't leave until I've corrected the disastrous decorating job Rachel's lover did to Zane's house." She grinned. "Call it my wedding present."

Carly stood and pulled her in for a hug. As much as she and Savannah liked to fuss at each other, Carly loved her and Emery like the sisters she never had. "Thank you for coming to cheer me up when I thought I'd lost Zane. And thank you for staying to help me celebrate this special day."

Emery came over and wrapped her arms around them. "This is a special day. Who would've thought that we'd all be getting married within months of each other?"

Savannah sniffed. "Stop that right now, Em, or you're going to have us all weepy and messing up our makeup. But you're right, it does seem like—"

"Destiny," Carly finished for her. They smiled at each other as the door opened and Becky rushed in. She wore a dress two shades darker than Emery's and Savannah's, and her brown hair was swept back in a mass of long curls. She still managed to look like a wild hoyden. There was a tear in the hem of her maid of honor's gown, and a few of her curls had come undone.

"Zane sent me to tell you that he's done waiting. Either be at the altar in two minutes, or he's coming to get you."

Carly drew back from her friends. She should've been mad about being ordered around. Instead, she laughed. She had fallen in love with a control freak, and there was no going back now.

KATIE LANE

Speaking of control freaks, Savannah turned to hyper-wedding-planner mode at Becky's words. "Sweet Baby Jesus," she breathed, as she grabbed the veil from Emery and placed it on Carly's head. Then she adjusted Dirk's bowtie, fixed Becky's curls, fluffed Emery's dress, handed all the girls their bouquets, and finally nodded. "Okay, we're ready. Line up behind me with Dirk and Carly last."

Becky shook her head. "Nope. Zane said that Dirk needs to stand at the front with him and Cole."

"But Dirk is walking me down the aisle," Carly said.

"All I know is that my big brother told me there was a change of plans."

Dirk gave Carly a shrug before he walked out the door. She didn't mind. She could walk down the aisle by herself as long as Zane was waiting for her at the end.

She followed Becky, Emery, and Savannah out the door. The chapel had been decorated beautifully in teal and white. As she moved toward the aisle, it all seemed surreal. This was the wedding she had dreamed about when reading the Tender Heart books. A storybook wedding in a little white chapel to a strong, handsome cowboy.

She waited for Savannah, Emery, and then Becky to head down the aisle before she stepped up to take her turn. She froze when a gray-haired man in a dress military uniform moved next to her.

"Dad?"

Without a word, her father held out his arm. Her heart swelled with hope as she slipped her hand in the crook and they moved down the aisle. He still seemed as unbending as ever. But he was here, and so was her mother. She sat in the first row with a bright, teary smile on her face. Carly smiled back before she turned to the man who had made all her dreams come true.

Zane stood at the altar, looking more handsome than ever in his tan tux and cowboy hat. Or maybe it was the love she read in his sky blue eyes that made him so handsome. He held out a hand, and she took it. When she was standing in front of him, she spoke softly.

"Thank you for the surprise."

He smiled. "You're welcome." He started to turn to the pastor who was waiting patiently, but she stopped him.

"Before this ceremony gets underway, are there any other secrets you've been keeping from me, Zane Arrington?"

She meant it as a joke, but grew concerned when he hesitated a little too long before answering. "You know that spider I killed for you the first time we met? Well, the thing is, I never did find that little ol' spider. You were so hysterical that I pretended to pluck something out of your hair and stomp it under my boot just to shut you up."

She bit back a smile and tried to look stern. "Are you telling me you aren't the hero I thought you were?"

"Uh-huh." He flashed his dimples. "But I am the man who's going to love you for the rest of your life."

She looped her arms around his neck and kissed him. "In that case, who needs a hero?"

The End

HERE'S A SNEAK PEEK AT THE NEXT
TENDER HEART TEXAS
NOVEL . . .

❦

FALLING FOR A TEXAS HELLION
Out July 2017!

SOMEONE WAS IN THE HOUSE.
    Mason Granger listened as the floorboards in the hallway creaked. If he were at his home in Austin, he would already have his gun in hand and pointed at the door. But he wasn't in Austin. He was in a Bliss, Texas. And the only weapon he'd brought with him was his hunting rifle.

Which was still out in his truck.

Damn.

He eased up off the bed, hoping that the old springs in the mattress would keep their silence. Once his feet were on the floor, he wasted no time moving to the wall next to the door. He might not have a weapon, but he had surprise on his side. He held his breath and waited. Another creak sounded. This one was much closer. Only a second later, a shadowy form entered the room. Mason didn't hesitate to pounce.

His intention was to tackle the invader to the

floor and beat him senseless. But once his arms closed around the soft body of a woman, instinct kicked in, and he twisted to take most of the impact. He landed on the shoulder he'd injured playing college football. That injury had ended his pro sports career before it began and turned his path towards law.

"Sonofabitch!" He rolled onto his back in pain but refused to release the intruder, even though she was fighting like a hellcat. A hellcat that he remembered tussling with before. He remembered the small breasts that brushed his forearm. He remembered the long legs that tangled with his. And he remembered the shapely ass that bumped against him in a rhythm that sent a shaft of sexual awareness spearing through him. He had no business being sexually aroused by this woman. Not only because she was the younger sister of a friend, but also because he liked his women submissive. And there was nothing submissive about Becky Arrington.

"Enough, Rebecca!"

He didn't know if it was the command in his voice or the fact that he knew her identity that made Becky hold still. Probably the latter. She didn't seem like the type of woman who took commands. She released an exasperated huff as her body relaxed against his.

"I thought you were in Austin," she grumbled. "I thought that's why you couldn't be at my brother's wedding."

It was the excuse he'd given Zane so as not to hurt his friend's feelings, but the truth was that he didn't attend weddings. Any weddings. As a divorce lawyer, he dealt with too many broken vows to think of a marriage ceremony as anything more than a farce perpetuated by starry-eyed lovers with no clue about the reality of married life.

He lifted Becky and plopped her none too gently on the floor before he got to his feet. He switched on the lamp, not caring that he didn't have on a stitch of clothing. She walked into his house unannounced, she deserved to be embarrassed. He should've known better. Becky didn't even blink when he turned around. She sat on the floor with her dress hiked up and her panties showing, staring brazenly. The dress surprised him. He'd only seen her in western shirts and wrangler jeans. But the lacy pink panties surprised him even more. He hadn't taken her for a pink lace kind of girl. She was more the boy shorts type.

"You sleep naked?" she asked.

He walked over and grabbed the boxer briefs he'd stripped off earlier. "Only when it's the hottest summer in Texas history and there's no air conditioning." He pulled on the briefs and turned to find her deep blue eyes filled with annoyance.

"If my house is too hot, then maybe you should leave," Becky replied.

He moved to the window, but there wasn't a trace of breeze to cool him. The night air was thick and humid. It was also peaceful. In the city, all he could hear at night through his open windows were the harsh sounds of traffic, downtown partiers, and sirens. All he could hear now were the soothing sounds of chirping insects and the occasional hoot of an owl.

Mason needed soothing. In the last few months

he'd felt restless and uneasy. He no longer got satisfaction from punishing greedy spouses in the courtroom. Nor did he get satisfaction from punishing submissive women in bed. His discontentment had prompted him to take a leave of absence from work. Foolishness had him believing that Bliss held the key to his cure.

"Your house?" he said without turning around. "Funny, I believe I'm the one who holds the deed to the house and land."

She jumped up and came striding over to stand behind him. Unlike most women, her scent wasn't manufactured perfumes or lotions. She smelled earthy . . . like fresh-cut grass on a cool spring morning.

"Only because Mr. Reed reneged on our deal when you sneaked in and offered him cash," she snapped.

He turned and raised an eyebrow. "You had a contract with Delbert Reed to buy this place?"

"Not a contract exactly. But I told him I wanted to buy it, and I would've as soon as I turned twenty-five and got my trust fund. I had plans for this ranch." She stepped closer and pointed at finger at his chest. "Plans that I'm not going to let some uppity lawyer from Austin ruin just because he wants a place to hunt and fish on the weekends."

"Is that why you snuck into my house?" He arched an eyebrow. "You planned to murder me in my sleep so you could buy the ranch from my beneficiary? I should warn you that I don't have a will so it could take some time for my estate to work its way through probate."

She sent him a smug look. "A lawyer without a

will? Isn't that like a doctor without health insurance?"

He couldn't help but laugh. She might be a brat, but she was entertaining. "My life has always been tumultuous. Why not my death? But we digress. Why did you sneak into *my* house?"

Her eyes flashed with temper. He had thought they were the same blue as her brother Zane's, but on closer examination, they weren't as dark. Rays of sapphire shone through the twilight irises. "I didn't sneak. I thought you hadn't moved in yet and I came to get my . . . stuff."

"Why would your stuff be here?"

She paused before she answered. It was a tactic he'd seen often in the courtroom—usually when someone was about to lie. "Because my cousin Gracie and I used to hang out here when we were teenagers, and we left a few things behind." Her gaze flickered to the corner of the room for a brief second. From what he could tell, there was nothing there but a few cobwebs and some dust. Which made him extremely curious.

"All the furniture and household items were included in the sale," he said. "But I wouldn't want to keep anything that belongs to Zane's sister." He crossed his arms. "So please help yourself."

Becky paused again, and her gaze returned to the corner just long enough to make him even more curious. "All I want is my grandma's quilt." She grabbed the quilt off the bed. He would've bet money that it wasn't her grandma's. Especially when she looked so annoyed to have it in her possession. "Well, thanks for the stimulating conversation, Mr. Granger. And the even more stimulating peep show."

He bit back a smile. "I'm glad you enjoyed it." He followed her out, simply because he didn't trust her as far as he could throw her. With her temper, he wouldn't be surprised if she torched the place just so he wouldn't have it.

He expected to find her candy-apple-red truck parked in front of the house. Instead, a white stallion was tied to the porch railing. The horse tossed his head and snorted when they came out the door.

"You're still riding that demonic horse?" he asked.

She grabbed her boots that were sitting on the porch and sat on the steps to tug them on, which pretty much proved that she had been sneaking into his house.

"Ghost Rider is not demonic," she said. "He's just high spirited." She got up and rolled the quilt tightly before securing it to the back of the saddle. The horse pranced and jerked at the reins, confirming Mason's assessment. And even though he felt Becky needed a tough lesson on the dangers of misjudging an animal, he untied the reins from the rail and took the horse's bridle to hold him steady.

"A high-spirited horse that would've trampled you to death that day in the barn if I hadn't pushed you out of the way."

"More like tackled me. You seem to enjoy manhandling woman." She jerked the reins from him and swung into the saddle.

There was something about the image of her astride the white stallion that momentarily took his breath away. Her long golden brown hair hung almost to the horse's rump, and her aqua dress was hiked up so far he could see a hint of lacy panties and a whole lot of toned, long leg. Unable to stop himself, he took her calf and guided her boot into the stirrup before he lifted his gaze to hers.

"I only manhandle the ones who step into my lair." He slid his hand up her calf. "Fair warning, Rebecca. Next time you come into *my* home uninvited, I won't be so nice." He brushed the soft skin behind her knee with his thumb before he released her.

"I don't think you have a nice bone in your body." She whirled the horse, forcing him to jump back or get his bare feet crushed beneath its hooves, before she galloped off into the darkness. When she was gone, he released his breath and gave himself a mental warning. *Be careful, Mason. That one's not for you.*

He turned back to the house. It wasn't a pretty place. The roof needed repairs, the front porch sagged, and the trim needed sanding and painting. Not to mention the broken air conditioner. But he hadn't bought the ranch for the house. He'd bought it for its location. And it had nothing to do with fishing and hunting. The same way Becky hadn't come for her grandmother's quilt.

He walked to his Range Rover and got his rifle. He didn't expect any more visitors, but he always believed in being prepared. Back in the bedroom, he set the rifle on the bed and walked to the corner. Just as he'd suspected, there were only dust and cobwebs . . . and one loose floorboard.

Getting a knife from the kitchen, he came back and popped up the loose board. The space beneath was too dark to see anything so he had to move the lamp closer. In between the floor joists there was a small wooden box. He leaned down and pulled it out.

When he opened it, he discovered the real reason Becky had snuck into his house.

OTHER SERIES BY KATIE LANE

DEAR READER,
   Thank you so much for reading *Falling Head Over Boots*. I hope you enjoyed Zane and Carly's story as much as I enjoyed writing it. If you did, please help other readers find this book by telling a friend or writing a review. Your support is greatly appreciated!

Katie

ABOUT THE AUTHOR

KATIE LANE IS A USA Today Bestselling author of the *Deep in the Heart of Texas*, *Hunk for the Holidays*, *Overnight Billionaires*, and *Tender Heart Texas* series. She lives in Albuquerque, New Mexico, with her cute cairn terrier Roo and her even cuter husband Jimmy.

For more info about her writing life or just to chat, check out Katie on:
Facebook *www.facebook.com/katielaneauthor*
Twitter *www.twitter.com/katielanebook*
Instagram *www.instagram.com/katielanebooks*

.

And for upcoming releases and great giveaways, be sure to sign up for her mailing list at
www.katielanebooks.com

71409301R00152

Made in the USA
Columbia, SC
29 May 2017